GWENDOLYN M. PARKER was born in Durham,
North Carolina, and lived there until her family moved
north to Mount Vernon, New York, when she was nine.
She was educated at Kent, Radcliffe, and N.Y.U. Law
School. After a decade working as an international tax
attorney on Wall Street and as marketing manager for
American Express, she left corporate life to devote herself
to writing. Ms. Parker currently lives in Connecticut,
where she maintains a small private law practice and is at
work on a new novel.

D0197323

THESE SAME LONG BONES

GWENDOLYN M. PARKER

A PLUME BOOK

PLUME
Published by the Penguin Group
Penguin Books USA Inc., 375 Hudson Street, New York, New York 10014, U.S.A.
Penguin Books Ltd, 27 Wrights Lane, London W8 5TZ, England
Penguin Books Australia Ltd, Ringwood, Victoria, Australia
Penguin Books Canada Ltd, 10 Alcorn Avenue, Toronto, Ontario, Canada M4V 3B2
Penguin Books (N.Z.) Ltd, 182–190 Wairau Road, Auckland 10, New Zealand

Penguin Books Ltd, Registered Offices: Harmondsworth, Middlesex, England

Published by Plume, an imprint of Dutton Signet,
a division of Penguin Books USA Inc.
This is an authorized reprint of a hardcover edition published by
Houghton Mifflin Company. For information address
Houghton Mifflin Company, 215 Park Avenue South, New York, N.Y. 10003

First Plume Printing, May, 1995
10 9 8 7 6 5 4 3 2 1

 REGISTERED TRADEMARK—MARCA REGISTRADA

LIBRARY OF CONGRESS CATALOGING-IN-PUBLICATION DATA
Parker, Gwendolyn M.
These same long bones / Gwendolyn M. Parker.
p.   cm.
ISBN 0-452-27428-1
1. Afro-American families—North Carolina—Durham—Fiction.
2. Afro-Americans—North Carolina—Durham—Fiction.   3. Community
life—North Carolina—Durham—Fiction.   4. Family—North Carolina—
Durham—Fiction.   5. Durham (N.C.)—Fiction.   I. Title.
[PS3566.A6786T48   1995]
813'.54—dc20   95–740
                                                                                                CIP

Printed in the United States of America
Original hardcover design by Anne Chalmers

PUBLISHER'S NOTE
This is a work of fiction. Names, characters, places, and incidents either are the
product of the author's imagination or are used fictitiously, and any resemblance to
actual persons, living or dead, events, or locales is entirely coincidental.

BOOKS ARE AVAILABLE AT QUANTITY DISCOUNTS WHEN USED TO PROMOTE PRODUCTS OR
SERVICES. FOR INFORMATION PLEASE WRITE TO PREMIUM MARKETING DIVISION,
PENGUIN BOOKS USA INC., 375 HUDSON STREET, NEW YORK, NY 10014.

FOR

MY

PARENTS

Heartfelt thanks to my family, for giving me the foundation; my friends, for their constant encouragement, especially Joan, Ronn, Alta, Margarett, David, Dawn, Karen, and Kjell; my agent, Marie Brown, who believed in me from the start and never wavered; my editor, Janet Silver, whose perceptive and skillful editing was a writer's dream; and lastly, the young ones — Jay, Cole, Sarah, Kate, Aaron, Shawn, Mariah, and Lena — who fill my life with their ineffable joy.

I

THESE
SAME
LONG
BONES

1

As if he'd been shaken, Sirus McDougald abruptly opened his eyes. There was a merciful moment of forgetfulness. The sheet was tangled about his long legs. He lay for a second at the center of a haze, moist and open from sleep, his limbs relaxed and peaceful, the recollection of a smile still puddled at the corner of his full lips. It was near dawn, and Sirus had been dreaming. He had dreamed that nothing would ever awaken him again. He had dreamed that he could stop life at his bedroom door. He had dreamed that he could force time to retrace its steps. But even as he turned to avoid it, the sun stole into his room, creeping into his sleep.

Sirus rubbed a broad hand across his face and looked drowsily around him. The dust in a beam of light that streamed through the blinds sparkled like fireflies near his slippers. Next to his head, on the small folding table he used as his nightstand, the light caressed the items he had laid out the night before: a small tortoiseshell comb, his pocket watch, his mother-of-pearl studs edged in gold, the loose pieces of paper on which he'd absently scribbled as he spoke to the reporter from the local paper. The light seemed to halt on the words on the top sheet of paper — "Brown, brown, 5'3", reading." What could the reporter he'd spoken to yesterday possibly print that would be news?

At once, Sirus's lingering ease was gone. His eyes widened, his chest swelled with air, and his mouth opened, gaping. He seized the piece of paper from the table, crumpled it, and stuffed it into his mouth.

A moan escaped. His daughter, his precious girl, his only child, was dead. Of what importance was the color of her hair and eyes, her height or favorite hobby, when even the paper boy knew more than that: knew that she liked to sit in the narrow tunnel made by the honeysuckles between their house and the Senates', knew how she banged out of the house with her skates already on, how she stopped on the grass at the edge of the walk to tighten them, knew the way she posed to wave good-bye, one hand on her hip, the other straight in the air, an elongated little teapot.

No, there was no news to convey, talking to the reporter was just a formality, one among dozens that were expected of him. So he rented all ten of Jason's cars for the funeral and he called people personally with the news, and he readied his house as if for a party. These were the things that were done, and he did each of them, when it was time, in turn. He knew that his neighbors and friends were similarly busy: the women baking pies and hams and fretting over who might not know and still need to be told; the men collecting money, arranging for their own transportation and clean black suits; even the children, bent over basement tables, cutting construction paper to serve as backings for paper flowers and poems.

Sirus forced his legs stiffly to the edge of the bed. Get up, he said to himself, spitting the paper onto the floor.

Outside, cars slowly traveled past his house. Some carried

strangers: a Northerner in search of a relative's home, vacation-
ers from farther inland heading for the coast, a delivery truck
with vats of sweet cola syrup. But most carried Sirus's friends
and acquaintances, unable to resist taking an extra turn past his
house in an attempt to catch a glimpse of him or to see the large
black and purple wreath hung on the door.

How was he holding up? Why was his wife, Aileen, sleeping
over at her mother's house? Had they, following the country
way, covered the mirrors with black paper? Like Sirus, the
people who had settled this part of town — the colored section,
which butted up against the white part of town and then turned
back on itself — were primarily the descendants and relatives
of farmers. As they'd spread throughout the city, one brother
and then one cousin following the next, they'd left the country
but brought their country ways: an unflagging belief in cause
and effect — after all, hadn't they always reaped what they
sowed — leavened by a large measure of fatalism bred by bugs,
fire, and a too hot sun, and bound together by clannishness
based on proximity, shared cheekbones, and common values.
For these farmers and their progeny, holding the line against the
sorrow of history, there was absolute virtue in hard work, an
education was a lifeline, and life was an inevitable mystery.
These things were givens, like the choice of good land, from
which everything else that was good would proceed. And to
these descendants of farmers, death itself was both sower and
reaper, an unreasoning though sometimes benevolent messenger
from God.

Sirus himself was born on a farm that produced three hundred baskets of tobacco a season, in a town called Carr, in
the upper coastal plain of North Carolina. It was a typical
pocket of life in the South, crammed with contradictions and
ellipses of time. There were the Cherokee and the Tuscarora,
who had lived on the land for always; the slave and the free

Africans, who'd settled beside them; and the Scottish farmers, who had worked beside the others. Sirus's parents, like those of his neighbors, were descended from these Africans, Cherokee, Tuscarora, and Scots, and these people, when they were not farmers, were blacksmiths, barbers, cabinetmakers, grocers, and traders. They built everything they would have one day from these skills. And Sirus absorbed in his greens and hog crackling and corn bread the peculiar mixture of building and dreaming that was the heritage of these people. Now, in the wake of death, he was as much a part of this town of some five thousand colored people as the red dirt that ringed the manicured lawns, or the North Carolina light that was at once bright and hazy, or the ash, willow, cedar, and pecan that were native to the land.

Sirus stood now, some thirty-five years past his birth, in the late summer of 1947, in this town of Durham, North Carolina, which bustled with progress, in a house on Fayetville Street that was one of dozens he'd built, wishing he were the one who was dead. From his bathroom, the sun streaming in the window, Sirus could still hear the cars as they slowed to pass his house. He stood his shaving brush on its base, bristles up, to dry, and carefully shook the last drops of water from his razor. He looked at his face, now clean-shaven, in the mirror.

There was still the familiar broad chin, the wide cheekbones, the long thick nose, the thick black hair that formed a sharp contrast to his unbearably light, almost pearl-toned skin. The cold water had restored some color to his face; his gray eyes were smooth and clear. He marveled at his own composure. How could his features reveal so little while he felt as if every aspect of him, every thought and desire, every feeling and habit, was hurtling inside him at such speed and with such force that he could be an atom exploding, shattering into oblivion?

From the moment he had learned of Mattie's death, from

each second that moved forward, he was dragged backward, caught in a great rush of time away from the present, away from the husband he'd been, the prosperous businessman the town had grown to rely on, the solid friend that so many came to for advice. And in his place loomed the specter of another Sirus, a youth, a boy he believed was long gone, a boy who was all quiet and softness. This boy, his eyes permanently wide, followed after him in his own house, relentlessly padded after him in his own shoes.

There had been nothing authoritative about Sirus as a child. He had been thin and too pale, his elbows always at the wrong angles, his energy too volatile, kinetic, as likely to lead him in one direction as another. But as the years went by his skin had gained a translucence and his energy had cohered, coalesced, so that it no longer erupted jerkily in his limbs but rode high in his chest, girded by his thickening muscles. As a man, he was loose-gaited, solid but warm. If he wanted to command attention, he had only to stand, releasing heat into the air like fire.

He dropped his gaze from the mirror to the basin and watched the spot where the water continued to run. A small green stain glinted at the bottom of the bowl. On any other day it was just green, a color, but today it summoned half a dozen memories: the color of new tobacco in the fields, the color of his mother's eyes when she stood in the light on their porch, the transparent color of an old penny, or the color, in spring, of all the land of his youth. The color, this green, came rushing up at him with its freshness and longing, setting off an embedded charge. Sirus doubled over, an intense wave of pain and nausea gripping his gut. He grabbed the sink, shaking.

Tears welled up and just as quickly receded. With careful steps he returned to the bedroom, took a clean shirt from his wardrobe, and slid his arms into the cool, crisp cotton. Then, slowly, he walked to the window. The starch in his collar was exactly as he'd requested, but now it felt like a gag. He watched the cars continue in an endless procession out on the street, until a black limousine appeared. It was Etta Baldridge's car, turning onto Fayetville from Dupree, already bearing down the road with that ominous cadence reminiscent of halting steps stumbling toward death. If its headlights had been on, it would have looked as if it were already part of the funeral procession.

As the car crept down the street, Sirus could easily imagine Etta's voice and her short, sharp fingers tapping on the back of the front seat right below her driver's neck. "Albert, Albert, slower," she'd be saying. From where Sirus stood at the window he could imagine Etta's head, peeping forward from the relative darkness of the back of the car, her mouth moving animatedly, her face nearly pressed against the window. "Albert." Etta had been the first person to call on him when he had moved into this house. "I'm Etta Baldridge. Welcome to Fayetville," she'd said, pressing her face against the inside screen at the front door, an unofficial welcoming committee. Etta was always one to be pressing.

He thought he heard his housekeeper's key in the lock downstairs. Thank God, he thought. Mrs. Johnson could talk with Etta if she insisted on stopping. He reached for his pants from his wardrobe and his suspenders from the back of the cane-bottomed chair by the window. He knew that if he went out to the porch, Etta would ask Albert to stop altogether, would wave her arms and hands frenetically until he came out to the car. Once he was there, she would clasp him with those same grasping hands, her eyes sweeping greedily over him, hunting for a stain on his shirt, a cut from shaving, some food left on his lips, some sign of his grief — anything she could carry away with her to the bank or the insurance office or the beauty parlor where she would find an ear in which to deposit her find. If Etta saw him at this moment she might also be able to spy the child who was hiding in his face. He reached for his suit jacket, feeling a wave of relief as the car passed.

Downstairs, Mrs. Johnson was at the back door, pushing it open with her hip as she always did. She held her key in one hand and, in the other, the bag with her change of clothes, her morning paper, and a pair of flat shoes. She was a sturdy, compact woman, with blunt fingers and short, thick legs, and when she hung up the light raincoat she wore, regardless of the weather, her roundly muscled forearms showed. Her face was diamond-shaped, a dark brown flecked through with magenta, crowned by a wide forehead and dominated by closely placed, expressive eyes. She had worked for Mr. Mac, as she called him, for over fifteen years, beginning when he first came to Durham from Washington after college, continuing through his marriage to Aileen Bryant twelve years ago, through Mattie's birth, and on up to the present day.

She tugged at the chain to the overhead light and lit the oven and the burner under the kettle in rapid succession. On any other morning, she would also have turned on the radio standing on the counter next to the sink, softly tuning in to "The Sunny Days of Glory Hour," which was broadcast from eight till ten. This morning, however, as she had yesterday and the day before, she went about her work as quietly as she could. She gently closed the catch on the cabinet where the coffee was stored, took her flat shoes from the bag without rustling the paper, and turned off the heat under the kettle as soon as it began to whistle. She thought of Mr. Mac upstairs, still asleep, she hoped.

If asked, she always described Mr. Mac as a firm but fair man to work for, though in the privacy of her home or among close friends she usually elaborated on his kindness with great pas-

sion. To her, this tragedy, which was the precise word she used
to describe Mattie's death, was not only God's will but also
the work of the devil, the latter having cruelly shut out the light
in Mattie's eyes, the former having blissfully caused them to
reopen in the temple of His everlasting love. As she construed
it, Mattie's death was also a test of a special and particular
nature.

Mrs. Johnson had been the one to find Mattie lying on the
ground in the backyard (a fall from her slide, the doctor later
confirmed), her neck at an impossible angle. As soon as the
housekeeper recovered her senses, her first thought had been,
oh, my Lord, how will Mr. Mac survive? Mattie was his treas-
ure, his precious girl. They blurred together in each other's
company, he and Mattie, an edging of the hardness that was
him into the softness that was her, until the exact point at which
one finished and the other began was obscured, as if they actually shared one body and one heart. Mrs. Johnson could not
begin to imagine how he would survive this loss. Certainly Mr.
Mac would need help — everyone did in such circumstances,
and Mr. Mac would be no exception — but she was hard
pressed to say where it would come from. He seemed to value
her opinion, but that was not the kind of holding up he would
need. There was his friend Jason, but she had never known Mr.
Mac to rely on him in that way. The logical place to look would
be to his wife, of course, but Mrs. McDougald's own collapse
had been immediate and complete. Yes, Mrs. Johnson concluded, this was going to be a trial, a difficult one, and she
would do what she could to support him. After all, hadn't Mr.
Mac helped her with her Cora's tuition? And with extra money
for shoes and pants for the two boys those three years in a row
when they both kept growing?

"Good morning, Mrs. Johnson," Sirus said, appearing suddenly in the kitchen. He was completely dressed; he looked

severe in his black suit, his light skin made all the paler by the contrast.

"Good morning, Mr. Mac," she answered. "You're up early. I'd hoped you'd be sleeping at least another hour." She ran her gaze over him methodically, as if weeding a garden, looking first at his eyes, then at the lines around them, then at the slope of his shoulders inside his suit.

"I didn't sleep well," he began. "Why don't you bring the coffee to the front room so we can talk for a minute." He waited for her nod before he left the room. Mrs. Johnson shortly followed with his coffee, careful to use his favorite cup and saucer. He definitely hadn't slept well, she decided, looking again at the shadows under his eyes and the pinched set of his shoulders.

"I think we have enough food now," he said as soon as she sat down. He sipped some of his coffee, holding it in his mouth until it cooled, and let her know it was how he liked it. "Every lady from the church will bring something," he continued, "and I don't want it to appear as if we're not grateful." He fastened his eyes on an old photograph of his father, which sat on the table beside her.

Mrs. Johnson continued to watch him carefully, encouraging him to go on.

"It's okay if you go ahead and fry up those last two chickens in the freezer, but after that I think we have more than enough."

Mrs. Johnson still said nothing. Of course there was too much food. There were three hams and two turkeys and pots and pots of collards and turnips and cabbage, not to mention rolls and pies and cold salads. On occasions like this there was always too much food. But no matter how much there was, it always got eaten. They both knew this.

"It's not as though any of these people will make their only meal here," he added.

"No, Mr. Mac, I don't expect they will," Mrs. Johnson said. "But it's always been the way to have more than enough, as long as a body can see their way clear to that."

Sirus pointed at her with his cup. "Just because I can afford it is no reason to waste both food and money," he said sharply. The coffee in his cup splashed up on one side.

"No, I didn't say there was," Mrs. Johnson said evenly. She sought his eyes, but they remained resolutely fixed on the point to the left of her. "I merely said it's usually the way, that's all. The food will keep, at any rate, and not go to waste; you can rely on me for that."

"Then you'll just cook what I said," Sirus said quietly, and drained the last of his coffee. He reached into his pocket for his watch, and Mrs. Johnson took his pointed hint, picked up his coffee cup along with hers, and left the room.

As soon as she was gone Sirus realized that he'd sounded foolish. He never talked to Mrs. Johnson this way. Yet the thought of all that food amassing in the kitchen nauseated him. It also made him think of another wake, at another time, at the home of a carpenter he'd known a long time ago in Wilson County, a man who had lost his wife and two of his three children in a fire.

The fire that killed them had erupted suddenly, its origin a mystery. The flames were already extinguished by the time the carpenter returned from a night of hunting with his youngest boy. He and the boy sat in his shed as smoke hung in the air, the same shed in which, in happier times, the man had often boasted he could make or repair anything made from wood: a wagon wheel, a table, a sideboard — anything that a use was known for. Now, ringed by the neighbors who had battled the blaze, he sat quietly. A thick layer of soot was everywhere: on the tools and chips and wood shavings that lay all around, on his clothing, on those of his neighbors. He sat precisely on the edge of the chair someone had dragged to the center of the shed. His arm was loosely draped around the shoulders of his son. Later, at the wake, with the food spread from one end of a table to the other, he'd held his son in the same slack manner, his eyes fixed on the three coffins that crowded the front of his house, taking up the space where a worn sofa and two chairs normally stood.

It was only later that it happened, what people referred to as "the change." First he kept his son home from school; then, when he allowed him to go out, he tightly buttoned the boy's shirtcuffs and layered both a vest and a sweater underneath his overalls, even in the summer. And later, or so Sirus heard his parents whispering, he rubbed the boy every night with a mixture of tar and pitch. It was so strange, so secretive, these private protections, but no one intervened. Nor did anyone step forward when it ended, finally, with the slaughter and ritualized eating of his animals. It was a story that even the busiest seemed loath to tell: how he had begun with his goat, gone on to the spindly-legged mule that drew the cart in which he delivered his work, and then to their dog, a mutt, with one brown ear and one yellow. It was rumored to have taken him weeks to finish this grisly task, and no one said a word to him about what he had done. Later, when the spring came, the carpenter and his boy simply moved away.

It was the carpenter and his son Sirus had been picturing when he spoke to Mrs. Johnson about the food. He thought about the boy chafing and sweating under the vests and the sweaters, about his mumbled excuses when he tried to explain his absence from school, and about what the boy's skin must have looked like after being covered with that stinging tar and pitch. Most of all, though, he thought about those beasts, their large, surprised eyes blinking shut against the spurting blood, their flesh cracking and smoking. Sirus never saw the flames that licked the animals clean; he only heard of their agony. But now he saw the animals multiplied, walking into the flames, two by two. And those images became mixed with others — of food piled high, stacked like a funeral pyre; of people eating so much that their bellies became distended; of a ladder made of food on which Mattie disappeared into heaven. Sirus was sure that he had to draw the line somewhere, anywhere, as a cordon of order and reason. Death and even his young self might stalk him, but he was resolved that he would not go the way of the carpenter, would not find himself, in the middle of the night, clinging to another body, his hands raw and stained, rubbing and covering and praying, and killing and consuming, doing anything at all that was necessary to keep from facing the truth, that he had lost the thing on earth he loved best.

A few blocks away, Etta Baldridge was back at her home, leaning against a pillow she'd bought on her last trip to New York. "I've got a stomach like a cast-iron skillet," she said to her best friend, Ophelia Macon. The remark concluded the conversation about food and digestion and bowels that Mrs. Macon had begun some five minutes earlier. The women left a respectful pause before launching into the subject they had gathered to discuss.

"I've never felt such a sorrow," Mrs. Baldridge began, interrupting the sound of her own breathing. "Never," she added dramatically.

Mrs. Macon nodded.

"Now I can't say how I would feel if it were my own Lily, but you know what I mean. Nobody outside 435 Fayetville loved that child more than me."

Ophelia Macon added a high sound of her own breathing, whistling up her nose.

"Wasn't I her godmother? Didn't I go to every birthday, every church play, every little thing they had at school?"

Mrs. Macon again showed agreement, lifting her chest so that her whole upper body shuddered. The two women sat at opposite ends of the beige and blue couch Mrs. Baldridge had had recovered only a month before. They sat in almost identical poses: their hands folded in their laps, large upper torsos perched precariously atop narrowly proportioned waists, hips, and legs, lips momentarily pursed against the torrent of words each always carried in her mouth. Mrs. Baldridge sat to the right, near the entrance to her dining room, her feet flat and even on the floor. Mrs. Macon sat to the left, near the archway to the front hall, her legs crossed at the ankles. On the low mahogany table in front of them sat two glasses of iced tea, with a sprig of fresh mint in each. The two women had had their hair dyed the day before, Mrs. Macon's a dark red, Mrs. Baldridge's a paler red, like new mahogany finished with clear resin.

"Have you seen them? Do you know how they're holding up?" Mrs. Macon asked, leaning in Mrs. Baldridge's direction.

"I've given them privacy, of course," Etta answered, thinking of her calls to Sirus, how he had ignored her hints for an invitation to come over. "I called, but there'll be time enough for them to lean on their friends. In the meantime I've been praying to the Lord to fill my bosom with comfort."

Mrs. Macon looked as if she too had been filling her bosom.

Mrs. Baldridge continued, "There're the days right through now, of course. Holding up Aileen. Being a post for Sirus so he can carry out his duties. But what grieves me to think about is later."

Mrs. Macon bowed her head.

"Remember Fran Farmer, her poor daughter, lost to TB?"

Mrs. Macon looked up, her eyes wide. "Oh, yes. Poor Fran Farmer."

"And remember how we took turns sitting with her? I mean her with no family, and only here in Durham five years."

"Oh, yes, she had no one."

"And we all kept coming, till a week after the funeral I think it was, and then someone said, 'Maybe we shouldn't intrude.' Why, I think it was Evelyn Knight who said it first."

"Was it Evelyn? Oh, mercy."

"I believe it was. I can't think who else would say something like that, can you?"

"No, I'm sure you're right. I'm sure it was Evelyn."

"Yes, I know it was. But we have to share the blame, too. Didn't we take what she was saying to heart? I mean, she put it so well. 'Who really knows her?' she said. And she had a point. She kept to herself pretty much all those years."

"But all and still," Mrs. Macon interjected.

"Yes, that's just what I was saying," continued Etta Baldridge, "but all and still. We should have kept going but we didn't, and who's to say if we had, why, that poor Fran might not have gone and followed her baby."

The women gasped simultaneously, as if the horror of Fran Farmer, found lying with her head resting — "like on a pillow," the preacher said — on the door of her stove, had suddenly pressed itself, for an instant, against them, and then, as quickly, had retreated, leaving them just that one image and a story to tell.

"You don't think?" Mrs. Macon began after a respectful silence.

"No, no, don't even mention such a thing."

But for a few long minutes both women imagined the worst. For Mrs. Macon it was one sorrowful scene after another: the wailing sound of the ambulance from Lincoln Hospital, ladies at the church wailing and fainting, the large, beautiful house on Fayetville once again draped in black and empty. For Mrs. Baldridge the images were much more far-ranging. She saw herself and her daughter Lily not exactly ostracized, but no longer occupying a place of importance. No more parties for Lily with the daughters of the other leading colored families of Durham: the McDougalds, the Gants, the Wilsons, the Gerards. She imagined a pall settling over the families, over all their hard work and their dreams of "progress for the race," until the whole fragile structure wilted and lay dead. She imagined an edgy despair spreading through the town, so that when some-one fell on hard times people turned away instead of coming by with a pot of greens or a pile of carefully folded clothes. No one lending money to anyone anymore. No eligible young men, with the right education and the right family connections, com-ing by for Lily when the time was right. In Mrs. Baldridge's mind, Sirus was the knotted thread that bound them together. As you ringed salt around a stain or stitched a wound with pig gut, you relied on Sirus to be the stanch, to keep the tear from spreading. Driving past his house today, Etta had asked Albert to slow down so that she could concentrate on this. She had seen it clearly, how he had to hold together, not just avoiding the way of Fran Farmer, but going beyond, going from bad to good. Sirus had to redeem this tragedy; that was how she saw it. He had to swallow it whole like a bitter root, not alone, but with the assistance of his friends and neighbors. And after the sweating from the poison was over and the shaking stilled, he had to rise up and be new. Mrs. Baldridge was as sure of this as she had been that her husband would die before fifty, and he'd died abruptly, as she had predicted, just two years before.

"Sirus will be strong," she said. "And with his strength Aileen will find her own. We just have to help him know his own resilience."

Mrs. Macon showed her agreement, staring at Mrs. Baldridge.

"I think we should arrive early. Not at the same time, of course, but within the half hour."

Mrs. Macon took a large swallow of her iced tea. "Are you going to read a prayer?" she asked.

"Well, nothing planned." Mrs. Baldridge let her shoulders fall against the back of the couch. "Of course I'll bring my Bible, and some subject may present itself."

"There are so many passages that bring comfort," Mrs. Macon observed.

In response, Mrs. Baldridge suddenly bellowed, "'And though after my skin worms destroy this body, yet in my flesh shall I see God.'"

"Oh, my goodness, yes. Amen," Mrs. Macon replied.

"'I will lay me down and take my rest,'" continued Mrs. Baldridge.

"Blessed be the Lord," echoed Mrs. Macon.

"'The Lord is my light and my salvation; whom shall I fear? The Lord is the strength of my life; of whom shall I be afraid?'"

"Praise the Lord."

"'Weeping may endure for a night,'" Mrs. Baldridge nearly yelled, lifting her hands from her lap, palms lifted. "'But joy cometh in the morning.'" She dropped her hands back into her lap with a loud clap.

"Joy, oh, joy, oh, joy," Mrs. Macon said softly, clasping her hands.

"Yes, joy," Mrs. Baldridge concluded, staring ahead as if the word were printed in the air.

Upstairs, in her room, Lily heard the word *joy* erupt like a dissonant chord. Oh, God, what was her mother bellowing about now? She sat at her desk and looked at the words she had written so far:

Mattie was my friend so dear
Her face so full of grace
And now that she has left us here
No one can take her place.

It was a poem she was writing to read at Mattie's funeral —
her mother's idea, of course. She would have preferred to sit
quietly in the back and do nothing, but her mother had insisted.
"You were her best friend," she said, "and I was her godmother.
How would it look if you didn't say or do anything while
someone like Cottie Moore sings a song, or Jane Henson does
a dramatic reading?" Lily didn't care what Jane or Cottie was
going to do; she didn't like them anyway. And even though she
was Mattie's best friend, she still didn't want to read a poem in
front of everyone.

She stared at the blank space under the four lines. She wanted
to say something about Mattie's hair, which was a thick bushy
brown, or her eyes, which were dark dark brown and always
alert, but she couldn't think of any rhymes for hair or eyes, or
any adjectives to go with them. Why couldn't she just sit at the
back of the church like she wanted to? She hated the idea of
everyone staring at her while she read her poem. Lily knew she
was what was called a funny-looking child. She looked like both
her mother and her father, but all mixed up in a jumble. She
had her father's nice full lips, broad nose, and thick kinky hair.
But she'd also gotten her mother's fair skin and light hair,
and together she knew she looked a little like a duckling, awkward and ungainly. The only feature that was truly hers were
her eyes, which were wide and round and sparkling brown,
and drew people to her. Lily knew, however, that up on the
podium, raised above the pews, she would only look yellow and
strange.

She shifted her gaze out the window, hoping to find an ad-
jective to describe Mattie's hair. Why couldn't she just show one

of the pictures she had sketched of Mattie? There was the one of Mattie sitting on the steps of her front porch, with acorns in her mouth. Or the one of the baptism, where she had drawn Mattie, Edie Senate, and Floyd Turner all sitting in a row at the back of the church altar, waiting for the preacher to call them down into the pool of water, where he would rest his hand over their noses and mouths and dunk them, fully dressed, in the water. Or even the one she had drawn of Mattie today, of the two of them, sitting on Mattie's front porch the night before she died. They put up flowers at funerals, so why couldn't they put up one of her pictures, like a little flower? And that could be that. It would mean telling about the drawings, of course, and if she did that, her mother would want to see them all. Maybe it would be easier to read the poem; at least it would be over quickly. If she told about the drawings, there'd be no end to it.

There was a quick rap on the door, and as soon as she slid a piece of paper over what she was writing, her mother was in the room.

"Oh, Lily, I'm so disgusted," her mother said, huffing from the flight of stairs. She dropped onto the edge of Lily's bed and immediately began picking at a loose thread on the bedspread.

Lily watched her mother's eyes frenetically sweep around the room.

"Really, I can't even begin to tell you," Mrs. Baldridge continued. "No one seems to have the vaguest notion of how to behave tonight." She stared at a pile of books on top of Lily's dresser and read the title of each one. She focused on Lily's shoes and then at the hem of Lily's dress. "And do you know what I saw today as I drove past the McDougalds'? No, of course you don't know. You couldn't even begin to guess." Her gaze at last rested on Lily's face. "Guess," she said sharply.

"I don't know, Mother. What?" Lily answered.

"A skate," she announced. "Do you hear what I'm saying? A skate."

Lily was puzzled. She was sure her mother could read her expression.

"You don't understand what I'm saying, do you?"

Lily shook her head slowly.

"It was her skate," her mother elaborated. "Right under the front bush."

Lily's eyes widened.

"Right," replied her mother; "that's just what I'm saying. It was as plain as day. I'm surprised Sirus hasn't seen it. But he hasn't. His mind has been too busy, I expect. But there it was and, I imagine, still is. Do you understand what I'm saying?"

"Yes, Mother," Lily said quietly.

"I mean, anyone could see it tonight. Sirus. Oh, God, poor Aileen. What a shock that would be."

Lily tried to imagine how the skate had gotten there. Had Mattie fallen, flung it there in anger, and then clumped into the house on only one skate? Or had she put it there on purpose; was there something wrong with the skate that she wanted to hide?

"I'm at a loss," continued her mother. "Completely. I can't very well go over there and pick it up myself. What if someone saw me in the bushes, for goodness' sake? And it can't be left there. What a cruel thing that would be."

Lily suddenly imagined running over to Mattie's house right now to pick it up, not so that it would be gone, but to make it hers.

"Well," Mrs. Baldridge said, leaning toward Lily. "Do you think I'm just talking to hear myself speak? What do you think we should do?"

Lily wished she had seen the skate first and had it now, under her bed, safely wrapped in a blanket.

"Can you really see it from the road?" she asked.

"Like buckshot in a deer's eye."

Lily winced. "Then I guess someone should pick it up." Her voice trailed off at the end of her sentence.

"Do what?" her mother fairly yelled. "Speak up."

"Pick it up," Lily said louder.

"Well, what do you think I've been saying? I mean, have you been listening to a word I've said?"

"Yes, ma'am, I'm listening." Lily made an effort to sit straighter in her chair and bring her eyes to her mother's.

"What have you been doing up here all this time, anyway?"

Lily wished they could return to the skate, but she knew her mother would not be satisfied with that.

"I cleaned my room," she answered, "and ironed my dress for tonight."

"Oh, really? Let me see it."

Lily took her dress from the closet and held it up to herself, holding it out at the hem so that the skirt flared.

"There's a wrinkle there, on the left side," her mother said, taking the material in her hand and balling it lightly. Lily knew that this would not only mark the spot that needed ironing, but make a new wrinkle as well.

"And your ears? Let me see them," she continued as Lily hung the dress back in her closet.

"Yes, ma'am." Lily returned and leaned forward so that her head hung just within reach of her mother's hands. Her mother took her chin in one hand and turned it first to one side, where she inspected one ear, and then to the other. "There's wax at the back of both of your ears," she concluded.

Lily backed her head away, willing herself to move it slowly. What was it her mother was moving toward?

"You might as well know, I'm worried about this whole thing."

"You mean about the skate?" Lily asked.

"That, and the whole thing." Her mother waved her hand listlessly in the air.

Lily wasn't at all sure what her mother meant. "You mean about the funeral tomorrow? What you're going to say?"

"No, not that . . . You think I'm worried about something so minor when this house, our car, all those fine things you wear, your whole future and mine is what's at stake?"

"No, I guess not," Lily ventured.

"No, of course not. Do I look like somebody's fool?"

"No, Momma, of course you don't."

"Oh, if your father were alive, it would be different. He'd still have his job, his position, and we'd have our place from his, but since he died, it's all dependent on everyone else. Did you know we get an allowance from the bank every month, something the bank board voted on after he died? Well, what do you think would happen if Sirus McDougald were not heading up that board? Do you think those others would be so generous? No, I don't think so. They'd just as soon forget we even exist; that's what I think. I wouldn't trust a one of them. And what about this house? Who do you think owns it? Do you think there's a deed with my name on it? Of course there isn't. And do you think it's anyone else down at the bank that argues for us to stay? Not for a minute. The rest of them don't think of anyone but themselves."

Lily had had no idea of any of this. It was the first she knew that everything they had wasn't really theirs.

"I don't understand, Mother," she began. "Why would anything change now? Is Mr. McDougald going somewhere?"

Her mother groaned loudly. "Don't you know anything? Must I spell everything out for you? Things change. Death changes things."

Lily still didn't understand. Of course death changes things.

It meant she and Mattie would never go to the beach together again, or ride in the McDougalds' car. It meant there'd be no one sitting on the porch or standing in the yard that she could yell hey to when she rode past on her bike. Oh, a hundred and one things would change. But nowhere was there the kind of change her mother was talking about, and she couldn't see, even for a moment, why it should be so.

"Why am I talking to a child?" Her mother looked around the room as if there were someone else to talk to. "I mean, here is a child who doesn't have the sense the good Lord gave her at birth, and I'm expecting her to understand something as vital as her own future? The good Lord must think I've lost my mind."

Lily lowered her head. She knew her mother would be through soon — she always was when the good Lord began to have an opinion.

"Be downstairs and dressed in an hour," her mother added as she left the room.

"Yes, ma'am," she said quickly. But her mother was already down the stairs by the time she got the words out.

Just down the street from Sirus, Jason Morgan, Sirus's friend and the leading colored undertaker, climbed behind the wheel of his hearse. His two young assistants, Lucas and Earl, were in the seat behind him, and the small coffin that held Mattie lay in the cabin beyond them. Jason pulled the car smoothly out of the driveway and into the right lane. It would not take long to drive Mattie's body the five short blocks from the funeral parlor to Sirus's house. When he and Sirus were boys, back in Carr, the distance between their farms had been nearly two miles along a pounded dirt road. But back then, even that distance had flowed like water. Back and forth, back and forth, one or the other of them made the journey. Those two miles seemed no more than these five blocks did now.

Throughout their childhood, they had been best friends. Jason was more uniformly muscled than Sirus, with knobby wrists that sprouted from the cuffs of his cotton shirts, large, knuckled hands, small flat ears, and a long skull that curved back and away, giving his head an elfin look that matched the sinewy shape of his body. Sirus, by contrast, was made of pieces that seemed not quite whole; his feet were too large, his legs thin and muscled only in the thighs, his chest narrow and sloping inward, his light skin delicate and easily bruised.

Jason was the one who played softball well, who won when they raced each other, who vaulted over any chairs and logs in his way. Sirus was uneven and distracted at sports, lost his train of thought when something upset him. At school Jason was considered the regular fellow, jovial and good-humored, emotional but unaffected, so quick to recover from easy tears that by the time anyone might have begun a jeer he was all smiles and jokes again. Sirus was more likely to be confused, to cry and fall silent, or to feign indifference and then brood over an event long after it was finished for everybody else. Sirus enjoyed Jason's easy fit with others, his sincerity, his uncomplicated response to things; Jason enjoyed Sirus's curiosity, quiet intensity, and his energy, which easily matched Jason's own.

Whenever they were together as boys, it was as if there were no space between them, until that time when it changed. One late July day, the air thick with wet heat, he and Sirus had lain in the tall grass behind Sirus's house, beyond the four stripping barns, next to the woods that ran the length of the road. Their heads were cushioned by the matted grass; their sneakered feet rested in the red dirt path. Sirus had brought with him his collection of dried skins: a copperhead, a flat mouth, an Indian moccasin, and a tiny field mouse, treasures he had found in the fields or woods and carefully placed on a broken stripping shelf in a barn to dry. Jason had brought his new Sears, Roebuck softball, a present for his birthday; his hand-stitched glove, made by the tanner in town, was propped under his knees like the bump in an old sofa. They had had a game of catch and searched fruitlessly for more skins, and then lay nearly stuporous in the shade.

It was Sirus who decided it was too hot for clothes. He jumped to his feet and peeled away his socks and overalls and tightly buttoned cotton shirt with one unexpectedly graceful motion, as if he were shedding his skin. It was just the kind of surprising thing, back then, that Sirus would do. He stood in the path next to Jason's feet, the sun bouncing off the right side of his body, casting a shadow on the ground between them. As he stood there, naked, the skin under his clothes paper white, he looked not so much like a boy of ten as like a newly hatched creature that had been deposited on the narrow path. Jason was too lazy to stand, but he kicked off first one sneaker and then the other as he randomly unsnapped and unbuttoned his clothes. While Jason undressed, Sirus seemed suddenly set free. Pretending to be a Cherokee warrior, he pranced in the path and the grass, waving his arms, hooting, cawing like a crow, kicking his legs and flapping his arms.

He carried on for five minutes, a mist of sweat covering his body. "You going to catch the grass on fire, you keep rubbing those stick legs of yours together like that," Jason said, laughing, still not undressed. Then he heard a crackling in the pine underbrush. He sat up and hooked his arms around his knees, squinting into the dappled woods. He searched the path that wound between a stand of cedars, but he didn't see the two men until the moment they emerged from the woods, their rifles nosed toward the ground. Startled at first, he was quickly relieved to see they were men he and Sirus both knew.

Ezra Carter, short and the color of cocoa, owned a small drygoods store and was a fanatical hunter. Hank Prinde worked in Ezra's store. Ezra wore a brown felt hat with the brim rolled up on one side, pushed back on his head. His mouth worked furiously on a large piece of chew. "Fool boy" was all he said as he gaped at Sirus, who stood frozen, his chest neither rising nor falling, his hands at his sides as if they were plumbed. Ezra spat on the path and shifted the heft of his gun.

"Looks like a bird; think I'll shoot it," Hank Prinde said, coming up behind him and laughing in three short bursts that sounded like a small dog barking. He raised his rifle from the ground, leveled it directly at the center of Sirus's thin chest, and cocked the trigger. He moved the barrel up toward Sirus's eyes, then down to his Adam's apple, which seemed to be shriveling in the boy's throat, and next to his private parts, which were indeed no bigger than a small bird. They stood like that for a full minute.

"Boy, put your clothes on," Ezra said finally. "You look like some goddamn savage." He motioned to Hank, who barked his laugh again, and they both turned, making their way back across the field, swaying with the weight of the rows of rabbits slung across their backs.

"Damn, nearly scared me," Jason said, turning to Sirus. Sirus stood without moving; the quiver in his lips had spread to his arms and legs, like a giant chill coursing from one end of his body to the other.

"That Hank's the one who's a savage," Jason said, "pointing his gun like that." He wiped his hands on his coveralls. "You'd think a grown man would have more sense than that."

Sirus continued to stare after the two men.

"C'mon, Sirus, let's start back." Jason stood and reached forward to swipe at Sirus's leg with his hand. Sirus jerked away. "Don't," he said quietly.

"Well, okay." Jason let his hands fall beside him. He wished that he could just tell Sirus again that it was Hank who was the fool, but Sirus's stillness inspired his own. He felt uncomfortable in his own skin. A second ago, Sirus's dancing had made him glad, and now the men had taken that away. It was as if some rule had been broken, but neither of them could say what it was. He fumbled with his own clothes, buttoning and snapping what he had undone. A chasm had suddenly opened between them, and he felt himself on one side, with Sirus on the other. Ah, just forget them, he tried to say with his hands, willing the gesture to be nonchalant, but Sirus wasn't listening. He harshly forced his legs and arms back into his clothes, as if he might tear off his skin with the rough corduroy and cotton. Those men, Jason thought as he watched Sirus dress, have snatched something away from us.

He and Sirus didn't talk about what happened, but the two boys were never again so free with each other. A stiffness, a small measure of furtiveness insinuated itself into their physical selves. Jason sometimes looked back and wondered how it was that that had happened. And whether there was anything he could have done to make it different. And what about now? What special part of his friend would death chase away? Would he fail Sirus now as, he felt, he had failed him then?

He thought about the work he had just completed on Mattie's body, which lay nestled inside the molded pink couch of her coffin, underneath a spray of yellow roses, at the back of the hearse. The hands that gripped the wheel — a little more tensely than he would have liked — were the same large and knuckled hands he had had as a boy. He had a mustache now, thin but nicely curved, and sideburns, which came to the middle of his sloping ears. Though he did not cry quite as frequently as he had as a child, he still cried easily.

Despite the smell of formaldehyde that clung to him like burdock, and the sometimes quizzical looks he got from someone new when he identified his profession, Jason enjoyed his work as an undertaker. He liked working with his hands, liked to be as respectful and gentle to the bodies as his work allowed, liked particularly to let his own deep capacity for tenderness and empathy find a rightful and appropriate home. Unlike some undertakers, who needed to conjure up a display of sorrow, Jason had sympathy that flowed as naturally as his love for his wife and three children. He loved them and his work freely, simply, without reserve or conflict. And because he loved so freely, there was nothing to hold back his grief.

When he first heard the news about Mattie, he was at the drugstore, talking to the pharmacist, Dr. Gerard, about the smelling salts he thought he might need for an upcoming funeral. In the middle of their conversation, Dr. Gerard got the call. Jason left everything just where it lay on the counter: the box of salts, aspirin for his wife, Edith, and two comics for the girls. He rushed from the store and drove without stopping. When he pulled into the driveway at Sirus's house, the sight of Sirus's own car in the garage seemed suddenly to make the tragedy real. He jumped out of his car, ran up the steps of the porch, and rushed into the house. Dr. Gant sat in the foyer, his large leather bag at his feet, filling out the death certificate. Sirus sat opposite him in a high-backed leather chair, his head frozen to one side, his shoulders hunched forward. Jason had never seen Sirus look so small or so pale.

In one swift motion, Jason grabbed Sirus's hands, pulled him up out of his chair, and folded his arms around him. Without even knowing that he did, he rocked his friend in his arms, and for a moment Sirus's full weight collapsed against him.

Jason now knocked at the front-door screen of Sirus's house as Lucas and Earl waited with the hearse at the curb. Jason strained to see into the darkened front parlor, but Sirus got to the door before Jason's eyes adjusted so that all he could make out was Sirus's broad frame.

"Hello, Sirus," Jason said, stepping back as Sirus swung open the door.

"Morning, Jason," Sirus said, nodding also toward Jason's two assistants, who now stood in the middle of the sidewalk.

Jason turned slightly to include Earl and Lucas in his statement. "We've brought her home," he said. "Do you want to go upstairs while we bring her in?"

Sirus didn't move. "No, I'll wait here," he answered, sliding the metal hinge that held the door open along its rod.

"Are you sure, Sirus?"

"I'm all right, Jason," Sirus said. "Please, just go ahead."

"Okay," Jason answered. "It'll take us about five minutes to get things all set up."

He turned and walked down the porch and sidewalk, motioning to Lucas and Earl to precede him back to the hearse. They swung open the heavy black door, one of them on either side, and pulled out a folded metal cart. Watching them, Sirus remembered that until a few days ago he had been able to carry Mattie easily, sweeping her up in a second, her arms around his neck, supporting her whole weight with one arm. Now it would take three men and five minutes to bring her inside.

"Sirus, why don't you roll back the edge of the rug?" Jason called from the steps of the porch.

The coffin rose up in front of Sirus like a whale breaking from the sea. For a second, if he closed his eyes, he thought it could be a month ago, at Highland Beach: Mattie's face breaking the water, her mouth spouting salt water, laughing, her thick brown hair holding the water and salt like a sponge so that it caught the sunlight bouncing on the surface of the ocean.

"Catch me, Daddy, catch me."

She had flopped toward him, her arms stretched out over her head, her legs and feet beating the top of the water like butter.

And he had caught her up, just under the ribs, swinging her around in the water so fast that there was, for a moment, only spray and motion, making a small circle in the middle of the ocean around them.

"Again, Daddy, again," she had called out in her high, breaking voice, pushing off with her feet against his thighs. She had flopped and smacked and dived and he had caught and swung and lifted until his arms felt there was nothing else they had ever done before but catch her and carry her and whirl her around deliriously in the midst of her zest and joy. When he asked Aileen that night to put salve on his shoulder, she had said, "Sirus, you spoil that child. Why didn't you just tell her your arms were getting tired?" "She's a lovely child, Aileen; we couldn't have asked for one better" was all he said in reply.

Jason cleared his throat.

"Of course," Sirus said, flipping back the edge of the carpet with his foot. Jason and the boys pushed the cart up the last step and through the doorway, steadying it carefully as the wheels ran over the threshold. So she was coming home, Sirus thought, stiller than she had ever been, with a stillness that felt more still than death.

"We'll put her here," Jason called, as they traveled across the living room like a small caravan, "by the window." By the time Sirus turned, the coffin was off its cart and resting on a pedestal the same color as the coffin.

"We'll be able to bank the flowers here nicely," Jason continued, spreading his arms out on either side like long sails. "And if we move these two chairs" — he pointed at the two wing chairs that flanked the coffin — "we'll have a walkway for people to spend their time with her to say their goodbyes."

Jason moved about the room, touching various pieces of furniture. There was something hypnotic in the way he spoke, as if the scene he was describing were not real. Behind his words, Sirus thought, another scene seemed to unfold. In that scene Jason's arms, raised and lowered, were a shepherd's arms; the square, slightly formal living room was a wide meadow; and Mattie's coffin contained not a dead child, but something magical, something created for a moment of worshipful celebration.

Sirus interrupted Jason, took him by the arm, and led him, Lucas, and Earl into the kitchen. There, Sirus pressed biscuits and coffee and eggs on them, encouraged by Mrs. Johnson. He left them there, Jason in the wide-bottomed oak chair he usually sat in, the boys scooted up to the table, their brown caps resting on their knees, as Mrs. Johnson turned to the stove and tended her biscuits, which were browning. Sirus, in the armchair next to the head of the coffin in the living room, could hear their voices.

"He's quite a man, that one," Mrs. Johnson said somberly as she lifted the tray of biscuits from the oven. "Not a better man to work for in this world." She dropped the tray on the counter, where the water beneath it made a hissing sound.

"He's a good man, all right," Jason agreed.

"You better believe it," Mrs. Johnson continued. "Don't let a person come anywhere near me saying anything different."

"Yes, indeed."

"Did I ever tell you about how my Cora used to do her homework, right here at this table?" Mrs. Johnson continued. "Mr. Mac would come in, take a look at it for her — I mean, sometimes reading a whole report, cover to cover, like it was an important paper from the bank — and when he'd be done he'd say, 'Well, Cora, that's really fine,' or 'You ought to try and change how you end it. I got a little confused along the way.' Whatever he thought."

"Umm-hmm," Jason murmured, taking a bite of the hot biscuit.

"And those Genene girls, didn't he have one, then the next, then the next, till all three of them lived here at one time or another, every one of those girls coming up from the country to go to school. And they went, too, every one of them, and their parents decent hardworking people. But you know what I'm saying, about the expense and all. And the whole time, Mr. Mac not saying a word to anybody, except something about how he needs help down at the real estate office. I guess there might have been something they could have done, but who could for the life of them say what a country girl would know about all that work Mr. Mac is always doing. You know what it is I'm saying."

Jason nodded, swallowing and chewing almost simultaneously.

"And don't tell me anything about loving that child," she went on. "Oh, mercy, think I'd like to die myself than have to live to see the day something happen to that child, then die again to keep from living long enough to see Mr. Mac have to go through it." She turned on the water in the sink full force. "He's been like something right out of the grave himself, walking and breathing, but not much more. Oh, Lord, I thought I'd never see this day."

Jason looked at her, soap rising from beneath her hand swirling under the stream from the faucet. His large eyes clouded over. "It's a terrible thing," he agreed.

"Terrible ain't even the beginning of it." Mrs. Johnson turned to face him and the boys. "If I weren't afraid of blasphemy, I'd talk about pestilence and flood; that's how bad this thing strikes me. Must be near on to hell and damnation."

Earl's and Lucas's eyes met across the table, their mouths motionless as they contemplated Mrs. Johnson.

"But I ain't saying nothing about that subject in this house." The boys resumed their contented chewing. "Got to remember the good times, especially now you've done gone and brought her soul's house on home." She stared at Lucas and Earl. "You boys brought her in here okay, yes? You been gentle and careful like with a lamb?"

They bobbed their heads.

"Good. I wouldn't want nothing more to disturb that child on her way to glory, and praise the Lord, I know that's where she's bound."

"Praise the Lord," Jason responded, bowing his head briefly as if in prayer.

Mrs. Johnson's words seemed to have caught up to her, and her eyes filled with tears. "Oh, Lord, that was one sweet child," she said mournfully.

"That she was," said Jason.

Sirus now heard silence in the kitchen. He had been aware of Jason's being there and of what his presence represented: the things they needed to discuss. But as long as he heard the voices, that moment seemed distant. Now, in the silence, it was a presence standing beside him. This was the moment he had been dreading, what he wished he could avoid, to face yet again this stillness that was supposed to be his Mattie.

When Aileen left the house yesterday, fled, really, she had insisted that she would never be able to sleep, knowing that her baby would be coming home in a box. She could not bear to see it, she told him. And she warned him, pleaded with him, not to let them make Mattie look like someone else. "They're always doing that," she said tearfully. "Remember my father's mouth, how they filled it with cotton and his cheeks were all puffed out so that he looked like he was pouting and angry? Or they get the color all wrong. She's our child, a bright chestnut, a happy child," she kept saying. And Sirus had promised that he would be careful, that he would handle this detail, make sure it was done right. But how on earth could he do it, he wondered. Where would he find the strength to look in the coffin, much less talk with Jason about anything else that might need to be done?

He looked around the room. The sun was streaming through the window behind him; he felt it hot on his shoulders, spreading a warmth that his muscles yielded to in spite of himself. If he closed his eyes, with the feel of that sun, he could escape this room, he could once again be a small boy on his parents' tobacco farm, the sun reflecting on the tall grass that ringed the house. In that imaginary field, lit by this sun, he could keep his eyes closed, and what he sensed was not this coffin but something else, something more closely resembling a mysterious presence. He felt that if he were to turn and approach this inexplicable something, it would be with anticipation, a feeling tinged with yearning.

Drifting with the sun's warmth, he felt himself sink deeper into this scene. He became aware of an altered sense of time, a feeling of long hours, long days, no, long years, bringing him to this point. He kept imagining himself as the boy in that grass, looking to this future, and if he were to open his eyes, then or now, what he'd see would hold all of the years that had gone by. He could feel all of the tension held in his body over the past two days flow out of him. Gone were all the times he had held himself in check, all the movements toward or away from someone. All that was left was this thing, this something. As he drew nearer in his imagination, his heart swelled so that it nearly burst with anticipation.

Yes, that was what he was feeling, he thought giddily, a kind of rejoicing. Things were not as they seemed, he wanted to shout. Look, look, something wonderful has occurred, and he was the only one who knew or was allowed to see it. Privately, secretly, he alone was going to be given a glimpse, permitted only once in a lifetime, of something he couldn't name. And almost joyously, he opened his eyes and turned his head, and as he did, the living room slid into view. What was visible was not this magnificent presence, but the coffin, suspended. The vision faded, not all at once, but as a dream fades. His giddiness slipped away, and then his trembling hope, and the overwhelming joy he had expected to taste. One by one his senses returned him to himself, and what he saw and heard and felt was exactly what was here in this room — and no more.

He was alone. There were no sounds around him. He rose from his chair and lay his hand atop the coffin. She was gone. He ran his hand along the curved top of the molded lid. It was both smooth and cool. If he were to lift the cover, she would lie before him, lifeless. Her smile, her laughter, her smell of leaves and tart apples, her plumply muscled arms folded over her painfully angular legs would be shrouded, still. They would never move again, never explode from the center of the room. The cool, quiet body lying in this box would never again hurtle toward him, take his breath away. Now they were at an end. Now they were removed to a region of memory and shadow. Now he would never experience her again.

He heard Jason come into the room and felt his warm presence beside him as distinctly as a bell pealing in his ear.

"We have a few more things to discuss," Jason said quietly, resting his arm across his friend's shoulder.

"Yes, of course." Sirus's voice was close to breaking. He reached into his pocket for something, anything, and his hand came out empty. "I need my glasses, my pen," he mumbled. He backed away from Jason and the coffin, then turned, stumbling over his feet. He regained his balance, hurried across the front parlor, and disappeared up the stairs.

2

LONG BEFORE THIS DAY, before his successes, his marriage, before Durham and buildings and struggle, there was just
Sirus, a young boy, and his parents, Eubie and Mattie, living
together in the small town of Carr. It wasn't this future that
beckoned then, but just the moment, captured in a land defined
by tobacco, cotton, sun, and trees, where what was coming was
all motion and movement. Sirus's childhood was like all child-
hoods, even for colored boys, and no matter how brief, it was
a place out of time, set into itself, a vivid dream. The orange
sun that dropped behind the hill across from Sirus's house
eclipsed all other sunsets; the patterned light that fanned across
his floor in the morning was light itself. In this dream there was
no other place than Carr; there were no other people than his
own. The facts, of course, were different, as facts always are,
but it wasn't the facts that mattered. What mattered was not
the truth but the dream. To Sirus, in that very rural and very
small town, places like Durham and Raleigh were little more
than names, without faces or smells or memories attached. His
family was the world, and all of the world was his family.

He was seven when the outside world first shattered the present. Up until then, talk of places other than Carr, or of people other than his friends and relatives, was so much background noise, the rattle of a plow blade turning. On this day, however, something was different. There was a tenseness in his father's voice, an urgency, even a hint of fear. "We've got to get Harold and Louise out of town," his father whispered to his mother in the kitchen. "I'm to drive them into Durham tomorrow." Sirus overheard from the porch, and his imagination was set ablaze.

He knew that Durham was a place; now, suddenly, it was a place with a meaning for him. Why were Harold and Louise to be taken there? Why was his father driving them, and not their own father, Festus? How long would they be gone? Sirus cast his mind back but could not remember a time when anyone went lightly from Carr to another place. People said, "I'm going into town," or "I'm going over to So-and-So's house." They did not often say, "I'm going to Durham." Most often, when another place was mentioned, it was in the past, an appendage, explaining where it was that someone or their people came from.

"Where's Durham, Daddy?" Sirus asked at supper, just as they finished grace. His father's lean face tightened. He was not a man comfortable with lies.

"It's about a hundred miles from here," he answered, the smooth brown of his face separating into a stream of colors: yellow at his mouth and chin, dark brown at his forehead, a blackberry patch of red spreading between his eyes. "You take the long road out of town past the church."

"Why are you going there?" Sirus persisted.

The golden light from the setting sun streaming in through the windows and open door seemed to falter. Eubie looked at his wife, Mattie, across the table. In the second it took their

eyes to meet, there was time for a hundred questions and answers. Where to begin to tell their child about what had happened? When is it too soon to take innocence away?

"I'm taking Harold and Louise Porter there," Eubie said, "to
stay with their Aunt Matilda."

"Why? Why doesn't their daddy, Festus, take them?"

Eubie's milkweed-shaped ears quivered, and so did his shoulders. The weight of Sirus's questions was an unwelcome burden.
He had hoped, irrationally, that he would never have to have
this conversation with his son.

He examined Sirus carefully before he spoke, looking at the
two O's of his eyes, at the width and breadth of his shoulders
and arms, and at his small hands, always smaller in reality
than he imagined. He looked, too, at the trust spread across
his son's skin like fresh honey. Then he thought ahead, to how
his answer would change Sirus, would rebuild him from the
ground up. Eubie knew that Sirus would be damaged by the
truth, as he had been, as his wife had been, as everyone he knew
and loved had been. For an instant he thought to lie, to carve
a cave to shelter Sirus in — deeper than the fields around the
house, deeper than the dense web of people among whom
they lived, deeper than the grave toward which they all were
heading. His wife's eyes, though, said what they had been saying all along: he has to know; it's the truth; he must begin to
know.

"There was something here that happened, Sirus," he started,
and he could see the coiled braids on each side of his wife's head
bobbing as he spoke. "You're too young to know the full of it,
but you need to know some so that you can start to understand."

Sirus pushed the food on his plate into a circle.

"I'm going to tell you as much as I can, what I think you
should hear. But I don't want you asking a hundred questions,

you understand? You have to trust that your momma and I will tell you what we think is right for you to hear."

Sirus nodded.

"There are lots of different people in the world. You know that; your mother and I have told you. "

"Yes, Daddy." Sirus tried to remember who these people were, but all he could retrieve was a jumble.

"And you know one kind of these people are what they call white people, and they've got white or light-colored skin, instead of brown or black or red."

"You mean like me and Momma?" Sirus interrupted. "Are we white people?"

Eubie and Mattie exchanged tight smiles.

"No," Eubie answered. "You've got some of their blood in you — lots of folks have a little bit of everything all mixed together — but no, you and your momma aren't white. You're colored, same as I am."

Sirus took a piece of bread from the basket on the table and plucked out the moist center with his fingers.

"How can you tell the white people then? How do they look different?"

Eubie looked at the food in their bowls, at the smooth pine boards of the table. Feeding his son, growing things, planing the wood of the table, these were the things he understood and knew how to explain. "It's not so much how they look, though that's part of it," he said. "It's really who they are. Some of them may look no different from somebody you already know. But basically, up till now, all you've really known are the colored, plus some Indian. The only time you see the whites is when we go to the other side of town. Other than that, we all pretty much keep to ourselves."

Sirus squirmed in his seat. "So they've been around and I just didn't know it?"

"Well, I suppose," Eubie answered. "We never said, well, there, son, there's one. Your momma and I decided there was no need. And it's still no need, for us to be talking, or for you to be going around them." Eubie walked to the porch door from the table and looked at the vegetable garden in the front yard and, beyond that, to the large maple that partly hid the road. "The thing is, about white people — most of them, maybe not all, but probably most you'd ever meet around here — they don't much like the colored." Here Eubie's voice rose. "And for no good reason." He tried to lower it. "I can't tell you why; you just need to know that that's what's so. It's something for them to settle with the Lord; nothing you or any other coloreds've done to make it so." He turned and looked at his wife, her arms and face and the skin at her throat the color of flour, her eyes burning from the center of her face.

"Now I don't want you to ever hate," Eubie continued, walking back to the table, laying his hand on his wife's shoulder. "But you have to know this about the whites. It's not a good thing about them."

Sirus looked at his mother's fierce stare and at his father's studied calm. A small storm rumbled in his stomach. "Why don't they like the colored?" he asked. "Why they got to settle up with the Lord? Is the Lord angry with them?"

"Now, Sirus, I told you," Eubie said abruptly, striding back to his seat, "you can't be asking a hundred questions. I don't know why they feel like they do; I told you that. And about the Lord, it's not right for me to even say. It's just my opinion."

"But, Daddy, have they done something wrong?"

"Yes," his father said, exasperated. "Yes, they are sinning against the Lord. They are breaking His commandment, to love thy neighbor as thyself. But like I said, that's for the Lord to know and judge, not us. What we have to know is how to live different — and to be careful of them when we can."

Sirus tried to imagine what these white people who were disobeying the Lord were like, how they could have gotten to be so bold. "Are they like Teddy Franklin, that boy you said never minded anyone?"

"That's a good way of looking at it, Sirus," his mother said, resting her hand on his arm. "Think of them as bad children who don't mind, and how you have to steer clear because you never know what kind of trouble they might bring."

"But why don't they mind the Lord?" Sirus persisted.

"I wish I could tell you that, Sirus," his father answered, "but I can't. But the thing I'm trying to tell you, what I'm trying to say is that some of these white people got Harold and Louise's daddy. They hurt him, and they kept on hurting him and hurting him until he died."

Sirus suddenly felt the whole room shift, so that everything tilted — all the plates on the walls — the ones from his Grandmother Sarah's house, and the ones that his mother had painted — and the shelves that held their books and the clothes that hung on pegs on the walls. He was in the middle of a wild turning. He wanted to crawl under the table, grab hold of his father's legs, and never let go.

"Now, I don't want you to be afraid," Eubie said, lifting his chair and moving it closer to Sirus. "Your mother and I would never let that happen to you; that's why we steer clear of them whenever we can. And most of them feel the same way we do, happy to let things stay separate. You understand?"

"Yes, Daddy," Sirus answered.

"I mean that," he repeated.

"So why are Harold and Louise going?" Sirus asked. "Are the white people going to hurt them, too?"

Mattie grabbed Sirus's hand.

"Nobody's going to hurt any of our children," she said. "Not you, not Harold, not Louise. That's why your daddy's taking them to Durham. We've got people there who can look out for them until they catch the people who did this and take them away. Then Harold and Louise will come back home and be with their momma and sisters and brothers, just like always."

Sirus suddenly worried that, despite his mother's tight grip, he might slide off the chair, through a crack in the floor, and never be seen again. What, he thought, if his mother and father were wrong? What if there were white people right outside the door, right now? What if they had been there listening all this time to his daddy say they were bad? Or maybe they were hiding in the outhouse, down that long dark hole? Sirus could think of a dozen places where someone could get him, and his parents would never know. How could his parents protect him from someone who could hurt and kill Festus Porter? How could his mother and father keep him safe from someone who could just grab and kill Festus? And what about how they looked? How could they look like him and his mother, and still be something else, this white-people thing? Maybe there were white people hiding out with the colored who would hurt him when no one was looking — and then go back to pretending to be colored. Maybe that was what happened to Festus. He felt like crying but his fear was stronger.

"Is there anything else you want to ask?" Eubie said. To Sirus it sounded as if his voice were coming from across the room. His own thoughts were much closer, and he grabbed at one randomly as it flitted by.

"Are you sure Momma and I aren't one of these white people? Is there any way we can tell for sure?"

His mother laughed softly. "Oh, sweetheart," she said, "white and colored don't live all mixed up together, at least not here. You don't have to worry about that, we promise. Anything else?"

Sirus wanted the room to stop spinning. "Nothing, I guess,"

he said. Suddenly he clutched at his mother's arm. "But I want to go with Daddy when he goes into Durham. Please, can I go to Durham tomorrow, too?"

Both Mattie and Eubie were relieved that this conversation could end with something straightforward, a question they could say yes to. The trip would bring more good than harm; there was no real danger traveling in the daylight. The trip itself might be just the thing to take Sirus's mind off what they had told him. And it was true; Sirus seemed excited and consumed by nothing more than the coming journey, which made them all the more sure that they had done the right thing.

But Sirus was not so much busy forgetting what had happened to Festus as he was transforming it. He took what he had heard and what he could imagine about a new place, and mixed it all together. And what emerged was no longer a picture of an ordinary town to which the Porter children would be taken, or even the frightening image of whites hidden in the corners of his room. Instead, Sirus let Durham banish his fears; he buried them in the town of Durham, and the people of Durham, and all that the place came instantly to represent to his young mind.

In the span of a few hours, Sirus's world expanded to include not just the fields around his house, the woods behind them, the one road that ran through Carr, and the small church and schoolhouse, but these fearsome people, white people, and their unpredictable violence, and an unknown place that was far away, with important people who would shelter and protect his friends.

In his young mind Sirus saw these people as a very dressed-up group, in their Sunday best all the time. He also saw them, wildly, improbably, singing and marching from place to place. It is difficult to say precisely how he arrived at this, but the picture he saw clearly was of him and his father and Harold and Louise on his father's wagon, approaching a town filled with finely dressed people in finely polished shoes, people who came toward them waving and singing and marching. Each time he played the image in his mind, he embellished it. They swayed and danced, their feet moved in beautiful patterns, and they sang in the most thrilling way. He held that picture in his mind as they all set off early the next morning.

The long trip to Durham was hot and dusty. Sirus sat up front with his father; Harold and Louise sat in back. They ate the food his mother had fixed: biscuits and sausage sandwiches for breakfast, and chicken and whole tomatoes for lunch and dinner. By the time they reached Durham it was late at night, and all of them, but particularly Sirus, were tired and worn from the trip. Though he had stayed awake the entire distance, now, as they passed first one house and then another, sleep began rapidly descending. It was hard, between the lengthening shadows and his closing eyes, to distinguish this town from any of the others they had driven through. He sleepily tried to count houses, then the posts his father told him held wires that carried electricity, and he vainly tried to read the street names on the signs at every corner. But nothing could hold back sleep. He was asleep before they reached Harold and Louise's Aunt Matilda's house, and he slept until they were already on the road returning to Carr the next day. Until he returned to Durham for a second time, the images he held of the town were the ones he had originally envisioned, much more vivid than the real Durham he had scarcely seen.

Sirus's second visit to Durham came when his father decided to send him there to work one summer. He was thirteen and eager for anything beyond Carr. He had just begun to recover (if it could be said that he ever fully recovered) from his mother's death from pneumonia two years earlier, his body was in the middle of its most violent and unpredictable changes, and he was squarely in that moment when he first realized that simple existence is no longer enough.

He had no name for this feeling. He knew only that something was missing, that sitting by the stream and watching the water flow by, lying in the fields and gazing at the clouds, or running along the edge of the tobacco plants was now only half a piece. Something was missing. He found himself watching adults — his father at the table in the stripping barn, his aunt in her vegetable garden, his teacher at her blackboard — attentively, and with sudden bursts of envy. He felt the urge to be helpful extending long past the point when his chores were done. Each activity seemed to sharpen the feeling so keenly that he felt it as a constant goading.

At times this restlessness drove him to tears. There were powers and forces he was helpless against. Sickness was one; drought was another. White people, whom he now saw more clearly at the edges of his life, were a third. He would sometimes wake early in the morning and lie in bed, staring out the window, hoping to see in the trees and rising sun an intimation of his future. At other times he was awake at night, agitated, minutely examining every interest, every activity or accomplishment, with ruthless precision. His tallies were dismaying. He was not the strongest nor the fastest nor the best at anything. His father finished grading a row of tobacco leaves before he even found his place on the sorting bench. In the schoolyard someone else always excelled at the sport they were playing. Even at chores, Jason was always quicker, so that he would arrive at Sirus's house before Sirus was even close to finishing.

Yoked to his new dissatisfaction was an unquenchable curiosity, a fervent desire to know the secret to others' success. His father and teachers answered his interminable questions with patient good humor, but no one he pestered had any idea how important their answers were to Sirus.

In Durham that summer, working in his uncle's barbershop, Sirus found the pieces he needed. Here in the middle of Hay-Ti, the downtown section for the colored, the whole town gathered at one time or another at the barbershop. Men sat and waited on benches along the wall; others lay stretched out in chairs with sheets around their necks fastened to tissue collars. Women made infrequent but dramatic entrances, delivering the last word in an argument, dropping off packages to be carried somewhere, or giving instructions on some task needing to be completed. At the center of it all stood Sirus's Uncle Reggie, a tall, red-skinned man with an easy smile and a disarming manner who seemed to stand outside the gossip and intrigue, at the same time subtly moving every bit of it along.

Where his parents had tried to shield Sirus from the harsher details of life, Aunt Viola and Uncle Reggie delighted in dragging them forth in all their variety. From his uncle he heard, late one afternoon when there was only one customer left in the shop, what had actually happened to Festus Porter, beginning with how Festus had leaned against a tree outside the white folks' church on Sunday morning, his hair and eyes wild from a night of hunting and drinking, how he hadn't budged when two white men approached him and told him to git, how the man who hit Festus with a board was rumored to have bragged that Festus's head had split open "just like a watermelon those coons love to eat." There was nothing his Uncle Reggie would not repeat. He would strop the razor faster, pump the chair up a little higher, and a slow steady drawl would stream from his lips. There was no malice in these tellings. He was like a cat or dog relentlessly dragging home whatever carcass it found in the woods, simply because it was his nature.

From others Sirus heard additional stories, stories of progress and triumph, and exciting tales of colored men who fought on the white man's battleground and won. There were the stories of the soldiers, the union men, and most of all, because this was Durham, the stories of the entrepreneurs who were fighting and winning a different kind of battle. It was Durham where one of the largest businesses owned by the colored now stood — the North Carolina Federated, founded at the turn of the century — and it was Durham that spawned the men who built it. There was Dr. Anson, who was a distant cousin to Sirus, always described as a philosophical man, a doctor, and a fervent believer in the uplift of his race, and he lived in Durham still, on Durham's most prosperous street for the colored. And down the street from Dr. Anson was the second founder, Ed Menton, always with the largest cigar you could imagine in his hand, while just a few doors away lived Tito Shepard, the third founder of the Federated, a butter-and-egg man who owned a string of dairy shops, who was rumored to have gotten the initial loan for the Federated building by pulling yet another fast one on the white folks. That too was a subject Sirus caught up on quickly. Unlike in Carr, where there was hardly a reference to them, here, in his uncle's barbershop, people mixed in lots of talk about white folks.

"She don't even wipe her behind 'less I do it," said a woman who worked for a retired white lady, as she stood by the door waiting for her husband's shave to be finished.

"He always telling me which way to go, and I drives just the opposite and he never know," said a man who drove for two different white men on alternate days of the week.

"They kids be sweet, till they get six or seven," volunteered Sirus's aunt, who said she'd collected this tidbit from friends of hers who knew.

Sirus greedily absorbed it all, turning one tale, then another, over in his head as he walked the fragrant streets in the evening. Along with the smell of lilacs and honeysuckle, he took in a sense of prosperity. The houses on Fayetville Street were twice as large as any in Carr, and he never tired of strolling past them, noticing some new detail he hadn't seen before. Dr. Anson's was a rambling three story with porches on both the first and the second stories; Ed Menton's was newer, with bright green shutters and an enormous stone urn by the front steps that was always ablaze with flowers; and Tito Shephard's was distinguished by the two long Cadillacs he kept parked in front. Sometimes Sirus would wander down to the lodge building that sat at the end of the block, where the Caddies and Packards stood out front, like patient horses, Sirus thought, some low and sleek, others with the squared-off rump of a hound. Watching the prosperous men through the lighted windows of the lodge, Sirus would wave his arms in the air in front of him, gesturing in imitation of their conversations.

These were the "race men," people said, colored men whose progress and success were never reckoned as an isolated prosperity. Colored men might be killed in the night on a country road, the Klan might still be riding, hundreds of colored might live in shacks on the edge of town with no running water, and still there were these men and the town they helped build. The gleaming building of the Federated, as large as anything the white man might build, may have been founded by these men, but it grew and prospered from all of the dimes that were spent on its insurance policies, and as a result, all the colored people regarded the Federated as their own. Every folded silk handkerchief its owners wore, every carefully polished shoe that walked across a marble floor in a white man's building, every shining car driven by a colored man, belonged to them all. The individual triumphs were the triumphs of colored men everywhere, and the individual successes heralded all the triumphs to come.

Without even knowing the impulse that drove him, Sirus decided one day to go where they went, see what they saw. He arrived at his uncle's shop early that day. The street, though not exactly empty, was less bustling than it would be by midmorning. He said hello to Dr. Gerard, the druggist next door, who was sweeping the walk in front of his pharmacy, and to the two men he saw every morning on their way to the bus stop at the corner. Inside the shop he quickly swept up the wiry black hairs that had eluded his broom the night before, then wiped the counters with a cloth moistened with disinfectant. At the front of the shop, he wiped the lettered plate-glass window and looked at the outline of the buildings that lay beyond the railway yard.

It was the white downtown, a solid mass of buildings, sloped like a pyramid on each side away from the tallest building, which stood in the center. Atop it, the name CORT'S was printed in big white letters. It was a large department store. His people, Sirus knew, could come and go to the downtown area as workers, they could shop at Cort's as long as they waited until there were no white people who wanted to be waited on, but if they were hungry, there was only one lunch counter that would serve them, and they would have to take their meal outside to eat, since they weren't allowed to sit down. And they were never to be seen there at night. He had learned this much so far. But he also had learned this summer that exceptions were made. Though the white downtown was probably no more than five blocks away, the barrenness of the railway yard and the tracks that lay in between, together with the light reflected from the concrete and glass of the buildings, made the buildings look as distant and unapproachable as a mirage. On all other mornings Sirus looked at the buildings without feeling, as if he were staring at a rusty tractor abandoned at the edge of a field, but this morning he silently calculated the distance from where he stood to the tallest building.

Rubbing at a streak that seemed to have been made by someone leaning against the window with a greasy hand, Sirus concluded that he could walk the distance and be back before the shop opened. He looked around and thought about his other chores: he had changed the blue water and disinfectant in the jars that held the combs and scissors; the floor was swept and the counters wiped; the rack that held the magazines was ordered and alphabetized.

I really could be back before I was needed, he thought, and impulsively, without thinking any more about it, he decided yes, he would go.

He felt for the first time he could remember a surge of confidence in himself. He locked the shop behind him and double-checked the hour on the clock over Dr. Gerard's drugstore. If that store, Cort's, was open, he would go inside and look around. If not, he would just walk through the streets quickly, maybe look in the windows, and then return. The railway yard was quiet as he crossed the tracks.

Why, it hardly looks any different from Hay-Ti, he thought at first as he approached the streets and buildings. Then he saw those things which were different: the streets and sidewalks were paved, not just pounded dirt; the light that reflected from the buildings was a grayish blue; and there wasn't a single person on the streets. Where was everybody, Sirus wondered, and then he remembered what his Aunt Viola had told him, that morning for the whites never began as early as it did for the colored. The colored who worked here, as janitors and cooks and dishwashers, were already on their jobs, while the whites who would later shop and bank and stroll here were still at home, having breakfast.

It was then that Sirus thought about white people and not just about the buildings they owned. He had been so intent on seeing where they lived that he hadn't even thought he might come face to face with one. What should he do or say? Perhaps there were areas that were off limits to him. And with that thought, the image of Festus loomed large. What, after all, had Festus done but stand in the wrong place at the wrong time?

He was suddenly afraid. Part of him wanted to turn and flee. At the same time another feeling spread through him, just as raw and unmeditated, a surge of stubbornness and defiance. He bit his lip, jammed his hands into his pockets, and continued along the sidewalk toward Cort's.

He passed a colored man in an alleyway, collecting trash. As Sirus went by, the man touched his hand to his hat in greeting. Beyond him, Sirus glanced through a screened back door of a small luncheonette, where a cook and a dishwasher, also colored, were at work inside. Farther along the block was a long, windowless building. Sirus trailed his hand along the cool but rough concrete. When he reached the corner where the department store stood, a shadow from around the corner told him that someone was approaching. Without hesitating, Sirus stepped forward, directly into the path of the other person.

It was a white woman, the first white person he'd ever encountered alone. She was short and rotund, all squeezed tightly into a flowery pastel dress. There were ruffles at the collar and the sleeves, and atop her nearly pink face was a mass of white curls, tinged in blue, so thin that Sirus could see her scalp. He considered dropping his eyes, but he held them steady. He had never seen blue eyes before.

To his surprise the woman's small dry lips broke into a grin. "Morning, son," she drawled in a voice that Sirus recognized as unmistakably foreign, dipping in places that jarred his ear, and ending in a whine he found almost grating.

"Morning, ma'am," he returned softly, because he could not think of anything else to say. The little pastel lady smiled again and continued on her way.

He was left adrift in the woman's wake: a sweet scent of lily-of-the-valley mixed with lemons, and an afterimage of flesh as pink and white as a rabbit's. He was befuddled. In the midst of her foreignness she seemed wholly familiar, common. He could imagine her hands on bread, on her grandchildren's heads. From blankness to terror to a thing he had been steeled against on the edge of flight, these white people — or at least this first representative — had melted like so much cotton candy in his mouth. All he was left with was a taste evaporating on his tongue. He wondered if he was too young. Was he unable to see what others could see? Had he missed something crucial?

He decided that the remedy was more white people. So he kept walking, farther into their streets, heading like a small bear in search of more berries or honey. He was determined to find more of them, to see for himself what it was they so uniquely possessed.

But all he found were more pale people, some smiling, some not, others absorbed in the details of their lives so that they hardly saw him. He was dumbfounded by their ordinariness, and by their similarity to people he had known all his life. Even the boy who fell in step with him as he hurried back toward Hay-Ti could have been any light-skinned boy he'd known from school.

"Got me an agate," the boy said, his wide, flat face slightly sunken. He pulled out a marble the color of sapphire and coal, rubbed it on the end of his T-shirt, and held it out to Sirus.

"Pretty nice," Sirus said, reluctant to venture more than a few words at a time.

"Got any marbles you want to trade?" the boy asked.

"Not on me," Sirus said. "I left them all at home."

"Where you live at?" the boy asked, jumping in front of Sirus to show off the way he could make his muscles move.

"In Carr, but I'm staying here with my aunt and uncle for the summer."

"Oh, yeah, where they live?" the boy asked, looking back

down at his marble. He squinted to inspect the colors more closely; and Sirus squinted at him. There was something about this boy that made him uneasy. Then he thought, well, this must be rare, this talking across the races. He decided it was probably important not to be unkind or rude.

"Over on Ferrenway Street," he answered, worried that he might be late getting back after all.

The boy hacked and spit.

"Ooh, shit," he said, screwing up his face as if something vile had exploded. "How can they stand to live so close to niggers?"

The boy seemed momentarily lost in his reverie of niggers known and smelled, and as Sirus looked at him, his face receded. At the same time, Sirus felt a squeezing sensation at the center of his chest. He had known hurt before, had known the loss of his mother like a constant ache or the blows of a friend falling in anger, but nothing he could remember prepared him for this type of pain. Under its weight, he felt his self shatter, and he was suddenly outside his own body, looking at himself with this boy's eyes. Where, he thought, had this boy, someone so slight and unexpected, gained such an awful power?

"What they live so near the niggers for?" the boy persisted.

"What?" Sirus asked.

"I said," the boy continued, talking slowly as if he thought Sirus might have difficulty following his words, "why your people live so close to them?"

He spat out the last word like so much tobacco juice, stretching it to nearly three syllables. And as the word sprang at him, Sirus suddenly understood, completely, not just this boy, but the whole day, as if a wet mist were being burned off the fields by the sun.

"I gotta go," Sirus said, throwing up his hand behind him. He ran woodenly down the streets, his feet moving of their own accord. He didn't slow as he approached the tracks, nor did he look up the tracks as he crossed them. He ran all the way until he was back in Hay-Ti. He reached his uncle's shop and threw open the door. Cool air from inside rose up to meet him. It would be at least another ten minutes before anyone would arrive. He pressed himself against the wall inside the door, wishing that he could sink into it and that the cool wallboard would tear away all of this flesh that no longer felt like his own. He traveled in his mind as he pressed, moving farther and farther away from anything that would tie him to the present. When he reached his destination, he took a deep breath, and, mercifully, the pressure and the pain began to recede.

3

JASON WAS GENTLE, and the conversation he had with Sirus, standing beside Mattie's coffin, was blessedly short. Sirus looked at Mattie without seeing her; thankfully, there were no major changes to be made. At least in this Aileen might find some relief. As soon as Jason left, Sirus hurriedly left, too. He drove across town, passing through the streets of Durham, which was essentially unchanged from the town he had known as a boy. There were more houses, more paved streets, more sidewalks, and the boundaries of the town had pushed out to claim more of the flat land that lay around it, but in its character and structure, the town was much the same. It was still tight-knit and insular, a solidly Southern town that prided itself on its purported modernity but was decidedly old-fashioned no matter how often or how far its citizens traveled.

Sirus's Durham remained the segregated town he had known as a boy. It was roughly four square miles, still cut off from the white section of town by the Southern Pacific railroad tracks and loading yard. As his parents had done for him, Sirus had shielded his child. Mattie never went to the white downtown,

never went to the white theater, where she would have had
to go through a side door and sit in a separate balcony, never
traveled on a bus, where she would have been forced to sit in
the back. Mattie's world, even as the town had grown, was a
self-contained one, with its own schools, banks, grocery stores,
drugstores, churches, lodge houses, and funeral homes. Fueled
by the segregation that defined all of the South, and the particular prosperity of the tobacco factories and lumber mills peculiar
to this region, their community boasted doctors, lawyers, den-
tists, bankers, pharmacists, day workers, nurses, cooks, teachers, porters, mill workers, builders, janitors, bartenders, barbers, gamblers, and members of a dozen other trades and
professions. These were the only people Mattie knew. For the
men, the most highly respected were still the business owners,
followed by the doctors and ministers; for the women, they
were the teachers, civic leaders, and nurses. The currency of
these individuals was the economic, physical, mental, and spiri-
tual health of the community, and they were viewed as inextri-
cably linked, a four-sided entity as concrete and palpable as the
borders of the town.

It was possible, Sirus thought, as he drove through the town,
to trace Mattie's whole life along these streets. Each home he
passed held a memory: of Mattie doing her homework in somebody's kitchen, two heads bent over the table, the room hot and
humid from cooking; of children's voices crossing the twilight
while he and Aileen sat on a neighbor's front porch, iced tea
cooling their hands; of a narrow hallway where Mattie's face
emerged from a room hidden in the back. The people Mattie
grew up with were the same people Sirus had grown up with,
or were related to them, from Carr or other towns just like
it. Mattie's whole world, like his own, flowed in a unbroken
stream, passed from relative to relative, moving from a common
past toward a common future. Until two days ago, this future

had protected her, held her up and away from whatever danger might intrude. But despite all his care, she'd been torn from him. The dream of safety was gone.

Sirus drove past the bank he had founded, where he was now president, then past the Federated, where he was an officer and member of the board of directors. The bulwark Sirus had created was considerable. He was a successful and powerful man. People not only envied but admired him, both for his material success and for the quirks of his personality that combined to effect those successes. People were intimidated by his bearing and reserve, but they appreciated his bawdy wit. They knew, too, that he could be playful or serious as he chose, and that he shamelessly used his light skin and his way with women to whatever advantage he could. When Sirus traveled away from Durham, when it suited him, he passed for white, and this bravado delighted his friends and enemies alike. He even enlisted for a short time as a white in the navy, until the trouble with his knees emerged, which kept him out of the war. And there was not a woman in town who did not go out of her way to find a private way to please Sirus.

Along with zeal and a propensity for hard work, which was shared by many of his colleagues, Sirus possessed some singular habits and traits: a certain passion and style, coupled with what could best be described as an intuitive method of processing information and events. His neighbors defined it by saying, "He's got a way," or, "That man sure can see," as if it were a particular divination they were responding to. But it was more than a habit of seeing that set Sirus apart; it was a belief in his own vision.

When he first settled in Durham after college he hadn't known how he would make his mark. He began by working at the Federated. Like so many young men, he was hired as a premium collector, making rounds to collect the dimes the laborers and day workers paid each week on their policies, ever alert for an opportunity to make a niche for himself. And when it came, not long after he began, he was on his way.

"Ought to have someplace to put this money other than just government bonds," he said one day at a meeting, referring to the insurance premiums that were held for investment. This made Ed Menton laugh, a soft good-natured laugh, horsey, showing all his teeth. Sirus saw in front of him what was coming as if someone had rolled a movie screen into the room. "We could buy a little land, put some houses on it," he said. After some discussion, Ed Menton agreed and told Sirus to take care of it, which he did. When the time came, in fact, and he found the land he liked, he took some of his own money and bought a small piece for himself. His daydreams had come to life.

Somehow, whatever he did, it turned to money. The land he chose for the Federated to invest in happened to be just where a new lumber mill was to be built, so it was sold at a quick and handsome profit. After that he built two shacks on the edge of town, encouraged Pete Paterson to put his barbecue pit by one and put a juke box in the other, and on Friday and Saturday nights those two shacks generated more than enough money for Sirus to buy two more pieces of land.

He went on buying land, sometimes losing but more often winning, at the same time steadily moving up at the Federated. He felt his ancestors stirring inside him. When he argued for something or navigated a risk others were wary of, the visions his ancestors showed him steadied him. He worked and prospered and saved until he had enough for the next step, which was building houses. He loved the smell and touch of the building materials, especially the wood. His parents' house had been a crazy patchwork of different woods in each room — cedar and oak and birch, which had a special green smell. As a boy,

Sirus used to oil the wood throughout the house with a paste of turpentine and beeswax, leaving each room with a soft glow. He knew that even the nails had their own smell, a coppery, acrid scent when newly pounded and, when old, the soft smell of talc.

The thick fragrance of jasmine and roses suddenly brought Sirus back to the present. Late bloomers of each lined his mother-in-law's driveway. Sirus parked his car there. Of what use were his successes now? He looked at Aileen's car parked out front, and, for the first time since Mattie's death, allowed himself to think about Aileen. They had both been knocked down, with nothing to hold them upright, and what comfort could they offer each other? When she fled to her mother's house last night, he had come to see her, but she could only lie in bed and cry, her back to him, a small quilt pulled over her head.

The first time he had ever seen Aileen, she was standing on the porch of this house. Although she was half in shadow, he could see that she was beautiful. As she stood there, she dropped her hand into her thick auburn hair, like a bird diving into its nest, and wound her hair around her hand once, twice, a third time, a gesture that seemed to entangle him, too, as he watched her, transfixed. In that time there was no halting, no hesitation. Their courtship, for both of them, began the second time he saw her. Making sure to put himself in her vicinity, he managed to catch her on the way to church on Sunday morning. He touched the brim of his cap; she looked his way and smiled and nodded in the briefest of ways. After that they spoke each time he passed, politely, formally, until at last he was officially introduced by his Uncle Reggie at a lodge dance. It was then respectable for him to stop whenever he walked by, and he did, to exchange a few words. "Nice day; going to be a hot one." "That evening rain was certainly cool." One day she said she'd just made some lemonade, and she invited him in for a glass with her and her mother. Once her mother seemed to approve, he was asked over for supper and told he could stop by in the evenings if he liked.

Up close, she was even more lovely than he'd first imagined. Her eyes were large and open, light brown, with flecks of green. When he looked into them it was as if she was, for the moment, translucent. Below, her cheekbones jutted out prominently, protectively. Their fragility always made him feel tender toward her, as if she were revealing some intimate aspect of herself through her skull. When he remarked on them, she said it was the Cherokee and Tuscarora in her, and showed him an old tintype of her grandmother, who was half of each.

Their evenings on the porch hardly seemed to have begun before he asked her to marry him. She was sitting next to him on the swing, her skin the color of a tree, her limbs as sinewy as a branch, her command of the space she occupied total and complete. He had marveled to himself: What must it be like to be so firmly staked to the earth, to stand or sit upon it so that the whole core of the earth boils upward in your veins and erupts, spraying through your hair like leaves? In her firmness, he thought, was shelter.

There was no shelter in her now. Last night, at her mother's house, it was as if she had come untethered, uprooted. Nothing was left staked to the ground through which they might reach each other. He watched her cry, embarrassed and angry that his own tears wouldn't come.

Now, as he walked up to her mother's house, he simultaneously cursed Aileen's decision to come here and was glad of it — cursed because there was no hope of their talking while her mother hovered about, and glad because this relieved them of the necessity to try.

"Sirus," Aileen's mother called from the front doorway, holding out both of her hands to him. She was a smaller version of

Aileen, the same facial structure and slim body, but paler, more wiry.

"Gertrude, good morning," Sirus said, wondering if Aileen was up or still in bed.

"Aileen's in my room. We were just having coffee," Gertrude responded as if in answer to his unspoken question. "She slept poorly last night."

It sounded to Sirus as if she thought him somehow responsible for this. "That's not good," he said. "She needs to get some rest."

Gertrude stepped through the door to give him room, sweeping her arm in front of him in an exaggerated fashion. As he stepped inside, she looked sideways at him, cocking her head. "I'll make you some coffee and bring it to my room," she said. "You go on back."

Aileen was sitting up in bed when he came into the room. Across her lap lay the same small quilt from last night, but the bed was fully made, with pink-and-white-flowered sheets and a white cotton spread, all of which she had pulled tightly around her. Her face shone with powder, and her thick hair was limp but neatly combed. So she had been out of the bed after all, Sirus thought. She was wearing one of the nightgowns he'd brought over last night. He waited until she saw him before he stumbled toward her in a thick, hurtling motion.

"Aileen, honey," he said, reaching for her hands as he settled himself on the bed beside her, careful not to disturb the covers with his weight.

She looked into his eyes and then away. He could see that her eyes were red and swollen, the skin of her face sallow. Her hands rested in his as if touching him was obsolete. He wanted to put his arms around her but didn't. For the moment they sat where they were, with nothing but the awkward silence holding them together.

"How did you sleep? Any better?" he asked, even though he knew the answer.

"About the same," she answered.

"No more nightmares?"

She shrugged her shoulders. "I don't think I dreamed at all. I slept as if I were dead."

Sirus felt he was being accused of something. Dead like our daughter? Dead as I wish you were instead? Dead like me?

"Aileen, don't," he said, rubbing his hand up her arm. Then he remembered how often she'd told him she didn't like him to do this. Where could they possibly go in this conversation? He began again.

"The Reverend Frankel is the one who's going to do the service. I've arranged for us to meet with him later this afternoon."

"Frankel? Why not the Reverend Martin?"

Sirus shook his head. "I don't know. I guess because he's phasing out. He hasn't done any services for a while now."

"But that man hardly knew Mattie. The Reverend Martin knew Mattie all her life." Aileen nearly wailed the last phrase.

"I know, I know," Sirus said, "but we can't force him. I asked him about it, and he just said he was sure the Reverend Frankel would do a fine job."

Aileen pulled her hands away. "Well, he'd better not give one of those fire-and-brimstone things."

Her eyes flashed angrily, as they used to, even when she was excited or happy.

"I'm sure he won't," Sirus continued. "We'll talk to him and explain the kind of service we want."

"No, Sirus," she said, "I can't." She twisted her fingers. "You talk to him, you do it, please. I couldn't stand it." Her voice thickened. "I don't know how I'm going to get through the day. I can't talk about it. I just can't."

"Of course," Sirus said, pulling back on the bed. He rubbed a thumb over the veins on the back of his hand. He had hoped that over this, the talk with the Reverend Frankel, they could begin the process of talking and facing this thing together.

"I mean, if you want me to," he continued, "but I thought, well, I thought it would do us good to do it together."

"Good?" Aileen said, squeezing up her face. She looked as if she'd been slapped. "Sometimes you are such a fool, Sirus."

Sirus got up and strode toward the window.

"I'm sorry, I didn't mean that," she said. "But really, you sound like my father: 'Oh, come on, Aileen, a little air, it'll do you good.' I'm sorry, Sirus," she said softly, "but I don't think anything's ever going to do me any good again."

Sirus turned and looked across the room. Her eyes were large and wet with tears. For a second he thought he could see Mattie peering from them. She had looked so much like Aileen.

"I'd love to have you with me," he said finally, "but if you prefer I handle it alone, of course I will."

Gertrude came in at that moment. No footsteps had preceded her. Sirus couldn't help wondering if she had tiptoed down the hallway and been listening at the door all this time. He started to check to see if the coffee she handed him was still steaming, but changed his mind. He took it from her without looking and blew on it absentmindedly.

"I'm going to have to leave soon," he said, aware that neither Gertrude nor Aileen was paying attention to him. Aileen was now crying in earnest, silently, and Gertrude was staring at her. She seemed to be inspecting her for any damage Sirus might have inflicted. "You know, the preacher, stopping by the florist, plus the chairs were delivered, and Mrs. Johnson and I will have to arrange them."

"Umm-hmm," Gertrude said, answering for both herself and Aileen.

"But I'll drop by here with the car to bring both of you over for the wake. What time shall I come?"

"Five is fine," Aileen answered. She stared at his face, taking in by turn his forehead, his eyes, his nose. Was she seeing Mattie's features in his as well?

"I'll be back then at five," he told her. Aileen didn't answer, and Gertrude began walking toward the door. He could still envision Aileen's eyes, searching his face for Mattie's, as he got into his car.

A few blocks away, the Reverend Leroy Washington Frankel was en route from his house to Ophelia Macon's. Ophelia was the choir mistress, and her daughter, Clorissa, the lead soprano. The three of them were to plan the songs for Mattie's service. Expecting refreshments, if not a full meal, the reverend had volunteered them the convenience of his coming to their home. As he made his way down the street, it was apparent that he could be called what was known as a spit-and-polish man. He alternated his black cordovan lace-ups with his charcoal wing-tips to give each pair a day to dry and breathe; he asked whichever lady of the church was kind enough to launder his shirts that week not to starch just the cuffs and the collars but the button plackets and the tails, too; and every Tuesday, Thursday, Saturday, and Sunday after his evening bath he carefully massaged a mixture of cocoa butter and Vaseline into his crusty heels, elbows, and knees. Walking toward the Macon home in his gray cotton preacher's suit without his preacher's collar, which he considered a trifle old-fashioned and wore only on Sundays and for funerals and the like, he unconsciously rubbed at intervals separated by four paces the top button of his suit jacket with the fleshy pad of his right thumb.

He was expected by Mrs. Macon and her lovely daughter at exactly two o' clock, which, by his watch, was only two minutes away. He felt a tasty anticipation. Not for Mrs. Macon, whom he considered vain and silly, but for her daughter, who had the smoothest brown skin he had ever seen, flawless teeth, and large liquid eyes, all adorning a spirit he felt was as sensual and determined as his own. Although he believed Clorissa both noticed and was flattered by his attention, he had thus far made his intentions clear to no one. He was only "of the town," as some of the more affected residents liked to say, the past two years, and as a junior minister was still an apprentice. Within a year, however, he expected the congregation to vote on whether he was to be permanently appointed to the post, at which time he would leave his current quarters in three corner rooms at the Weavers' house and move to the small second parish home — the elder Reverend Martin and his family occupied the first — two doors from the church. He felt reasonably confident that it would be only a matter of months that he would occupy those new quarters alone. The lovely Clorissa, he was sure, would soon join him there as his wife.

It was Mrs. Macon who saw him first from her seat on the porch. She sat to the left of her front door, in a yellow-and-green-upholstered gliding chair, apparently having changed neither her pose nor her dress since her visit with Mrs. Baldridge. A glass of iced tea was on a small brass and glass table in front of her (the table was from a catalogue, ordered from New York). Her hands, before they flew up in a florid wave to the reverend, rested like two lazy kittens in her lap, and her head was still perched, angled to the right rather than the left, above her ample chest. Without Mrs. Baldridge as a point of comparison she looked less imitative and more authoritatively content. This was, after all, the porch of her own home, shared with her living husband and a daughter quite a bit older and prettier than Lily. And though it was not located on Fayetville, it was, after all, on Lawson and near the college, a favorably regarded spot.

"Yoo-hoo, Reverend Frankel, yoo-hoo," she called out shrilly. As she did so the clergyman imperceptibly slowed his pace. Her greeting, intended to seem gay and high-spirited and to coincide with his turning into her walk, fell short of its mark and instead filled the space between them with evidence of her overeagerness and lack of precise social grace.

"Mrs. Macon," he boomed as he took possession of the porch, bowing his head deeply in her direction.

"Reverend Frankel," she repeated, as if she were announcing the name of a hymnal selection.

"A lovely day," he allowed.

"Yes, indeed," she began animatedly, since she truly loved to discuss the weather, particularly during this changeable time of the year. But he cut her off.

"'Tis a pity it comes with such a heavy burden laid upon our hearts."

"Yes, how true," she said, feeling the vaguest twinge of embarrassment over her initial jolly humor.

The reverend, glad to leave the swing free for Clorissa, took the seat Mrs. Macon proffered across from hers. He leaned his broad back against the chair and glided it gently to and fro, suffused with pleasure as he awaited both his glass of tea and the appearance of Clorissa. Though only eighteen, Clorissa was already, he believed, possessed of the woman she was bound to be. She was mature in her bearing, confident of her looks without being vain, and not afraid to express her abundant curiosity in the world. These were qualities he liked, qualities he thought would make her an agreeable wife. But they were not the ones that made him feel so certain of his claim toward her. Already thirty-one, he was neither especially handsome nor young. Even in his youth, the best that could be said of him was that he was sturdy, with something of a chunky build, and always fastidiously well groomed.

No, what he expected to win Clorissa with was what he

called his sphere of influence. He had given this considerable thought, not merely with respect to Clorissa, but as a factor in his becoming a minister. He was not a gambling man, he preferred sure steady things to long shots, and to him, born in a small town of hardworking but not particularly distinguished or ambitious parents, he perceived his route to a comfortable station in life to be through the church. He saw quickly that even in the smallest and poorest Negro communities, the minister was always well fed and cared for, had a house or a comfortable room, wore clothes that were cleaned and pressed, and was welcomed at anyone's table with honor. While in divinity school he had carefully followed the tales coming from those towns which showed prosperity, and Durham, dubbed the home of the Negro middle class, was a mecca. It had taken him nearly ten years to reach the point of his current post at the High Rock Baptist Church, but he was sure that, with further persistence and luck, and the fortunate consummation of some business matters he'd undertaken, all he desired would be his.

Clorissa, emerging from the house with her mother, carried a small silver tray holding three fresh glasses of tea. The glasses were tall and wide mouthed, with a border of gold around the edge. Stenciled on each were the initials C.M.D., with the M in the middle like a spire. A sprig of mint bloomed from each glass like a tiny tree, and as soon as Clorissa sat she took the sprig from her glass and twirled it between her fingers like a parasol. She liked to imagine herself in special places and scenes, and this moment was one of them. She had insisted that they use the monogrammed glasses, and she had pulled the silver tray from its place in the back of the china cabinet before her mother had time to object. She noticed as she sat in the swing that her green-and-white floral print dress fanned out gracefully on each side of her, and that the reverend held his glass with only three of his fingers, the other two acting solely as a counterweight.

At first glance, a stranger would have found Clorissa much less prepossessing than the reverend's assessment. Her figure, pertly drawn in by a thin belt covered in the same fabric as her dress, was indeed small and appealingly girlish, though the fullness of the dress accentuated her hips, which went beyond what would have been, strictly speaking, aesthetically pleasing. Her mouth, too, though a crushed berry color and nicely plump, could have been improved had it been wider. When she smiled there was hint of a shadow, a narrow space between her two front incisors, which marred in barely the slightest way her otherwise flawless teeth. Still, she did indeed have the smoothest brown skin, as unblemished as the surface of a fresh pecan. And her eyes, the color of dark walnuts, shone and sparkled like sugar. She was amused as she watched the reverend pretending to watch her mother as she, in turn, pretended not to notice he was looking at her. She shook her hair, which she was quite proud of, as she saw him looking her way again, so that it bounced and caught the sun, she hoped, alluringly.

"Don't you think 'Nearer My God to Thee' will be perfect?" Mrs. Macon was saying, having thumbed her way, or rather pinkied, as that was the finger she kept moistened to turn the pages of her hymnal, to the end of the book.

"Umm-hmm, Momma, that's so beautiful," Clorissa murmured, leaning her head in her mother's direction as her eyes darted toward the reverend.

"And you could sing the lead," Mrs. Macon continued. "Oh, nearer, nearer my God to Thee," she trilled in the high voice she felt approximated Clorissa's.

"Nearer my God to Thee," Clorissa added in her own lovely voice, which was actually more a contralto than the soprano her mother affected.

When they were done they both looked at the reverend as two children might stare at their father in the hope that he had penny candy in his pocket.

"Will it complement your sermon?" ventured Mrs. Macon, who was pleased to see the satisfied look on the reverend's face.

"Yes, I believe it will," he answered.

He sat back smugly and silently in his chair, imagining Clorissa standing before the congregation in her crimson and white choir robe, looking for all the world like a vibrant cardinal serenading from a tree. He already felt a sort of family pride. Mrs. Macon and her daughter exchanged glances.

"What will be . . ." began Clorissa.

"Have you decided on . . ." chimed in Mrs. Macon.

"Your theme?" each concluded, laughing. The reverend laughed, too, amused by what he saw as a charming synchrony of mother and daughter. In fact, even in their laughter, a series of overlapping muffled hiccoughs, there was a surprising similarity. He wondered, with some discomfort, how he could not have noticed it before.

"Well, yes, ladies, I have. It is to be on the theme of the Prodigal Son. But I intend to call it 'The Prodigal Daughter.'"

Both ladies were puzzled, but neither wanted to admit it. Mrs. Macon nodded and intoned "Mm-hmm." Clorissa began nibbling at the leaves of her mint.

"You know in the parable how happy the father is when his son returns?" the reverend prompted. The two ladies indicated yes, they certainly remembered. "Well," he continued, "in my sermon I shall liken Mattie to the son, but she has now returned to her Heavenly Father to do His heavenly business. Her visit here with her earthly father was that of a prodigal, far, as we all are here in this sinful life, from the Lord's business."

Neither Mrs. Macon nor her daughter replied until the silence began to feel awkward. Mrs. Macon then said she was sure his words would bring comfort to the family. Inwardly, she felt a chill, as though the ice from her drink had somehow lodged in her throat.

"That's very clever," Clorissa concluded, looking at the small gold and garnet ring the reverend wore on the last finger of his left hand. As she stared, he stroked the underside of the ring with his thumb, seeming to try to turn it, though the fit was too snug to allow any movement. "I purchased it in New York," he said, acknowledging her stare. As he began a tale of his last trip to New York, Mrs. Macon excused herself from the porch.

"Don't let the reverend forget his meeting with Sirus," she called from inside the house. Her voice seemed humorless and dry, with none of the liveliness and girlishness that had so animated it upon his arrival.

As Sirus drove toward the High Rock Baptist Church, he allowed himself to wish, as Aileen had wished, that it was the Reverend Martin he was meeting instead of the Reverend Frankel. He wanted the comfort the Reverend Martin's familiarity might bring. After all, it was the Reverend Martin who had baptized Sirus here in Durham the summer when he was thirteen; the Reverend Martin who had married him and Aileen; who had baptized Mattie just two years before. Sirus understood that his glaucoma and gouty arthritis and heart trouble were forcing him to phase out, but if he had to have this conversation about Mattie's funeral with anyone, he could imagine having it only with the Reverend Martin, not with the Reverend Frankel.

In fact, he really didn't know Frankel at all. He knew others were watching him for his suitability to take over the Reverend Martin's job, but he left that kind of surveying and assessing to the other parishioners. To the extent that he paid him any mind, he did think the Reverend Frankel somewhat pompous, and it was clear that he was out to get somewhere, but Sirus knew he'd be a hypocrite to begrudge him that. Of course there was that business deal with Dr. Gant with which he disagreed, but that wasn't what disturbed him either. There was something else that he couldn't put his finger on, something that was unsettling about the man. Maybe it was just that he was being forced into an intimacy with him that he didn't feel. Or maybe it was his feeling that, whatever a man did should be from a natural feel for the thing, as a prizefighter has a natural affinity for his fists and the ring. To his mind this was not the case with the Reverend Frankel. When he spoke of God, at least outside the pulpit, he always gave Sirus the impression he had some other conversation in mind that he would prefer to be having. Similarly, when he ate, it was as if it were his last meal, hungrily, but at the same time with restraint, which gave his eating a whiff of the hoarder. And when he sat in the sun, it was with that same greedy attitude, as though his body had a special need for the sun, like a hothouse tomato.

Still, Sirus wanted to support the Reverend Martin in his choice. "You have to give a man a chance to prove himself, the way God does," the Reverend Martin always said. He had first said that to Sirus over twelve years ago, on the day of his wedding. He'd pulled the young man aside when he arrived at this very same church and spoke softly but seriously. "Marriage is one of man's proving grounds for God," he told him, holding on to his arm. "But it's more, much more." He brought his face close and whispered, "It's a hint of God's love, that's what. The love you and Aileen will find in each other, the love you'll have for your children; it's just a taste of what God has in store."

The reverend had then released his arm, and Sirus had repeated the words to himself as he stood with Jason in the back room of the church, waiting for the ceremony to begin.

Jason had peeked out into the main part of the church. "There's a full house," he declared. "Nervous?"

"No, not really," Sirus answered.

"You look as cool as, what do they say, a cucumber?" Jason said. "Not me." He wiped his brow with a sky-blue handkerchief.

"Do I look cool?" Sirus asked. "That's funny; it's not how I feel."

"It's the big day, all right," Jason said.

Sirus stared at the closed door that led to the church. "It is, Jason, that's the truth there."

Jason walked back and forth across the small room. "Aileen is a beautiful woman," he said.

"She is," Sirus answered. "Absolutely beautiful."

Jason broke into a large grin. "Yes siree, my man."

Sirus looked at Jason. "But you know, Jason," he said, stepping toward him, "that's not why I'm marrying her."

"Of course not, Sirus," Jason said. He took a small step back. "Man's got to look for something beneath the skin."

"I know, I know," Sirus said, "but it's not just because she's sweet or agreeable, either."

"Well, no, of course not. Besides, who said agreeable is always a good thing?"

"Want to know why I'm marrying her?" Sirus interrupted.

"Sure," Jason said, "if you want to say."

"I do, I want to say," Sirus declared. He looked at Jason fondly. "You know you're my best friend. Have I ever told you that?" Jason shook his head and darted his eyes toward the communion chalice on the shelf behind Sirus. "Well, you are. And I should have told you before now if I didn't. So now you know."

Jason looked directly at Sirus. "I consider it an honor."

"I know you do," Sirus said, "and that's why it's also an honor for me."

The two men stood face to face, the embarrassment thick between them. Sirus felt it, too, as keenly, if not more, than

Jason. But something drove him past that feeling, made him want to hold and extend the moment.

"See, Jason," he said, grabbing at his friend's hands, "see how hard it is for us to say this? And it's such a little thing." He looked into Jason's face as if there were a hundred faces there. "Look at you," he continued; "you're dying to turn and look at the door. You're begging for the service to start, for someone to tap on the door and say, ready. And so am I," he concluded.

Sirus dropped Jason's hands and walked across the small room and looked out the window that opened onto a narrow courtyard. "Why should we know each other fifteen years, and that's what's so?"

Jason stood on the same spot, looking at Sirus's broad back. "Well," he began, "sometimes you don't need to say a thing, Sirus. Sometimes you just know it."

Sirus spun around and nearly shouted, "But didn't that feel good to hear me say it? Didn't it?"

Jason burst into laughter.

"Of course it did, my man, of course."

Sirus clapped his hands, and they each stepped forward and threw their arms around the other, slapping and banging at each other's backs like two large bears. They separated and Sirus laughed. "Okay," he said, "now we've said it."

Jason nodded.

"But see," Sirus said, "that's what I was about to say about my marriage."

Jason waited for him to go on.

"See, I want that, on a regular basis, what we just had, somebody saying something. And somebody listening. Have you ever had that, regularly?"

Jason looked puzzled. "I'm not sure I know what you mean."

Sirus lifted his arms and held them out at his sides. "What I mean is this. When I was little, I could be close to anything, a dog, the tree that grew out in the yard. I followed my dad around when he'd be sitting up on his tractor, with those big wide wheels, and I thought he was a god who'd just landed on earth. I thought my mother was a queen; the clothes she wore were like robes. And you, I used to watch you and think, oh, there's the earth and the stars. I mean it, it was just like that. And somehow, little by little, it changed. It got so when somebody was near I couldn't quite know what it was I was feeling. Or I'd know and then I'd forget, until they were gone, and then sometime later, I couldn't remember at all, until maybe the next day or the next week. And then I'd look up, and whole weeks or months would have gone by, and I'd not have felt anything. Until somewhere along the way it was mostly gone, and there were all those conversations about other things — who went where, when to do what, what way to go to get to something. You know what I mean?"

Jason had a faraway look in his eyes, as if he, too, were remembering a bright part of his life he was suddenly aware of losing.

"It just went away, all those times, smelling, and lying atop things to feel their shape along the whole length of yourself, and breathing deeply. All the times when I'd feel, you know, close to things and people, and the sad part, the part that really kills me, is I don't even notice that it's different. It's like half the time, or maybe more, it never was."

Jason again nodded.

"So with Aileen" — Sirus moved closer to Jason — "with Aileen it's going to be different. That's what I was just standing here thinking. That we'll have that together, find it and keep it with each other."

"That sounds wonderful, Sirus. I know you're going to have what you're looking for."

"I know it, too. And you'll find it, too. Maybe with Edith. What do you think? Think I'll be standing here with you some-time soon?"

Jason nearly blushed

"I think so, maybe, if she feels the way I think she does."

Sirus realized as he climbed the steps of the church for his meeting with the Reverend Frankel that it was years since he'd recalled this conversation. And it was that long since he'd let himself even consider what he'd hidden and forgotten over all this time. Or even all those things he'd forgotten before. Like the loss of his hopes, not just for his marriage, but of the naïve hopes he used to have as a child: that people, even strangers, would always love and value one another; that each day follow-ing another would be more beautiful than the one that went before; of his hopes as a young man that the road for his people would not always be hard. And especially of the hopes for the kind of world he would make and leave for his child.

But nothing had gone as he'd expected. From those bright dreams he'd turned more and more into himself, and so had Aileen. The secrets they tried to share with each other got lost, so what he said and what she heard were often not the same. "Are you listening?" he'd ask her. "You think I'm a bad wife," she'd say. And he would say, "No, you're a fine wife." And she'd wonder if he meant it. And by the end of the night, or the by the next morning, he too would wonder if he meant it. And they would repeat themselves, and another night or morning would finish with false assurances and regrets.

Even when they both thought they'd stopped hoping, the dance around each other never ceased. Their proximity drew them, often unwittingly, toward each other, and then, as blindly and instinctively, pushed them away. He might ask something with an edge of anger in his voice, and Aileen would hear his anger and tell him what it was he wanted to hear, would say yes when she felt he wanted to hear yes, would say no when she thought he wanted to hear no. Or she might be frightened, and his desire always to be brave would push her away. "If you like" became a favorite expression, or, "Of course, dear." Each grated on the other's nerves like the point of an umbrella on the soft top of your foot.

There was no end to the compliments each received for the other, however. What a devoted husband he was, how lovely she was, and how spotless and beautiful she kept their home. He knew all of the contentment in their marriage was supposed to lie in those phrases, those *whatever you say*s and *whatever you want*s and *of course*s. These shut him out more effectively than if she'd screamed she hated him. The Sirus he wanted to be to her was the Sirus he couldn't reveal, the Sirus who felt things passionately, who needed time to get his thoughts together, who sometimes saw things in a flash, who, as a young boy, had lain in the fields and daydreamed, who loved the smell of wood and of houses. No, he had become the Sirus McDougald he'd willingly created: a good catch, a hard worker, a wealthy, powerful man. And Aileen Bryant, with all her passion and fury, had become the complaisant and dutiful wife.

So this was what they had become to each other. And as he worked harder and made more money, she became more obedient and solicitous. He closed the church door behind him, and the darkness rushed up to envelop him. He could feel Aileen and Mattie and all the memories they'd shared, as a family, in this church. He reached out to caress the darkness. From outside, he could hear the Reverend Frankel softly humming as he came up the walk.

4

THAT EVENING, as people arrived for the wake, they settled themselves in different areas of Sirus and Aileen's house. In
the kitchen, along with the empty plates piled precariously on
every surface, were guests intent on laughing and eating. At the
center of that group was Sirus's Uncle Reggie, his short-cropped
hair lightly sprinkled with flecks of wiry gray, his frame no
longer as taut and lean as it had been in Sirus's youth, but still
poised and charged with vitality and good humor. Not even his
dark suit could detract from the ruddy color of his skin, the
wide sparkle of his smile, or the hearty clean scent of cloves and
Sen-Sen that was his trademark. He had cut the hair of every
man in the house at one time or another, and there was something familiar in his hands even now as he clutched the small
tip of a chicken wing, as if their soft touch along all those scalps
and astringent-tightened faces and necks still lingered. He completed one circle around the morsel he held before he continued.

"And did I tell you about the time Mattie told me she was
going to turn herself into a flower?"

His audience — his wife, Viola, her hips folded gleefully over the sides of the kitchen chair she sat in; Willy "Bat" Gates, so named because of his wide, flapping ears, which hung astride a small peanut-sized face; Mrs. Johnson's sister, Thelma, who kept house for the Candlesses; and Ida Turner, the college registrar, as rail-thin as Viola was corpulent — rolled back to him their encouragement. "Mm-hmm, but let's hear it," they said, or "No, that's a new one."

"Oh, tell that one," his wife insisted, her voice shaking the life out of the word *tell* before making the last two words dance. Her whole frame shook, a shiver of flesh as she spoke, and her eyes seemed to swim with the pleasure of remembering.

"Okay, here's the one," Reggie said, waving the finished chicken wing with a flourish, as if he were sweeping away with his hand the last impediment between his listeners and a true moment of joy.

"It was in this very kitchen," he began, motioning toward the seat Viola sat in. Both Ida and Bat leaned forward, as if they could peer back into time. "And I was waiting for Sirus to finish dressing." There were chuckles. "You know what a finicky dresser that man is," he added.

"Don't we know it," Bat joined in, his own dandy looks — the silk dotted bow tie, the studs at his collar — a comical counterpoint.

"Well, in comes little Mattie Louise from the backyard, and I can't tell you what a sight she was."

The warmth in the room from the stove, from the half-eaten food, from the bodies standing in a close circle, seemed to arc and lift them out of the time they stood in. Mattie became a presence as real as the chairs, the table, the pots and pans, the glasses lining the drainboard, stained with lipstick. Reggie leaned over as if he were about to chuck her under her chin.

"She was covered, now I mean covered," Reggie continued, "from here" — touching one side of his head — "to here" —

sweeping his hands to the other side — "to here" — swooping both hands nearly down to his shoulders in the back.

"And that child had hair," Viola added; "not like this old coot."

"With honey," Reggie finally concluded, to a chorus of "Oh, my goodness," "Don't you say," "Now don't you tell me." Viola expanded her husband's tale. "Umm-hmm, honey," she said. "Child put it all over herself; thought she was going to be a flower if she did. Now you tell me how a child gets a thing so mixed up in their head?"

Viola and Reggie, then the others, looked out of their enclave — out past the dining room to the living room, where the coffin lay — as fondly as they might have looked across the room to a smiling, breathing Mattie who had come in to hear their tales. Viola got more greens from the pot on the stove, Bat refilled his glass with ice water from a pitcher on the counter, and they went on, another story about Mattie continuing without pause.

In the dining room, next to the kitchen, there wasn't any laughter, only the somber weight of mannered good intentions. Here, labored respect was the goal, and in order to display it, people held their bodies tightly and spoke in hushed whispers. The Reverend Frankel was one of those talking, whispering actually, into Etta Baldridge's ear, droning on about the details of his last trip to New York, his manner solicitous and eager, as if he would deliver as much pleasure to her in the telling as he had derived for himself on the trip. Mrs. Baldridge's attention, however, was on Sirus and Aileen and her daughter, Lily, who were all in the next room. Sirus stood by the mantel, his arm loosely encircling Aileen's waist as the Arthurs squeezed Aileen's hands, offering their condolences. Both Terry and Frank Arthur were short and round, neither of them tall enough to obscure Etta's view. Etta watched as Aileen attempted to rouse herself, to acknowledge the Arthurs' soft words; yet even from this distance, Etta could see the thick haze that engulfed her. She had felt like that, she remembered, two years before, when her husband suddenly died, as if life were a pulsing, welcoming thing, but she was frozen and rigid, clamped off like a vein, at the edge of its warmth. Across the room she could see that Lily, who had headed directly for the coffin when they arrived and had stood over it for a few seconds as if in a trance, was now sitting, seeming chained at every limb, in a chair beside it. Lily, Aileen, Sirus: all three of them seemed bound to the other, weighing down their places in the room, heavier than anyone else, as if grief were a stone pulling them under. If she could, Etta thought, she would clear everyone from the room, would rouse them, would rouse even Mattie, if she could, make her live for them, if she could, even for a moment.

"Has anyone thought of a suitable memorial?" she asked when there was a large enough opening in the reverend's tale through which she could escape. She addressed her question not only to him but to the whole small group that crowded the dining room. Everyone turned around: Dr. Gant; his wife, Muriel; Ophelia Macon and her daughter, Clorissa; and the Butler sisters, Emma and Satha, the younger of whom had been afflicted with polio when she was a child.

"Mattie loved to read. Perhaps some new books, or chairs for the library," Satha Butler volunteered from her wheelchair.

Satha Butler's speech was thickened, as if her tongue were weighted inside her mouth. Her words often came in clumps separated by long pauses. Mrs. Baldridge hoped she would not say much more, because she was wearied by the effort to understand Satha.

"Lovely, lovely idea, Satha," Etta murmured, patting her on the shoulder. But she was irritated. Of course Mattie loved to read. Lily did too. And so did Jane Henson and Marjorie Oates and half a dozen other girls their age. Did people's lives always come down to this, some common fact that rendered them indistinguishable? Wasn't there any way to hold on? Or was that impossible? Did people always slip through your hands like so much water, the way her parents had when they died, the way her husband had, the way her own child would if she should be so unlucky as to live to see that day? Satha jerked her chair backward with a twitch at one large wheel.

"Or perhaps a tutoring program," Satha continued. She lifted her arm, its thin outline visible beneath the gauze of her dress sleeve. "'It is an Ancient Mariner,'" she began to intone softly, struggling to move her arm gracefully to the beat of her words, "'and he stoppeth one of three.'" She swung her arm in a loop that ended in an unintended jerk. "'By thy long gray beard, and glittering eye, now wherefore stopp'st thou me?'" She smiled when she finished.

"Mattie's recital. Weren't you there?" she asked Etta by way of explanation. "The ceremony at the college, the day the elementary school children visited. Don't you remember?"

"Yes, of course I remember," Etta answered. Mattie had read the first two stanzas, and then each child had followed, two verses a child. But only Mattie had seemed transfixed, as if the ancient mariner were real to her, as if she had more than a notion of what the poem was about. "I was there," Etta continued. "In fact, all of the children read, now that you so eloquently recall it."

Etta rolled the word *eloquently* in her mouth as if it were her own personal invention, but her final stab fell far short of its mark. Satha returned her gaze and then turned her wheelchair and rolled away. Her sister, as always, loyally followed.

"I know Satha can be tiresome, with her little idiosyncrasies, but really, Etta —" Muriel Gant began to scold but Etta stopped her. "Oh, she is just plain rude," she said. "And that little performance. It was disgraceful. Just because she's afflicted. Did anyone ask her to recite poetry? And at a time like this? Both of them and their bootlegging father. They've always acted as if they don't have to answer to a soul, and I for one am sick of it."

"I don't see why you're getting all fired up, Etta," Dr. Gant commented. "It was only a suggestion, and not a bad one at that. I think Aileen and Sirus might feel —"

"What do you know about how Aileen and Sirus feel?" Etta interrupted. "You're never the one waiting for news in a hallway, watching a doctor walk toward you with his eyes turned away, speaking so calmly you're sure you must be dreaming. Oh, no, you're always on the other side, always the one handing out the news. How would you like to be on the other side for a change?"

Ophelia and the reverend moved in almost simultaneously on either side of her. "Sister," intoned the reverend. "Etta," crooned Ophelia. They were not a bit of comfort to her, but Etta was tired, so she let them quiet her down. Besides, she had other things to attend to. She returned her gaze to Lily, still seated next to the coffin.

Lily stirred in her chair as if she felt her mother's eyes on her, and stretched her leg to ease the cramp she had been persistently trying to ignore. This was the first time she had moved in twenty minutes. She had willed herself to be still, not, as some might have supposed, out of depression or grief, but rather in sympathetic solidarity with her friend, who lay unnaturally quiet and stiff.

She hadn't expected to be so frightened by seeing Mattie's body. She had seen dead bodies before. The first was Mrs. Butler, who looked at the wake, Lily thought, like an impostor, in a pink dress no one had ever seen her wear, with her hair in a series of flattened curls through which you could see her pale pink skull, and grasping a bouquet of flowers in a gesture that seemed the most uncharacteristic of all. Lily had half expected her to rise up from the coffin, throw off her absurd pink dress to reveal a stark and more fitting navy one, disdainfully toss the small bouquet at some simpering woman like Mrs. Macon, and dismiss all of the mourners with one brusque wave of her hand. That would have been like the Mrs. Butler she knew.

And then there'd been her father's funeral, which she still couldn't let herself think about. This death, however, Mattie's death, was different. Mattie was nearly her age and size. The dress she had on was the one she normally wore to church. Her hair was braided in three braids, the way she always wore it. And Lily could still see the scar on Mattie's arm from the cut she had gotten when they were skating together one day. All that was so familiar, and yet nothing was the same. Her eyes were closed, not squinted shut as they'd be in the pool or if she'd got dirt in her eye, but closed as if she were sleeping. And when had Lily ever stood over Mattie when she was sleeping? Lily had an urge to pull up the satin that covered Mattie's legs and take a peek to reassure herself that her friend's legs were the same, long and skinny, her bony knees covered with scabs. But what would that prove? Mattie wasn't going to laugh again or ride her bike with her or sit out on the porch drinking lemonade or do any of the hundred things they used to do together, and it was going to be that way always, forever and ever. Lily felt sick, thinking about it. She couldn't hold *forever* in her head, not when her father died, not now; it all felt too sad.

She stretched her other leg and looked again at the coffin. What if that was me, she thought for a second. What if I could never move again, never open my eyes, never see my mother or my teachers at school, or any of my friends? She suddenly felt that she was choking. How awful, terrible, horrible that would be. And then the renegade thought came. Lucky me. Lucky me.

She rejoiced in the feeling. Her legs stretched out in front of her, where she could see them, her eyes, open and able to look all around the room, her heart beating, and her breath going in and out, and all of her memories and plans and dreams still intact. She wanted to run around the room and sing. Lucky me. And suddenly she was on her feet before she knew it. Up and next to the coffin before she was even aware of any intent to stand. She rocked back slightly on her little patent leather heels and grabbed the side of the coffin to steady herself. It was so quiet and hot in the room. She wanted to reach down and touch Mattie's face or her hand, something, but her friend's body seemed to keep floating away. Lily's stomach turned, and she felt a clammy chill spread from her chest to her toes, and the room spun away into darkness.

"How are you feeling now?" Lily heard a familiar but unrecognizable voice. She looked down at her hands, or thought she did, to see if they still gripped the coffin, but she realized her eyes were closed. Her hands lay loose and empty at her sides. She sat up and felt her body grow light again. "Lie back down," the voice said. She opened her eyes and stared. She was on a bed, with her feet up on a small cushion, in the narrow McDougald guest room that lay off the back hall. It was Emma Butler who was talking, standing over her with a linen napkin in her hand. She folded it and placed it on her forehead.

"You gave us quite the scare," she said, patting the cloth into place as if it were on a table and needed smoothing. "Your mother is upstairs with Mrs. McDougald. She'll be right down."

"What happened? How did I get here?"

"You fainted. It was awfully close in there." She waved her hand toward the front of the house. "Dr. Gant says not to worry." She sat down on the bed and smiled at Lily.

Lily tried to return the smile, but it was more than she could manage. "What's my mother doing upstairs?" she asked.

Emma hesitated, as if weighing whether to tell the truth.

"You seem to have set off a little chain reaction. You know how people can get." She made an airy motion with her hand. "One after another. I guess the strain was just too much."

Lily sat upright with a start, her sallow skin nearly green. "You mean Mrs. Mac, I mean Mrs. McDougald, she fainted?" she asked. She looked panic-stricken.

"Well, no, not fainted," Emma said. "She just got upset, and the doctor took her upstairs."

Lily fell back onto the bed with a groan. In a flash, the whole scene was clear. She had fainted, right beside the coffin, and it had upset everyone. Oh, God, how awful, she thought. She could not believe she had done something this bad. Her mother would be furious.

"Did my mother say when she'd be back?" she asked anxiously.

"Just rest, dear," Emma said calmly. "She'll be back any minute."

"No, that's okay," Lily insisted, trying to get up from the bed. "I'm fine."

Emma laid one arm across her. "Oh, no, you don't, young lady. I promised your mother and the doctor I'd make you rest."

"No, really, I'm fine. I feel fine," Lily insisted. She sat up again and rolled her head as if this were proof. "See, I'm not dizzy. Everything is working fine."

"It's okay," Emma said, sensing her embarrassment. She spoke more softly. "You did what everybody else was probably feeling."

Lily burst into tears. "No, I didn't," she wailed, hot shame coursing through her. "I wasn't feeling like that at all."

Emma reached up and wove her fingers inside Lily's thick

hair, lightly scratching at her scalp. Lily sank back against the headboard.

"You know, when I was once your age," Emma began, a sharp tingle of her own shame bringing the incident she was about to describe as close as if it were only moments away, "I was supposed to be watching my sister, Satha."

Lily's lips quivered, her shoulders jerking with each sob.

"And she was probably about the same age to me as Mattie was to you. Anyway, this was right after she first got sick, and none of us were used to it the way we are now." As she spoke, she remembered precisely how Satha had looked in those days: thin but without the steeliness she had developed over the years, the muscles she had had as a child only beginning to waste away. "So I guess there's an explanation for what happened, just as there is for you, but let me tell you, I didn't feel it at the time."

"What happened?" Lily asked, hiccoughing between each word.

"I left her out in the grass," Emma said evenly. "I was so tired of always watching her. And she got bitten up by ants. Red ones. They were all over her when I got back."

Lily gasped both with horror and with pure surprise that Emma should have told her this story. No adult had ever told her anything like this.

"Oh, how awful," she said. She could picture precisely in what parts of her body Emma must have ached, and for how long.

"Yes, it was," Emma said quietly, pulling her fingers from Lily's hair, "but the important thing was that I was sorry. And that Satha forgave me."

Lily wanted to throw her arms around Emma's neck, but she sat motionless, still hiccoughing.

"Here, lie in my lap for a minute," Emma said, smoothing

the wrinkles from her dress as gently as she had the napkin on Lily's head. Lily dropped her head into her lap, and curled up her body like a small child. For the moment, as she lay there, she was aware of nothing except the softness of Emma's dress and the scent of her light perfume.

Upstairs, it was quiet. Mrs. Baldridge had just tiptoed down the front stairs. The sounds of laughter and of glasses tinkling with ice continued to float up from the back stairs, and hushed voices floated up the front, though the sounds were muffled, as if the bottom half of the house were a ship that had been unmoored and was now gliding gracefully and noiselessly out to sea. Sirus stood over his wife, sleeping in their bed, her mouth open, her arms, as arranged by Mrs. Baldridge, in the disarray she obviously felt. He heard her breath puff out in despondent gusts.

It was clear that there was no hope for either of them. The shore, the other side, the safe harbor, had moved away from them — or they from it. They were irrevocably, hopelessly, lost at sea. He longed to touch the side of Aileen's mouth, the corner where it seemed her lips might crack, where her drowsy drugged breath was softly blowing, but he knew his touch would be like sandpaper. Nor, he realized, would it relieve his own despair.

How had this happened? How could grief have taken him so far from shore? He thought of Mattie's face, and suddenly even that no longer served as a bridge. Even if he willed himself to suspend reality and imagine her alive, in her going she had taken something and shattered it, and even her return could not repair it.

Sirus thought of all the phrases he knew, things people said in times of crisis, stories people told to explain life and its problems, but he could not retrieve a single one that seemed to fit. A home is never the same when you lose a child. Was that one? If not, would it now become one, would that be what people would say, long after he and Aileen were dead and buried? Would this very house be a reminder to people of what can happen when a child is lost, of how fragile is the bond between a husband and wife — no, more; between a man and his friends and neighbors, even between a man and himself — that one small child's untimely leavetaking can shatter it all?

Why had no one ever told him this before? Why were there proverbs for everything else, but not for this? Perhaps there was no purpose to having a phrase if there was nothing to be done. Maybe the sayings he remembered were only about things from which you could, with time, recover. This one was left out because it was, at bottom, incurable. He tried to summon God and could retrieve only blankness. Mattie had been his god, his sun, his moon, his reason for rising in the morning, his reason to sit on the porch at night with Aileen. How much of their conversation had revolved around her, what she liked, what she'd done that day, what hopes they had for her future? She was his reason for going to church — for the saving and preservation of her soul. There was nothing on the other side of her, he concluded, and with this thought, even tears wouldn't come. If he ever felt anything again, he was sure it would be a monstrous fury.

Aileen stirred, and he pulled the comforter over her shoulders. He could do this much, he decided. With or without feeling, he could continue to do the things he should. How many gestures, how many words, he wondered, would there be left to perform?

The voices from downstairs swelled and broke through the fog surrounding him.

"She's afraid of you, you know." That was Emma Butler's voice.

"That child, she's afraid of her own shadow." That was

Etta Baldridge. They must be at the bottom of the steps, though no sooner had he heard them than their voices moved away.

He thought of Etta's Lily, a poor rabbit of a child, and with a lion like Etta for a mother. Sirus sighed. Etta couldn't stay out of a thing if she tried. How often, he thought, had she been the one pushing, always at the front. "We should just get the day workers to all stay home; that would show them." "We have nearly enough for the whole year. Now who's going to volunteer more?" That was Etta — collecting, organizing, driving. When she had pushed into the room with him and Aileen and Dr. Gant, he knew another man might have said, "Now, Etta, go on back downstairs where you belong," but he hadn't. He had always liked Etta, even when she annoyed him. But now, as he thought of her, she seemed to pale and recede like all the rest.

"Sirus, Sirus?" He heard Dr. Gant's voice on the stairs. He left the room and stepped into the hall.

"Melvin?"

"Just need one moment more with you." The doctor's voice was smooth and composed. His hand was cool as he laid it on Sirus's hand, near his wrist. "Let's step in here for a second."

He motioned toward Mattie's room at the end of the hall. Sirus went with him, oblivious. He felt capable of anything now.

"Muriel and I are about to go. How is Aileen resting?" he asked.

"Fine," Sirus answered. "Her breathing's a little heavy, but I expect that's from the shot."

"Just a little something to help her sleep. She should be fine in the morning."

"Not too groggy?" Sirus asked, and Gant shook his head.

"No more than from a few Jack Danielses," he answered.

Sirus looked at his slim brown face, the dark hair with a neat part cut into the side, the thin tortoiseshell glasses. They had known each other for nearly sixteen years.

"I know this is not the time, Sirus, but I doubt there will ever be a good time soon, if you know what I mean. Besides, Muriel and I have to leave after the funeral tomorrow. Down to her sister's. She's just had her first child."

"Go ahead, Melvin," Sirus said.

"Well, I know you've made up your mind. About the development. And if you reconsider, that's fine."

"You were right; now is not the time, Melvin."

"I know that, but I wanted to tell you that I hope you won't believe a word that you hear. What some people are saying. About the timing and all."

"What do you mean?"

"I'm a man of science, Sirus; you know that."

"Of course."

"And we may have disagreed, but both of us, we're logical men."

"I suppose."

"So neither of us is the type to let his imagination run wild."

"Melvin, please."

"Well, what I want to say is just what people are saying. That you should know. The talk."

"About?"

"About Mattie. And the thing with the white folks, what's been happening over the summer."

"What?"

"The timing, Sirus. The timing."

"The timing?"

"What people are saying. What the white folks wanted you to do. Your stubbornness. Mattie's fall."

A sea of white faces rose and fell. It washed over Sirus and drifted away.

"Anyway," continued Dr. Gant, "we have differed in the past, probably will in the future, but on something like this, you should know it's not so. If it were just myself, no reason to say another word, but I'd hate you to hear from other quarters."

Sirus wanted to scream. Melvin had spent his whole life planning to be a doctor. He must have practiced this studiously blank look for years.

"What are you saying, Melvin?"

"It's just the coincidence," the doctor replied. He took Sirus's arm near the elbow. "You know how our people are always putting things together."

"A coincidence?" Sirus repeated blankly. A coincidence was bumping into someone you'd just been talking about. It was a word without weight. How could it have anything to do with Mattie?

"Right. I mean, some of our people are bitter. After all, there have been lynchings; there have been people beaten to death. People say, what's one small child to a people like that?"

Sirus thought he saw Mattie's face for a second, her eyes lit up, as if in panic.

"What are you saying, Melvin? I mean, just what is it you're saying?" Sirus felt a rush of air around him like a sudden storm, and the touch of Melvin's hand on his skin had the same dry, electric feeling.

"That it's nothing, Sirus; that's exactly what I came up here to explain."

Sirus felt as if dark clouds might explode at any second. "Are you saying some white man threw Mattie off the edge of her slide, Melvin? Is that what you're trying to tell me?"

Dr. Gant laughed dryly. "Of course not," he answered. He squeezed Sirus's arm.

"Then what are you standing here saying? I mean, you're the one who was arguing for those people; you're the one who was working behind the scenes; and you come up the stairs of my house and bring me into my dead daughter's room, and you tell me a thing like this. And then you say of course it doesn't mean anything, not anything like what you just said it meant. What is this about? I want you to tell me what you mean."

Melvin stepped back from Sirus, who was yelling, but he kept his grip on Sirus's arm. He was accustomed to hysterical patients. And relatives. He had not expected this of Sirus, but he knew how to handle it.

"I'm saying there was nothing out of line, Sirus," he began in his most soothing voice. He was careful to keep his sentences short. "I am only telling you the facts. There was one thing, and now there is this horrible other. And some people want to put them together. That's all I'm saying. I didn't want you to hear it first somewhere else, where it might take you off guard. The thing I'm saying is, yes, the timing might make a person wonder. But personally, I know it doesn't mean a thing. I know it happened just as I said it did. I'm sure of it. I simply wanted to be sure you heard that first from me."

He let go of Sirus's arm. "Coincidence is just something our people want to hold on to," he added. "It's a whole lot easier to take than the truth."

Sirus stood without speaking, the blood gathering at his heart. He could take Gant and hurl him out of this room or, with one shove, push him down the stairs. Or lift him above his head and sweep him like a large stick, clearing his house of all these people whose presence was more than he could bear. What kind of God forced him to live in this moment?

"Go, Melvin, go," he said, waving his hand. The doctor hesitated until he saw the full extent of the fury in Sirus's eyes. "Just go," Sirus repeated. Gant wanted to say one last word, then decided against it. Of course he's upset, he thought, as he gathered his wife and his suit coat from downstairs. People began crowding out of the house just as he was leaving.

Sirus remained upstairs with Aileen for the rest of the wake. He was unaware of the time that passed. Eventually, the house became silent.

The day of the funeral came and went. Some had dreaded it, fearing exposure; others had anticipated it, eagerly awaiting the display of emotion like trinkets at a fair. Etta Baldridge had heard about the reverend's topic from Ophelia and worried that Sirus would be furious, or worse. Lily was afraid she'd forget the words to her poem, and prayed to Jesus to keep her from fainting again. Satha and Emma Butler took their seats at the very back of the church, where Satha's wheelchair would be out of the way.

"This is our child, a child of God," the Reverend Frankel began, his voice dancing over Mattie's lifeless body, "one of the Lord's little lambs. And He has called her home. "

Two of the more devout women who always sat in the front row echoed the reverend's words. "Home, yes, Lord Jesus, home," they said in unison, clapping their hands.

The reverend continued. "Now why, the father shouts in anger, why was my child taken from me? And why, the mother wails, why was the light of my life so cruelly shut out so soon? And the only answer, the only answer the Lord will make, is that I've taken from you nothing that was yours."

Etta Baldridge didn't like the sound of the sermon already. She strained to catch a glimpse of Sirus's and Aileen's faces from her place a few rows behind them. As she did, Ophelia Macon caught her eye. See, this was just what I was worried about, Ophelia's look seemed to say. Satha Butler, ignoring what went on throughout the church, read silently to herself from the Bible.

"Now some may say," the reverend continued, "oh, preacher, that's cruel. What about some words of comfort for the grieving family? What about some soothing balm for their grieving souls? But what I'm saying is that the truth is the light, in the truth lies comfort, and only the truth can set you free."

Aileen suddenly moaned and Sirus put his arm around her. Ophelia Macon saw it all and had a good mind to just go up there and stop the Reverend Frankel now. What kind of sermon was this to give? She looked up at Clorissa in her choir robes. Did Clorissa take the reverend's intentions toward her seriously? And if she did, what kind of a husband would he make her?

"Now what is the truth?" the preacher went on. "Whose child was this Mattie Louise McDougald? To whom did she belong? Was she Sirus and Aileen's child? Did they make her? Did they give her the breath in her lungs, and the fire in her eyes, and the sweet smile that played upon her lips? And some will say yes, she was their child. Why, didn't she have Sirus's same long bones and Aileen's pretty smile, and eyes and bearing from the both of them? But I would say no, no, this child may have had every tooth and gene of these two people, but she was not theirs. For is the body the child? If so, then the body still lies here before them and the child who was theirs is still here."

Lily squirmed in her seat. She hated all of this talk about Mattie's body; it made her feel hot and flushed. Satha, however, along with her sister, looked up at the reverend for the first time since his sermon began.

"Isn't this the hair and lips and eyes and legs and lungs and heart and forehead they gave her," Frankel went on, "still lying in the box before us? And if that's so, then why are we grieving? If this was the child who was theirs, then why do we mourn? I'll tell you why. Because the light of her soul, the heavenly breath of life that was breathed in and out of her lungs through her sweet lips, this is what we are now missing. This was the Lord's. And what the Lord giveth, He may take away."

Satha Butler put down her Bible.

"Because the Lord has called His child home, He has called His child back to His bosom. And we might ask, oh, Lord, why have you done this?"

Etta suddenly forgot about Sirus and Aileen. She could think only about her husband's funeral, just two short years ago. How many times had she asked herself the same question: Why?

"But what right do we have to know that answer?" the minister asked. He looked down at Mattie's body as if he were seeing her for the first time. "Did any of us ask, when she was sent, why are you sending us this gift, why are you sending us this heavenly package? No, we let this light come into our lives and we took it for granted as we do the miracle of the sun and the moon, the earth whirling in its firmament. And now the Lord, in all His mysterious ways, has taken this child away — just as He gave her, without a word of explanation to us. Because the Lord works in mysterious ways, which is not a way of saying oh, don't even think about it. It means ponder all you will, but we may not always know all the whys and wherefores. The reasons are the reasons of God and not of man."

The reverend paused and shook his head, lightly, from side to side. Everyone, except the Butler sisters, looked up at him with surprise.

"I am grieving today with the family," he concluded. "I am grieving today with the friends. I am grieving today with all the children who will miss their classmate. But I am standing here in the pulpit to say I know the Lord's will has been done, that Mattie Louise is sitting now with the Lord in all His glory and is basking in His love. And for that I say hallelujah, hallelujah, and amen."

This was what the preacher said, though the truth was it was not at all what he had intended to say. He had intended, all along, up until he'd finally uttered the words, to be clever and iconoclastic and, yes, in fact, to show off. But something had stopped him. People cried at the end of his sermon, and even the choir sang with greater feeling than usual. Satha told her sister later that she wasn't surprised. What had happened, she explained, was that the Holy Spirit had finally taken this occasion to speak inside the Reverend Frankel's soul.

11

STEADIED
AND
SECURED

5

THE JUNE before Mattie's death was like most Junes in the South: thick with heat. The paved roads were soft and tarry; dust from the unpaved ones filled the air with a fine red powder; and peonies, roses, and early tomatoes were ripe or already past their bloom. It was a time when windows were open and noises competed in the heavy air: birds rustled through the trees, chirping and squawking; katydids and crickets raised a high-pitched buzz; at night, horned and black toads croaked to their beloveds. Painted fans with pictures of Jesus' hands flapped against dark skin, and anything that could be folded was pressed into service to bring the breeze with a brisk snap of the wrist toward the flesh. Those who liked the heat were in their glory as rivulets of sweat snaked down their bodies — cotton against their skin suddenly sodden and, for a moment, cool, their hands wiping those streams they could reach and flicking the wet away like so much sweet lemonade flung down a parched throat. They sat on their porches, these heat lovers, glistening, or stood in their gardens like short dry wicks, plumping in the heat. Those who found the air's thick measure too heavy to breathe, for whom summer was another curse in a long line of curses, mopped angrily without end and prayed for a breeze.

It was against the backdrop of these sodden days, tumbling one after another, that Mattie's last weeks passed like mist rising from an empty road. There were no trumpets to presage her passing. Her life blazed on, a small spark in the midst of the heat, and then she was gone. Each day toward death passed innocuously, uncounted.

One of the hottest days of that summer was a hazy day at the end of June. It was the day of a dinner in honor of Sirus, who had been named Man of the Year by a half-dozen civic groups who awarded the honor annually. For the first time in nearly a decade, they had chosen someone who lived right here in the town, instead of giving the award to a distant though much-admired civic leader. It fit well with the mood of the town. The men were home from the war. Truman had finally signed an order integrating the troops — too late for the war's glory, but the order seemed a sprig of the sense of liberation that was so thick in the air.

Dr. Gant had been one of the men instrumental in choosing Sirus. Others had suggested one of the two Negro leaders who had been invited to the White House this year, but Gant lobbied hard and long in the veterans' group, of which he was the head, for the town to "bring it home," as he'd put it. "We have outstanding, brilliant men right here," he'd argued. "Why does it have to be some national leader who's going to swing in for one day and then out the next? And what kind of message does that give the white folks here? That none of us are good enough?" He was looking forward to the day when it might be his turn to be honored, but in the meantime, he started a groundswell for Sirus that spread through the clubs and civic groups: let's bring it on home, they echoed, and it was almost a rallying cry, not just for choosing Sirus, but for everything that was in the air. Let's bring home the peace and freedom and justice men had fought and died for overseas; let's bring the prosperity that was booming everywhere to our own streets; let's even, though it was never said, only hoped for and hinted at and blooming in people's hearts like an indomitable weed, let's yank the glory and the promised land, snatch them out of the sky and set them here, aground for once, right here on earth. The NAACP might still report lynchings, but change fairly crackled in the air.

Now, on the day that Sirus was to receive the award, Dr. Gant was lobbying on another matter, trying to persuade Bert Candless from the bank to join the Reverend Frankel and himself in a new business venture. The three of them sat in Gant's small office at the hospital, in the basement, where all of the hospital staff were located.

"We can build on this, I'm telling you," Dr. Gant was saying.

The Reverend Frankel fingered the buttons on his shirt. "Tell him about how much we might make," he added.

"Don't jump to that," Dr. Gant said. "Let him think about the concept first."

"I understand the concept," Bert Candless interjected. He was a tall skinny man and looked awkward in the low-ceilinged room. "How much are we talking about here?"

"See, you don't understand the concept," Gant said. "If you did, you wouldn't be asking about the money right off the bat."

"Well, that's a big part of it, isn't it?" asked Bert.

Dr. Gant snapped his fingers. "It's that much. Hear me? That much. Since when has money been the beginning and the end? After all, the reverend and I have money in the bank. Even if we had to save it a nickel at a time. But none of those nickels are going to get us a glass of sherry at a white tablecloth in a restaurant downtown. Or what about you, Bert? If you and

Elaine said, hey, it's a nice evening, let's take the kids, go for a drive, and you keep driving, enjoying the stars, and one of the kids says, 'Daddy, I gotta go,' and you haven't paid attention, and there's no colored restroom around, just a white gas station, and your little girl ends up having to squat in the woods, what's your money for then? Toilet paper in the woods?"

"What's your point, Melvin?" Bert asked, unfolding and refolding his legs.

"My point is that this will give us some power. Some respect. The white man is coming to us."

"We're still not sure Sirus will go for it," the Reverend Frankel said, "but Dr. Gant thinks he'll come 'round."

"Sirus will do what he believes is right," Bert said.

"My point exactly," said Dr. Gant. "And if he hears it from the right quarters — from the Reverend Martin, or from others down at the bank — he'll be convinced it's the right thing to do."

"I can hardly wait to see his face tonight," Bert said.

Upstairs, standing behind the hospital admitting desk for the last hour of her volunteer shift, Aileen was dreading the sight of Sirus's face. They had argued again that morning, and though it seemed they rarely needed a reason, this time it had been about the award dinner.

"Oh, Sirus, please don't," she'd said.

Sirus was stretched out on the bed, naked.

"Please don't what?" he asked.

"Please don't embarrass us," she replied.

Sirus pulled the sheet up over his legs. "I didn't say I wasn't going to mention hard work. I just said I was also going to mention love. I just don't think you understand what work can mean to a man."

"I know what work means," she said. She sat at her dressing

table in her bra and slip, finishing her makeup. "And you do a fine job in your work — I'm not taking that away — but you sometimes put too much faith in other people."

Sirus interrupted her. "And you sometimes put too little. Not everyone is out to get you when you turn your back."

"And not everyone is like you," Aileen replied, "believing everything will always work out for the best. That's all I'm saying."

Sirus got up and walked slowly to the bathroom, almost flaunting his nakedness, that his skin looked like a baby's, glistening, as if he didn't care what kind of fool she worried he might make of himself. It enraged Aileen that he could be so collected and impervious to her views.

"You think you're going to change the world," she yelled at him in the bathroom, "or this little piece of it, and I'm telling you, people couldn't care less. They want food on the table, a dry place to sleep, clothes on their children's backs." She slapped her hand loudly on the wall next to the mirror so that he'd be sure to hear it. "This is just plaster, Sirus. And there's wood behind that. That's what this house and all of the others are made of. They're not indestructible. And neither are you."

Aileen wished now she could take back her words. As soon as she said them she wanted to slap herself, bite her tongue, but she couldn't find other words to put things right, and neither could he, and they'd left the house that way, with the bitterness between them.

"I believe I've completed this," said the woman across the counter. She slid the admitting form toward Aileen and opened her purse. "How much do I have to pay?"

"We'll bill you later," Aileen answered. The woman looked surprised, as they all did. No hospital that admitted colored ever let them in without cash up front. But this hospital was one of the few colored hospitals anywhere, and the first in the state, and almost everyone paid his bill, even if it took a year, dimes sent in an envelope a few at a time.

The woman closed her purse and waited. Aileen knew she was not from around here, not only because she didn't recognize her, but because the woman didn't fit into any of the obvious categories of the people here in Durham. She didn't look poor, nor was she particularly well dressed. Her dress was something a matron would wear, she was without makeup, and yet she was a young, attractive woman with a good figure. It was as though she didn't care how she appeared, and she leaned against the counter, as Aileen finished the paperwork, with the same nonchalance about her carriage as about her clothes and her looks. Aileen silently contrasted her own makeup, so carefully applied, and the colors of her clothes, which she took such pains to choose, and her almost regal bearing, which had taken her years to achieve. This woman looked as though there was little in life she took the time to worry about.

"It's my boy. Shall I call him over?" the woman asked. Without waiting for an answer, she called to a bundle stretched out on a chair near the door. Aileen had hardly noticed him; the two had come in when the waiting room was already full. He walked over slowly, obviously in pain, but his steps were careful, with a precise grace. He came and stood beside his mother.

Like his mother, the boy was beautiful. He stood slightly behind her, but he peeked out. Aileen could see that he had thick, tightly coiled black hair, large brown eyes, a nearly perfectly shaped head, delicate but masculine, and full, sensuous lips. His handsomeness, however, was more defined than his mother's, and it was clear that he had inherited good looks from both sides of his family.

Of course the father must be handsome, Aileen concluded. That a good-looking man might choose a woman who was so careless about her appearance seemed to Aileen an embarrassment. How could a man expect to get anywhere if his wife wasn't scrupulous about what her attire conveyed?

It was precisely ideas like this that led to many of her arguments with Sirus. He thought her concern with appearances was petty. But wasn't much of what they had achieved built on exactly this kind of concern? What would the whites in the town think of their successes if they let themselves grow careless about any detail?

"The doctor will be able to take him in a moment," Aileen said, directing the woman toward a row of chairs behind the desk. Usually, she pointed people toward the row of chairs right by the door to the examining room, but she thought the upholstered chairs near her would be easier for the boy. They were normally used by the nurses on break, but today's was a short midweek staff, and Aileen knew the chairs would be empty for most of the afternoon. The woman shrugged and sat down, her legs stretched straight out in front of her, while her son folded himself into his chair. "Are you from here?" Aileen asked once the woman had settled herself.

The woman laughed a soft, almost ironic laugh, as her face lit up, just briefly. "No," she answered, "not for a long time. I was born here, but my husband and I moved away." She said it as though she were glad of the fact. "We're here on a visit." She looked down at her son. "Alfred hurt himself since we've been here."

"He's a beautiful child," Aileen said. The woman chucked the boy under the chin, and he burst into giggles despite his pain, and his mother giggled back at him, oblivious of Aileen.

"Yeah, I suppose he is," the woman answered when she was ready to take the time to look back toward Aileen. The boy was quiet now, but he leaned slightly against the side of her chair, and his mother rubbed his head absentmindedly.

Aileen looked at the two of them and tried to think of a time when she had leaned as securely against someone as this boy did now his mother. Had there been such a time? She wasn't sure, but then she remembered coming home from the hospital after Mattie was born, when Sirus had arranged for his driver to pick them up, and the three of them, she, Sirus, and Mattie, were in the back seat. She was more tired that morning than she could ever remember being in her life, and Mattie was asleep in her arms, as light as a small package. She had leaned against Sirus that day, her full weight against his side, with nothing held back, and he had supported her in a way that she had never felt supported before.

She suddenly felt giddy. It came back to her at once, not just the deep ease that she and Sirus had once shared, but the joy and the pleasure they'd once had. She remembered how, when she'd first seen Sirus, when he'd passed the porch of her parents' house, she'd thought him the most handsome man she'd ever seen, how much pleasure she'd taken in just the sight of him. She'd heard of him before she met him, of course, about how he was from the country, but had gone away to Washington, D.C., for college; how he was a distant cousin to Dr. Anson; how he was going places, and fast, at the Federated. She'd heard it all, but that and the other fine things she'd heard didn't add up to anything until she saw him. She hadn't expected to like his looks — he was very fair, she'd heard — but it was hard to imagine any man looking better. The first thing she noticed was his height: he was tall, very tall, and she liked that in a man, and he had a thickness to him that she also liked. But what reached down and rocked her hip bones back against themselves was the shape of his face: it was as broad a face as she'd ever seen on a man who wasn't fat. Sirus was lean and strong-looking, even though he was big, and something about his high broad forehead, wide chin, and that mouth as wide as a river, well, it was a face to hold in your hands and never let go. This she could see about him right away, and she'd set her sights on him just that fast. She dropped her hand into her hair as he passed, and sure enough, that caught his eye.

And when they came face to face, she saw more, more that carried her out into what felt like the chilliest, fastest-moving water she'd ever felt, a ride that would forever have her heart in her throat. His voice was soft and rich, not his calling-out-to-people voice, but the one he used when they were close together. It was a voice that sounded as if it was meant just for her. It was a voice as soft as anything she had ever heard, and with it he wove such a web — oh, the things he would say. She felt exposed and new, as if here was someone who could see her for the first time in her life, and the sight held a promise of both strength and gentleness that she found almost impossible to bear. He had felt something too, she could tell; and that thrilled her. She was thrilled that it should have been so easy, that there wasn't all the awkward fumbling and groping about, not with words, and certainly not when they touched each other, which they did as soon as she dared let him. There was nothing about him that said to her, now you have to pretend not to like what you like. And she had loved that, loved him for that, right away.

Now, nearly shaking, Aileen was aware that she rarely remembered how she'd once felt. She looked at the woman across from her, sprawled, dozing, in her chair. Taking life's pleasures obviously came easily to her. She wouldn't worry that danger might find an opening in the small things. Sirus was like that, too. Aileen remembered an evening, shortly after Mattie was born, when she and Sirus were going out to dinner with some business acquaintances. Aileen had been worried about what dress to wear. She tried on a couple for Sirus, and when she modeled a third, he had laughed. It wasn't a mean laugh, just a chuckle, but Aileen had suddenly felt as if she were seven again, back in her parents' home, where what she wanted or cared about was belittled; and it was such an infinitesimal thing, but she had felt betrayed, as if Sirus's promise to her had been broken, as if he were not someone new, with his own special rules, but was just like all the rest, a person she had to be wary of, a person she had to protect herself against. And it was then that she'd begun to hold something back, to back away, just to be sure, and the retreat became so strong a habit that it had its own momentum, so that even when she wasn't angry or hurt, she still held herself apart from him, never again being sure about giving her all.

She remembered the night before with Sirus, the pattern as familiar as her name. He had wanted to make love, and she'd wanted him to, but a simple yes was impossible. Standing between her and pleasure was the pain, this pain which he could and did hurt her with, that he might be like her father or her mother or even like the young white child who had laughed at her on a bus once when she was a girl, because she'd been careless dressing that day and her socks didn't match. There were so many little things that she couldn't even begin to remember them all, and more and more it became necessary to go through the pain to reach the pleasure. She was convinced that Sirus could simply lift her in those strong arms of his and carry her across, if he would. Unlike her, he was hopeful and free; he didn't worry as she did; he had more hope in him in a day than she had ever felt in her life. But as much as she needed this from him, he refused to give it to her. She had said last night, "Well, I'm a little tired," her words less a statement of fact than an invitation: help me, lift me, carry me over to where you are. Sirus had merely turned away, his face toward the door, his arms at his side. "Why is it you always choose times that you know are bad?" she'd continued, and he'd returned, "Since when does it matter what times I choose?" He'd concluded, coolly, "Perhaps you'd prefer it if I slept downstairs." Even without looking, in the dark she knew he must know how much this hurt her. His body next to hers was essential. She could no more imagine life without his body than she could imagine deserting her own.

The young boy shifted in his chair. She looked up to see the flashing red light that told her one of the examining rooms was free. She called to the woman, who woke up with no effort, and directed her and her son toward the empty room. "Thank you for your concern," the woman said to her just before she and the boy disappeared into the room with the nurse.

Sirus was on the road back into town from Pete's shack, where he and Jason had stopped to have lunch. What he recalled of the fight with Aileen bore little resemblance to Aileen's thoughts. He did not know of her physical dependence on him — or of any dependence, for that matter — and if told of it, would have found it hard to believe. Desired him, yes; he could believe that he gave her pleasure (as she did him). But as far as he could tell, for her it was an uncomplicated matter: she reached for him as easily as she did for a good meal.

What was on Sirus's mind instead was the thought of leaving. He drifted over it idly, no clear picture of where he might go, just somewhere, away. He knew he'd never really do it, but it gave him relief to imagine it. He thought of what it was that he wanted: love; what it was that he had: anger and bitterness and constant fighting; and he saw himself away. It was a three-part picture, like a hinged mirror: love, disappointment, away. The only disturbance in his daydream was Mattie. He had no illusions about taking her with him if he should leave. So he would tell himself that it was because of her that he stayed.

"You're mighty quiet," Jason said, riding back into town with Sirus while his assistant took his own car in the other direction to be serviced.

"What?" asked Sirus.

"I said, you're mighty quiet."

"Yeah, I suppose."

Jason licked at the edge of his mustache. "What are you thinking about so hard?"

"Oh, just things in general, nothing special."

Jason looked out the window and watched the trees go by. "I bet everybody at your house must be buzzing. Getting all ready for the dinner," he said.

"It has been pretty busy."

"How long did it take Aileen to decide what to wear?"

"What? Oh, Aileen, what she's wearing? No, not long. She showed me something I think a day or so after it was announced."

Jason laughed. "And hasn't changed her mind since?"

Sirus frowned. "No, that's not something Aileen would do."

"Yeah, she is pretty set once she gets going." Jason laughed again. "I was just thinking of my Edith. Oh, she'd have chosen something too, but you'd better believe I'd have seen it a hundred times between now and then. Paired with something different each time. 'Is this one better than the blue? Is this green better than the red?' And heaven help me if I don't remember the first dress and stick with that all along. 'But you told me the blue was best, right from the start. What don't you like about it now?' Enough to drive you out of your mind. Aileen doesn't do that?"

"No, not Aileen," Sirus answered.

The silence was filled by the sound of the tires across the road and the hum of Sirus's car. Jason pulled out a small notebook and began turning the lined pages. Sirus accelerated to pass a slow-moving truck. He watched it disappear in the rearview mirror.

"Sometimes I think of leaving Aileen."

Jason stopped turning the pages of his notebook. "What?" he asked.

Sirus repeated himself.

"What do you mean, you mean leave, as in separate, divorce?"

A billboard for Camels and then another for Lucky Strikes whizzed by.

"Well, leave for good. I don't really think of divorce. We could stay married if that was what Aileen wanted. For the sake of what people might say and for Mattie."

Jason twisted on the front seat so that he could more nearly face Sirus. "Sirus," he said, "come on. You don't mean it."

Sirus looked again in the rearview mirror and saw only the road disappearing behind him.

"Yes," he answered, "I think I might mean it."

"But why? This is crazy. Are you two having some kind of trouble? Hell, that happens all the time. Edith and me, we fight all the time; all couples do. If you're having trouble, you just wait, wait until it gets better. It always does. You don't just up and leave."

Sirus took his eyes from the road for a second, long enough to glance at his friend. "Why not? Why don't people just leave when they don't see any more reason to stay?"

Jason slapped the seat beside him, hard. "Because there's always reasons," he shouted. He hit the dashboard now, just as loud. "Don't be stupid. You know that. Even Bob Jefferson. He and his wife don't speak like two human beings more than two days out of the year, and you don't see him talking about going somewhere. You stick in. That's a reason. Particularly if you've got kids. How can you even talk about leaving your own flesh and blood?" He stared at Sirus. "I don't believe you. You wouldn't just up and leave Aileen. You couldn't. And even if you could, what about Mattie? Are you telling me you could leave your child? I don't believe it, not a word."

Sirus accelerated, for no reason. "That's the one part I can't get through," he said softly. "Mattie. That's the one thing I know I couldn't do."

Jason leaned back against the seat, exultant. "Of course you couldn't. And you couldn't leave Aileen either." His shoulders relaxed. "This is just some kind of nonsense. Now what happened. You and Aileen have a fight?"

"Of course."

"And you both said some pretty terrible things. Am I right?"

"Right."

"Well, see, that's what I mean; that doesn't mean a thing." Jason warmed to his subject. "I mean, married folks are always fighting. You say one thing, she says another, next thing you know, you want to hear that door slamming behind you for good. You may think any kind of crazy old thing, but it's just a feeling; it's not something you go and do."

Sirus's voice rose. "You keep saying that."

Jason yelled louder in return. "You damn straight I keep saying it, because it's true. And you know it. This is just craziness talking."

Sirus persisted. "But why not, I mean, if you want to leave, feel like there's nothing left to make you stay, why don't you go?"

Jason was exasperated but patient. "Look, you said it yourself already: there's kids, and what you have to promise and do for them. They didn't ask to come into the world, and once you've brought them here, you can't go running off at the first sign of trouble."

Sirus bristled. "I think you know me better than that."

"Of course I do," Jason said soothingly. "I know you wouldn't talk like this over some little thing. It probably feels pretty bad. What was the fight about?"

Sirus paused as if trying to remember. "It's not what it's about. I don't even know if I can remember. It's more the feeling, like, oh, sweet Jesus, we can't keep going on like this."

Jason probed more gently. "Look, I don't mean to pry, but you know, are things okay between you in the love department? Sometimes, if a wife gets tired on you a lot, you can start thinking crazy things, believe me I know, but you've got to be patient. You know what I'm saying? Hell, go into Raleigh one afternoon if you know what I mean. But you don't talk about leaving just over that."

Sirus accelerated a second time and the car's engine whined. "You know," he began, an edge to his voice, "my mother and father loved each other till the day my mother died. That's what I believed, what everybody said, the whole time I was growing up. Eubie and Mattie, Eubie and Mattie. No one ever heard them argue, never heard any angry words. But just last year, I was down in Carr visiting my father, and we sat out on the same porch where they lived forever, where I grew up, and you know what he said to me one night, just before I was going to leave the next day?"

"No, what?"

"'Your mother was a very angry woman, Sirus. Just like your Grandmother Sue. I hope I did the right thing to stay, but I can't tell you what's it's like to be so lonely.'"

Jason didn't reply.

"Do you hear what I'm saying?" Sirus continued, his hands turning pale at the knuckles. "It's like all my life I've thought this one thing, that my parents were happy. Hell, I would have gone to my deathbed swearing, oh, yes, they were as happy as any couple could be. And then, just like that, sitting in the dark, some stupid crickets going at it, a whole swallow of good bourbon about to let slide down my throat, and all of a sudden, it's completely different. Just like that. Changed. In a second. And you know what made me feel that I was losing my mind? It's that as soon as he said it — I mean, just as the words were coming out of his mouth — I thought to myself, I know. As if I hadn't known a thing before, nothing, and then, out of the blue, it's changed and I see I knew all along it was the way he was now saying. I can suddenly remember a lot of things I never even knew I'd seen, like my father staring off into space — he used to do that a lot. I thought he was drunk, and probably he was, but I must have seen him a hundred times, on the porch or in their room. Again, if you'd asked me, I wouldn't have known that I knew a thing, right up until then."

Jason seemed undisturbed. "Well, every marriage has got its ups and downs. Your father probably didn't mean he was lonely all the time, that it was all bad. Why, hell, I know the two of you were probably sitting there drinking on that bourbon till God knows when, and maybe what he's thinking is how lonely he is now. But instead, out something like that comes, and maybe it's not even true, or if it is, maybe it's not the whole story. Like with you and Aileen right now. I bet what you're thinking right now is something that's making it all worse than it is. You might just be confused, like your dad."

Sirus's voice got angrier. "And maybe I know exactly what I'm talking about."

"Maybe," Jason said slowly, "but as long as either one is possible, then you owe it to yourself and to Aileen and little Mattie to stay till you're sure."

"Oh, what the hell," Sirus said.

"Exactly," Jason answered. "What the hell." He clapped his hands together, but he was already thinking ahead about what he would say if this came up again. He'd talk to Edith tonight, maybe have her say something to Sirus. She was good with things like this, good and practical; no one could make a thing clearer than Edith. It looked as if the worst was over, but if it wasn't, then Edith would be able to patch things back up. He'd keep his eyes and ears open and see what else, if anything, one or the both of them needed to say.

"Mattie. Mattie Louise. Mattie Louise McDougald."

The voice that called to Mattie across the McDougalds' backyard was Mrs. Johnson's. She stood on the back porch steps, the air in the yard cool after the heat of the kitchen, and raised her voice with each yell. Where is that child, she thought. She spoke without premonition; she stood on the porch and called as casually as she had across this same yard a hundred times. The squat branches of the pecan tree that grew in the corner next to the back fence rustled — the leaves in the lower limb stirring despite the lack of a breeze — and she was at the tree in ten quick strides. Mattie's legs emerged over her head as she looked up into the thick branches.

"What are you doing up there, young lady?" Mrs. Johnson asked, her hands on her hips, looking up past the sneakered feet and dangling legs into a face partly hidden by the leaves. Oh, Lord, this child is always up to something, she thought. Just then, Mattie leaned forward, and there was a sudden flash of hickory skin framed by dark pigtails.

"Look," Mattie said, waving a white handkerchief she had tied into a bundle. "I picked them." She dropped the white ball, then turned in midair and swung to the ground with both hands. She dangled for a second before she let go and landed at Mrs. Johnson's feet.

"You know they're not ripe," Mrs. Johnson said, picking up the pecans and holding them out to Mattie as she wiped the dirt from her hands. "That's why they haven't fallen yet."

"I know," Mattie said, taking the handkerchief by its tied end, "but I couldn't wait. They taste good even when they're green."

Mrs. Johnson waved her arms to get Mattie moving. She followed her across the yard, watching her untie with her teeth the knot she'd made in the handkerchief. Her legs gangled beneath her, as if they operated on their own. She was a slender child, tall but wiry, and she was busy emptying the pecans into a bowl from the cabinet by the time Mrs. Johnson came into the kitchen.

"You've only got a little over an hour to get cleaned up and dressed for your daddy's dinner," Mrs. Johnson reminded her. Mattie stood at the bowl, rearranging the pecans. They were pale tan, and the stripes, which would be thick and dark by the end of the summer, were now only a hazy charcoal with no more than an intimation of a line.

"Did you hear me, Mattie?" Mrs. Johnson repeated. "It's already quarter to four, and your father and mother plan to leave at five."

Mattie turned and looked at Mrs. Johnson, finally satisfied with her arrangement.

"Do you think they feel different?" she asked, seemingly absorbed by a scab on her knee. She jerked her head toward the bowl. "The pecans, that is. I mean, if they could feel, do you think they'd know they're no longer up in their tree?"

"Heaven knows," Mrs. Johnson answered, laughing. "They might've noticed a change in altitude, but I'd guess that would be about all."

"Bet they felt it when I dropped them."

"Yes, I expect they didn't like that one bit."

Mattie widened her eyes and made a trail with her fingers through the air, as if she were following the pecans' flight to the ground. Then, mimicking their fall, she flopped into a chair at the table, propping her head up in both her hands so that her braids poked through her fingers.

"You know, I've been thinking . . ." she began.

"Really, about what?" Mrs. Johnson asked. Mattie's three braids stuck out like barely plucked chicken wings.

"About Amelia Earhart," Mattie said.

"Amelia Earhart?"

"Umm-hmm." Mattie lifted her arms and dipped them from side to side. Mrs. Johnson could see the flurry out of the corner of her eye. "You know, the lady pilot."

Mrs. Johnson stood at the sink and rinsed the bowl she had mixed the tuna salad in earlier. "Oh, right," she said, "the one who disappeared somewhere halfway across the world. I think it was the year you were born that she was trying to make that flight."

"Right, I know," Mattie said impatiently. She tapped on the table with her fingers. "We learned about it in school last week. And I was looking at a book from the library today, and it said it was 1937. They said it was in all the papers."

"Oh, that it was," Mrs. Johnson continued. "For weeks, months really, it was all you heard. People were calling up on the radio from everywhere, all over the world, little towns, remote places. There were hundreds of reports about some-where she'd been or someone who'd seen her. Or her plane. Everything that was silver people thought was a piece of her plane. Seems like the whole country just went plain plumb wild for a while."

"Yeah, I know," Mattie said intently, and then fell silent.

Mrs. Johnson looked over at her, her eyes focused on a point far in the distance, her shoulders hunched forward. She began to tap on the table again with her fingers, softly at first and then louder and louder.

"I want to be a first like that," Mattie said determinedly. "Not to disappear! But to be the first to try something. To fly around the world. I don't think I'd like to fly, though, maybe, but something." She leaned forward and spun a bowl of fruit on the table so that it clattered on each turn.

"Well, there's nothing to stop you," Mrs. Johnson said. "Probably your only problem will be trying to decide which thing it is you want to do first."

Mattie stopped the bowl in midspin. "Really?"

"Why, of course, sweetheart. I can't see why not."

Mattie began to chew on her bottom lip. "Do you think there'll be any left?" she asked.

"Any what left?"

"Any firsts. Maybe by the time I'm all grown, maybe there won't be any firsts left."

Mrs. Johnson thought to herself, how could the world run out of firsts, particularly for the colored?

"Oh, honey, there'll be plenty of firsts for a long, long time."

"Good!" Mattie exclaimed. She jumped to her feet and began to dance around the kitchen. "One two three, one two three, one two three," she said, holding her arms out in front of her as though she had a partner. "Jimmie Knock-kneed is supposed to be my dancing partner in dance class. He steps on my toes all the time."

"His name is not Jimmie Knock-kneed."

"I know."

"He is a perfectly nice young boy."

"I didn't say he wasn't nice; I just said he's knock-kneed. I don't see why he has to be my partner."

"Well, who would you prefer?"

"No one." She suddenly ran into the living room as she heard a car pass, and then ran back again. "I thought that was Daddy."

"Speaking of your daddy, you have exactly one hour to get cleaned up and dressed for his dinner tonight. Now enough of this; upstairs with you."

Mattie frowned and bit her lip again. "Is my daddy the first to win this award for building things?"

Mrs. Johnson quite honestly didn't know. "I think so, honey, as far back as I can go. It's been more famous people, people in the NAACP, or like that, if I'm remembering right."

"So this is a first?"

"I guess it is."

"Well, that's something I could do, build things like my daddy. Maybe I could build the first house that's a combination house, plane, and boat, that you could put on land or fly or go out into the water."

"Enough!" Mrs. Johnson said. "Upstairs with you."

Mattie groaned.

"Okay, okay," she said. Halfway across the dining room she stopped and yelled back to Mrs. Johnson, "Will you come upstairs and brush my hair when I'm ready?"

"Yes, as soon as you're dressed to your slip. I put out what your mother picked for you to wear. Now hurry and get going. I let you talk, so now you've got to get at it."

"I'll be ready in fifteen minutes," Mattie called from the stairs.

The noise of her voice and feet faded abruptly after she reached the top and disappeared into her room. There was a sudden stillness. It never ceased to amaze Mrs. Johnson, this phenomenon of children, the energy that clung to them like static electricity, setting off random sparks. You reached for them expecting one thing, and you got another. Mattie was like that, so hard to pin down. For a week now it was the special people she'd been learning about in school. Last week, nothing at school was right; it was horrible and boring. Next week it would probably be something that happened between her and a friend.

The water ran in the bathroom upstairs. When Mrs. Johnson

heard Mattie go back into her room, she went upstairs to keep her moving along. She was there with Mattie when Sirus and Aileen arrived home, talking as they came through the door. With even a little effort Mrs. Johnson could have easily made out what they were saying, but out of long habit, she made it a point not to listen. She'd decided long ago, when she first came to work for Mr. Mac, that what she didn't hear, she didn't have to be concerned with — and being concerned about things she could do nothing about was nothing but a burden.

"I don't know all of who's going to be there," Sirus said. "If you have to know so badly, you could call Etta or Melvin. I'm sure one of them would know."

"I didn't say I have to know. It would just be nice, that's all. I hear some white man is coming from the city council," Aileen answered. The broad straps of the lime sundress she wore intersected the freckles across her back, and her hair seemed more red than auburn in the late afternoon sun. Her dress billowed behind her as she disappeared into the back hall toward the kitchen.

Sirus stood in the front room, watching the flash of color behind her. His own face was flushed and his light suit and shirt were wrinkled from the heat. He hesitated for a moment, then followed Aileen into the kitchen.

"Iced tea?" Aileen asked, standing at the refrigerator.

"Yes, thank you."

"Look, Sirus," she said, "it's your day. And I'm pleased for you. Really." She poured out a tall glass of tea and handed it to him. He took a deep swallow. She poured herself a glass and sat down at the kitchen table. "I really am." She picked over her words. "I just think you have to be more careful. If there are going to be white people there, that's a thing I think you'd want to know." She took a sip of her tea and then another, watching him between sips.

"Why?" he asked. "Is this white man going to steal my soul while I'm eating? Should I wear a special tie to please him? Why the hell should I care if some white councilman wants to come to my dinner?" He sat down in the chair across from her, scraping its legs across the linoleum. "Is there something you know that I don't?"

"You are being difficult on purpose," Aileen said. "You know what they think of us. Someone with some sense would want to be aware of that."

Sirus looked at her and suddenly wished she would disappear for a moment. He wished a cloud, like the ones he saw in the sky when he was out all day, would drift by and hide her face. He knew he'd never leave; he loved his daughter too much, and this house and the land and the town. And Aileen as well, despite how angry she made him. He wanted to stay but make Aileen's angry face drift away.

"Look, Sirus, I'm upset," Aileen said. "I can't stop thinking about that white councilman." She got up to fix him a fresh glass of tea. "What's his name?"

"Phil Burnett."

"Right, Phil Burnett." She sat back down. "I was thinking of him at the dinner, and what he would take back to his friends. You know, how he'd probably say, 'Yeah, I went to that award dinner for that colored businessman, and don't you know the thing he talked about was love.' It would be a joke to him. I'm thinking of others, too. It might hurt some people's pride."

Sirus knew that Aileen was worried about her own pride, but perhaps she was right. Maybe this wasn't the time or the place.

"I may say it, or I may not," he said at last. He looked at

Aileen to see if she would have a further response, but she took their glasses to the sink. He could hear the ice cracking against the sides of the sink before he was out of the hall.

Upstairs, as she wiped at her patent leather shoes with a rag, Mattie could hear her parents' voices as clearly as Mrs. Johnson had. And like Mrs. Johnson, she was determined not to listen. She called their arguing, to herself, "that whistling sound," and to block it out, she made other sounds that were louder in her head: songs, poems she'd memorized, the snuffling roar of cars when they drove on the highway, the surf pounding. She had a hundred sounds she liked better than her parents' angry voices, and she used them alone or, if needed, in random combinations. Today she sang and recited a poem and heard the sea crashing. She also kept up a nonstop chatter.

"Shall I wear my hair with three bows or one? Will my daddy be sitting on the stage? When you were my age, did you wear your hair in pigtails too?"

Mrs. Johnson simply nodded to most of her questions. It was the end of the day and she was growing weary. It would be a very late night for her, going on to the dinner and all, and her mind was on her own children, who would eat at a neighbor's tonight.

Sirus's voice boomed from the hallway as his large feet pounded up the stairs. "Where's my pumpkin?" he called. Mattie flung herself at him before he was hardly through the door.

"My pumpkin, little pumpkin," and, "Daddy, Daddy," mingled together like an engine approaching and leaving at the same time, a high thin whistle traveling away, a louder roaring noise approaching. Mattie's feet almost clattered against the furniture as Sirus swung her around once, twice, a third time.

"How's my girl been today?" Sirus asked, glancing over his shoulder at Mrs. Johnson.

"Good as gold," Mrs. Johnson answered, motioning Mattie back toward her so that she could straighten her dress and hair. Mattie stood in the circle of Mrs. Johnson's arms, her face looking up at her father's. It was clear that, for Mattie, no moment on earth but this one existed. Sirus's face, his hair, the scent of him, the damp cotton of his suit, his big hands lifting her, then setting her down, his eyes looking at her filled with love — all of these things expanded and became the world.

"Ready for the dinner?" Sirus asked, sitting on the edge of the bed to watch Mrs. Johnson brush Mattie's hair.

"Umm-hmm," Mattie answered.

"So do you feel pretty proud?"

"Yes, very!"

"Think you'll like it when I get up in front of everyone and talk?"

Mattie nearly squirmed out from between Mrs. Johnson's legs. "I love it when you talk," she answered.

Sirus raised his arms and clasped his fingers together behind his head.

"I have to tell everyone thank you for honoring me, and then say something else." He stared intently at Mattie. "I think maybe I'll talk about what my work has meant to me. What do you think?"

Mattie followed first the look in her father's eyes, then the line of his arms spread out above him like the limbs of a tree. She could imagine herself sitting safe and happy in those branches. "You mean, like why you do it, like that?" she asked.

Sirus let loose a broad grin. "Exactly."

Mattie suddenly saw hammers and nails flying, piles of lumber stacked around him, his foot resting on a stump poked in the ground and filled with concrete. Men wearing broad leather belts with glinting tools crowded around him, glistening with sweat and speckled with red dirt. Mattie often visited his sites with him, and he would point things out to her, tell her things she sometimes had trouble understanding. When she lost the words, however, she would follow the movement of his eyes and the tone of his voice, and somehow the things she said would always please him.

"Like remember those houses out by Cooper's stream?" he went on. "There have got to be twenty children living up there now. I get such a kick, seeing all of them out there, fishing and wading in that stream."

Mattie nodded, seeing nothing but her father's big eyes.

"Nothing wrong with a man saying how much he loves the people he does the work for," he concluded. He rode his finger off the end of Mattie's nose. "Is there, you little nut face?"

Mattie shook her head vigorously, then a second time to be sure.

"You wouldn't be embarrassed, would you?"

Mattie tried to imagine such a feeling and shook her head vehemently again. "I rode my bike all over town today," she said, "and I looked at everything you built, and I took a stone from each place and put it at another. I had cards on my spokes so they were flapping and everybody looked when they saw me coming. It was like a cavalcade. Except not with cars."

Sirus and Mrs. Johnson exchanged glances and laughed.

"You mean motorcade, honey, don't you? When they drive to honor somebody," Sirus corrected gently.

"Right, I mean a motorcade," Mattie answered, her voice chiming like a collection of cowrie bells.

As she sat at her dressing table, her brush poised over her head between strokes, Aileen could hear Mattie's voice. She was looking at her reflection in the mirror. The image that returned her gaze was precisely as she pictured herself, a honey-colored woman, still handsome, but stern. She listened again to Mattie, laughing now. Her voice seemed to chirp and warble. It was full of such sounds when she spoke to her father: trills, gales, filled with delight, pierced through with love and admiration and an eagerness to please. Sometimes it seemed to Aileen that the whole house was alive with those rippling sounds.

Aileen thought again about that boy at the hospital and his mother. They were just like Sirus and Mattie: no space between them, no hesitation or fumbling the way there was when Mattie was with Aileen. With Sirus, Mattie always found exactly what she wanted and needed, and her joy echoed throughout the house. Aileen could not help comparing Mattie's childhood with her own. Where was the parent who had so delighted in her? When she heard Mattie laughing with Sirus, unpleasant memories were caught up in that high pealing voice: crinolines so starched they scratched her legs, and still no one noticed how her dress stood out; row upon row of neatly drawn letters on green-lined paper that always went — always, even when it was stapled and done — unexamined; sentences begun with so much thought and care that sometimes they were swallowed in the throat, to which someone always said, "Speak up, speak up! What's the matter with that child; cat got her tongue?"

The good Reverend Bryant, her father, and his wife had been deaf to her own bell-like tones. A sober countenance is more pleasing to your God, her father used to say, catching her sometimes, unaware, smiling at nothing more common than the sun. He believed in hell and original sin more than he believed in sunlight. As a child, Aileen had told herself countless times that no God she could imagine would make a world for humans to sneer at, just as no God would make people in His own image and then brand them as bad. And she held out for a sign that she was right and her father wrong. She had waited for that sign as patiently as she waited for her time to leave the house, as her sisters had done when they were married, though she had sworn that, when her time came, she would do it differently, that she would leave to go to a house filled with love. She dragged the brush harder through her hair.

In her mind's eye, she saw all that was now a part of her life: this house they owned, the good work she did at the hospital, the clubs, the luncheons, the handsome and successful husband, the pretty and precocious child. She could find no fault anywhere. She had made it happen just as she'd intended, had arranged her life with care, yet despite it all, some form of terror seemed to be only a hair's-breadth away.

She couldn't begin to say why it was she sometimes heard her heart beating louder than any other noise in the house; why such gloom and dismay settled onto her that it often took days to lift. Why she sometimes felt like a balloon from which all the air was deflated, and why, as desperately as she wanted her husband to come to her, she occasionally felt nothing but rage mixed with panic when he did.

This dinner, for example. Why had she carried on the way she had? As soon as she'd heard about it, she felt both proud and afraid. Sirus seemed to think his large hands and broad face and open heart were enough for anything, that he could protect them all, no matter what. But she knew this wasn't so. At bottom, always, was the fear. Just this small opening of their lives, even in this small public way, might be enough to open the floodgates. You go before people, and anything can happen. And Sirus didn't seem to know how careful one always had to be.

As a child, the youngest of five girls, Aileen knew about being careful. She had arranged everything; it was her job. "The youngest is the one with the energy," her mother said, and it had been like that with each of them: her next older sister anxiously awaiting her birth, just as the older one had awaited hers. Her sister had tended her as an infant, bringing her sweets at night, biscuits soaked in milk and honey, feeding and cooing to her so that she would grow strong — and quickly — to take her place. And take her place she had. It was Aileen who, from the age of five, made the tea; at seven, washed the cabinets and lined them with fresh paper; at eight, ironed the collars of her father's shirts and scrubbed the tub out every morning. It was Aileen her mother called when she wanted her feet rubbed or the fingernails cut on her right hand. And to ensure that she didn't cause more work than she could lighten, Aileen was allowed only three toys, so there'd be less mess. She put each on a shelf labeled with its name: doll, teddy, book. Her mother had saved the labels and given them to her when Mattie was born, but Sirus had forbidden her to use them. "Child's going to have a lot more toys than that" was what he said. But in her home, no one had argued in her behalf. And no child came after Aileen to relieve her of her duties.

She finished her hair and began her makeup. Mattie would come in soon and beg to use the lipstick. No matter how many times she told her no, at every big occasion she asked again, as if she had never heard no before. It was unimaginable to her, this straight-out contest. As a child, Aileen had rebelled only in little ways: saved the nail clippings and put them in her sisters' talcum powder, cut paper for fourteen shelves an inch too short, burned a collar twice a year. She had thought of, but not done, more. More was too dangerous. There was the strap and the hand and, of course, the deadly silence.

She finished penciling her eyebrows just as there was a knock on the door.

"Mommy, may I come in?"

"Yes, come in, Mattie," she answered.

Mattie stopped just inside the door, shyly looking at her mother. The boldness and flurry with which she approached her father were absent, and in their place was a furled tentativeness

— her eyes cast downward, her shoulders hunched protectively over her chest. The sight of her, timid and halting, unleashed in Aileen a guilty fury. At the same time another feeling, like red berries in a thicket, spread through her. The same high cheekbones as her own, the blush of brown color, the familiar aquiline nose and slender hands — every time Aileen looked at Mattie, she saw her own young self, only slightly changed, stamped onto the girl's features. And as she saw that face, a small opening would wedge between her ribs, and a rush of air, like a gasp of hope, would escape and fly toward Mattie, ensnaring her in a tangle of love and longing. Aileen stretched out her arms in spite of herself, and Mattie, seeing her opening, rushed to fill it. Aileen felt the small, intense heat of her daughter, like a warm brick pressed to her bosom and throat, and she held her as long as she could, until the heat began to rise to her face, taking away the cool air, so that she finally had to raise her head to breathe.

"Let me look at you," she said as she disengaged herself and placed Mattie at an arm's length. "Are you all ready to go?"

Mattie nodded, still pressing against the space between them.

"Ten more minutes," Sirus's voice boomed from his shower.

"Go on, we'll be downstairs in a minute," Aileen said to Mattie, shooing her toward the door.

6

"Pontificate," announced Claudia Holmes.

"What?" asked Theresa Hunter.

"*Pontificate*. That's the word."

"The word for what?"

"For what it is these men like to do when they get together."

The women who were setting up for Sirus's dinner criss-crossed the room like ants. Claudia took three stalks of hybrid daisies — fuchsia with marigold centers — from the cardboard box balanced on her hip, clipped their ends, and deposited them in the vase on the table in one smooth flourish. She grew these daisies and over thirty other types of flowers in a backyard no bigger than a foyer, and because of her expertise, she was in charge of flowers for the dinner.

"Blah, blah, blah, blah, blah," she elaborated.

"Oh, hush up, Claudia, and get those flowers on the tables," Theresa ordered from across the basement room.

"Well, you know it's true," Claudia continued. "By the end of tonight, they'll all be complaining their voices are hoarse" — she paused dramatically, reaching into her box for a bunch of hyacinths — "and we'll be the ones with the sore behinds."

"You'd better stop talking and get finished before the old buzz saw gets here," interjected Flora Gayle.

The buzz saw was Etta Baldridge.

"Oh, who's afraid of that fast talker?" Claudia asked. "Remember, I knew her when she didn't have the Cadillac to ride in."

"She may not be riding in it much longer," Theresa said matter-of-factly. The veins in her neck stood out. She was a thin, steely woman who had worked hard for everything she had. Now, as the head of the ladies' volunteer nursing at the hospital, she was nearly as active in civic affairs as Etta.

"What are you talking about, Theresa?" Claudia asked, neatly filling another vase. There were two tables left, and people would be arriving at any minute.

"Yeah, come on, Theresa, tell us what you heard," added Flora.

"You'd have to be a baby not to know," Theresa replied.

Claudia pretended to suck at the stem of one of her flowers. "Well, we're babies then. Tell us what you know."

Theresa was setting out place cards behind each setting, lettered in brown ink in a straight up-and-down script. She had sat up last night until nearly one, painstakingly lettering each card until all were perfect.

"Well, you know how Etta's been since Charles died," Theresa began; "talking about her money problems as if she's the first one to have them. And I don't know about any of you, but I said to myself, come on Etta, stop the show." She completed her precise circle around one table and moved to the next. "I mean, I thought to myself, no way a man like Charles Baldridge, with not one good job but two, and one of them down at the insurance company, well, no way I saw him going and not leaving a good little something behind."

"Well, of course," added Claudia. "I don't even think they let you work at the Federated without having at least some kind of policy. It'd be as if you were a butcher and you never ate your own meat. Now, how would something like that look?" She retrieved a lady bug from one of the daisies and held it poised on her finger before it flew away.

The others agreed noisily.

"Well, that's what I thought too," continued Theresa. "And it's true; he did have a policy, just as you said."

"Well, what happened? Did he borrow against it?" asked Flora.

"Even if he'd borrowed against it," interrupted Claudia, "they wouldn't have let him take the whole thing, so there still had to be something left."

"As I live and breathe," Theresa suddenly said harshly, "that man had a wife and a ten-year-old girl, and he didn't leave them hardly nothing more than his good intentions."

Claudia threw down the bunch of daisies she was holding and shifted the flower box to her other hip for good measure. "What is this, Theresa?" she spat out. "Twenty questions? Now, did the man have a policy or not?"

"Had it. Didn't leave nothing in it to them," Theresa said.

"No."

"No."

"No."

Flora, Claudia, and even Bertie Barter, who up until now hadn't uttered a word, each let fly a separate cry of disbelief.

"Yes," Theresa said. "Changed the beneficiary. In fact, changed it just two weeks before he died."

"And left it to who?" Claudia shrieked.

"A woman named Phoebe Tucker." Theresa was finished with another table. "From Mobile. You know, that's where he was from. Turns out there were five little ones down there who looked a whole lot like him, and I hear tell any one of them is cuter than that one he got from Etta."

"Theresa, you are lying and you know it," Flora yelled.

"God is my witness," she said, raising her hand in the air. "Man disowned his flesh and blood here for some more of it somewhere else. Guess he just counted up the numbers and decided they had the weight in their favor."

The women were now nothing but questions falling over one another.

"How long did he know her?"

"When did they have their first child?"

"Did Etta know what was going on?"

It appeared that Theresa had all the facts, and she doled them out like candy.

"Charles grew up with the girl. Seems they were sweethearts even before he got into long pants. I think Etta even met her once. But I hear she knew for sure that Charles had had one baby with her before she and Charles got married. I guess she thought she'd won him, would make him a better wife and all. This Phoebe was doing day work from since she was only ten, and you know how much Charles wanted to get somewhere. Well, he did, with Etta, but still looks as though he couldn't cut loose that other one altogether."

"How do you know all this?" asked Claudia, suddenly suspicious. "Did somebody over there at the Federated tell?"

"No, in fact they kept this the quietest of anything I ever heard. Charles just changed the beneficiary on his own policy copy. The one in the files he took over to Chapel Hill and had the changes notarized. Only three people down there knew: Tito, Dr. Anson, and Sirus Mac. And all three of them chose this time to be as tight as a drum. Didn't tell a soul, I hear, not even their wives."

"Oh, I bet not," Claudia added bitterly.

"I only heard because I got relatives down in Mobile who know this Phoebe, and she suddenly let just one person know after all this time, but even there, it's not as if it's all over town. Supposedly she feels real bad about the child here, and even offered Etta some of the money. But Etta wasn't having any of it. She had a little something else left from Charles, some kind of bonds or what. And they're giving her some more money, those three that know. They voted her some sort of special pension."

The women, almost in unison, let loose with a collective shudder. Their shoulders and mouths were all set in motion at once. It was as if chaos had been let free in the room. It was hard enough, each of them thought, holding on to and preserving the bit they managed to pull together; hard to have the babies and then have to worry over each one; hard to worry if whatever job you or your husband had might not suddenly go away; hard to seem as though you weren't concerned with money, which is how everybody acted, when not a one of them ever ceased to worry. They had all seen it, the fall from good times to bad, an accident, a factory closing, a second dry year following a first, in and out of grace at the drop of a hat. It went all the way up and down the line: doctors who got into trouble with a licensing board, porter on a line that was cut back, a child sick — and there went all your savings. But this was worse; this was your own flank dropping away when you least expected it, leaving you with nothing between you and the cold night and a pack of hungry dogs but your own alert senses and your lips moving in a fervent prayer.

Theresa had dropped this thing like a hot stone, and they all knew, without saying a word, what had driven her to tell. They knew how the words had probably been bubbling inside her since she'd heard, and even — what made it dangerous — no matter what it might do to Etta for others to know, how hard to keep this kind of thing a secret from others. Look out, Theresa was saying. Look out not just for the weather, and bugs in the garden, and babies getting sick and dying, and stories of white folks getting riled, but look out for your men, probe every corner, not only where it is they might be resting their bodies, but find out if their hearts and souls might have strayed. Etta was a loudmouth and a showoff, but no woman deserved this, on that they could all agree. In their minds each vowed to close ranks around her.

"Don't say a word to Etta," Claudia said, speaking for the group. It was a solemn pact each knew the others would keep. Falling on something as hard as this was the most a body could take, and they did not intend to stretch her reserves any further. If, when Etta arrived, she noticed any difference in the greetings she received, she pretended otherwise. So did the other women. Once the room began to fill with people, it was as if the women's secret evaporated into the air, burned off by the fat yellow candles placed on every table to keep the mosquitoes from climbing through the thick meshed screens.

The dinner was held in the basement of the church, the room used for nearly every civic function and for the choir practice every Wednesday night. It was a big room, lit by one large chandelier, which hung in the middle, and three sconce lights along each of the long walls. The room was both formal and informal: the low ceiling, the ornate chandelier with its crystal pendants, the round tables spread with tablecloths set out in a circle on the finished wooden floor. There were flowers at the center of each table, which gleamed with silver, china, and crystal. Each sponsoring organization had a table, headed up by one member who organized the collection of the tableware and the serving of the food at that table. Many of the women who were to serve worked in one or more of the houses, except for Mrs. Johnson, whose place was with the McDougalds at the center table. There were ten tables in all, with settings for ten at each table. Sirus's table, around which the others were circled like a wagon train set in the

prairie, was in the center of the room. By the time the guest of
honor arrived, the air was thick with the competing smells of
pot roast, turkey, venison, and wild birds.

Sirus stopped Aileen and Mattie at the threshold to the bright
room. He looked around slowly, taking in each face that was
turned toward him. The aroma made him almost dizzy. Re-
flexively, he stretched his fingers, as if to extend his very senses,
and then let his hands relax, his fingers dangling, at the ready,
by his side. At just that moment Aileen reached for his hand,
and her perfume, a musk and fruity smell combined, reached
his nose. He closed his fingers around her hand. It was Emma
Butler who saw them first.

"They're here," Emma said to Satha as she waved to catch
Sirus's eye. Satha pivoted her wheelchair smoothly, following
Emma across the room. They were joined by Etta Baldridge and
Lily before they finished their short trek.

"Sirus, Aileen, Mattie," Emma said, reaching them first,
Satha right on her heels. Sirus kissed them both.

"Emma, Satha, how are you?" Sirus boomed, his voice deep
and rich. His thick black hair gleamed and he looked strong
and vigorous in his deep navy suit. The bright white of his shirt
reflected the light.

"The room looks simply beautiful," Aileen said.

"Do we have you to thank for all this, Etta?" Sirus asked.

"Me and at least a dozen others."

"Well, let me begin with you." Sirus opened his arms a third
time and swallowed Etta up in them, his lips pressed heartily
against her powdered cheek.

"Are you ready to say something in case they ask?" Lily
whispered to Mattie, the two of them standing apart, their arms
entwined, just out of reach of their parents.

"No, they won't ask me," Mattie whispered.

"They might," Lily said knowingly. "After all, you're his
daughter."

"Well, I know that," Mattie answered, her voice just a shade louder.

"Bet you have to talk," Lily countered.

"Bet I don't," Mattie shot back. Her voice was loud enough for her mother to hear.

Aileen whispered, "Hush up, you two," a finger to her lips for good measure.

Etta continued. "I hear nearly three hundred are expected for the part upstairs after dinner."

"You could have knocked me over with a feather when I heard," Sirus said, laughing.

"Oh, Sirus, don't give us that," Etta answered. "If you weren't working hard to get it, then just tell me who was."

Aileen looked away from them, out toward the room.

"Just trying to make my contribution," Sirus said.

Dr. Gant and his wife joined the circle.

"Sirus," Dr. Gant said, extending his hand to Sirus. He then turned to the women and added, economically, "Ladies," nodding at them all at once. His wife, Muriel, hung behind him until her name was actually said.

"Melvin, Muriel," they all said simultaneously.

"Well, this is quite the night, isn't it?" Dr. Gant asked. His eyes shone behind his round glasses. The small bit of envy he felt he hid well.

"If you don't say something, and they ask you, you'll look like a jerk," Lily whispered.

"Will not, " Mattie whispered back.

"Will too."

"If the two of you don't stop it, we'll have to put you at separate tables," Aileen said without letting her eyes leave the circle. Mattie shook her hips at Lily as if to say, fine by me, and Lily returned the gesture.

"Let's all get seated," Etta said, leading the group, which had swelled considerably, across the room.

By now, everyone who was to attend the dinner had arrived. The room was alive with noise and activity as Sirus
moved toward his table: voices calling out, perfumes mixing
and clashing, the clatter of plates, the rustle of waxed paper, the
door to the kitchen opening and closing; a hundred different
sounds and smells mingled and swirled, an assault on the senses.
Splashed across the room and cohering them into a whole, like
a pigment with which they'd all been stained, was the display
of the clan's assemblage. "Aunt This"; "Cousin That"; everyone
was related to at least a dozen others, and the blood lines
carried from one side of the room to the other, repeating like a
choral refrain, here a long nose, and there, and there, repeated
in shades from cream to red to brown, and everywhere, hair
the color of trees: mahogany, ash, maple, chestnut. The long
fingers curled around a cane were the same long bones as
those which leaned, decorously, against a table, or strode pur-
posefully across the room. Without knowing that they did, they
all danced together, an in-the-bones-and-blood dance, called out
by the patterns of movement and intonation stamped invisibly
alongside the nerves of every body, with the gathering light of
the sun of another time and place palely imitated by the one
burning chandelier.

"So how does it feel?" Gant asked Sirus, indicating all of the
people and the food as they paused to let Sirus shake more
hands.

"Just perfect," Sirus answered.

Gant privately smiled to himself. He was the only one here
who had learned — body by body and bone by bone — not to
trust the appearance of perfection. For Sirus, however, perfection was not only the present but the past and future. In the
time it took them to travel from the doorway to their table, the
earlier part of the day and the night before evaporated into the
heated and fragrant air around them. Buoyed up by their neighbors, he and Aileen and Mattie moved like a pleasure boat

pulling into harbor: Sirus leaning his tall frame like a wind-filled sail as he stopped and spoke to people, Aileen like a headlamp piercing out beyond where they stood, and Mattie, the breaker, tapping and swaying to the tempo of the talk that cascaded over her. For their neighbors, they were a stunning family — one broad, one supple, one electric — with a shared energy flowing from one to the next, in an unbroken circle, altering its form as it alighted on each one, while remaining, at its core, unchanged.

When they reached their table, they were joined by Sirus's Uncle Reggie and Aunt Viola, Jason and Edith, and Mrs. Johnson. Etta and Lily, Sirus and Aileen and Mattie, took their places behind their chairs.

"Can you believe this is the same boy who acted as though he didn't know which end was up?" Uncle Reggie asked his wife.

"Doesn't look like the same boy to me," Viola returned. "I thought your father was one strange boy," Viola said to Mattie. "Dreamy, dreamy boy. Used to bump into things, never watched where he was going, acted as though he didn't hear a word you said. If somebody had told me we'd be here tonight, and for his putting something together that didn't fall down no less, I'd have said, well just go ahead and dig my grave now, because I know I'll never live to see that day."

"I was not that bad," Sirus said to Mattie. "Don't listen to them."

"Oh, you listen to us, sweetie pie," Viola said. "We are telling you the gospel truth. And you just remember that, in case his head starts to get too big."

Mattie laughed and felt as light as a cloud. Her mother beautiful and smiling, her father laughing and huge, her relatives teasing as they always did, all the people she knew nearby; this was as close to heaven as she could imagine. If heaven wasn't filled with the people you loved, then she didn't want to ever go there, she decided. She looked again at the faces closely gathered around. She didn't even know that she had believed in Jesus until this moment, but she felt that if things were this perfect, then He must be real — and more, He must be here among them. She felt like hugging Him and thanking Him for giving her these people to belong to.

Sirus leaned over to kiss Mattie's cheek. Under the table, he squeezed Aileen's hand. The afternoon and last night were far away. He felt a great golden glow covering his wife and his child and his friends. He led the table in grace.

"Look what the wind blew threw the door," Uncle Reggie said when the grace was through. Sirus followed his gaze across the room. Just inside the door, talking to Theresa Hunter, who had intercepted him, was the white councilman, Phil Burnett. Theresa took his hat and disappeared with it to the cloakroom. While she was gone, Burnett stood precisely where she'd left him, looking awkwardly around the room. The people closest to him began whispering among themselves first, but their hushed voices alerted everyone else to Burnett's presence. One after another, heads turned, and then, as rapidly, turned away.

"I see him," Sirus told Uncle Reggie. His uncle shrugged as if to say, I've already told you everything I know. And of course he had, but it didn't change this moment. This was Sirus's night, these were his people; and yet there this white man stood, uninvited, but free to come and go among them at will. Theresa returned from the cloakroom and motioned to Burnett to follow her. The two of them made the same journey across the room that Sirus had just made, but the ripple flowed away from Burnett, different from the one that had risen up to greet Sirus. No one welcomed Burnett, and many looked down or away as he passed. Behind and in front of him, the whispering grew.

He was an unremarkable-looking man to create such a swell:

short, with loose fleshy skin, in his early fifties, with that pink undertone to his skin which set whites apart from even the lightest blacks. His hair was sandy brown and thinning, and it clung to the top of his head like wet thread. He wore what appeared to be his less than best suit, the lapels slightly frayed and shiny, and a button sewed back with a thread that didn't match.

"Sorry I'm late," Burnett said as slipped into his chair. Everyone shifted chairs to make room for him, but at the same time they pointed away from him, their arms shielding their bodies. Only Sirus turned toward him.

"How was your drive over? Any trouble finding the place?" he asked.

Aileen half-expected him to say, "You colored are easy to find," but he responded, jovially, "No problem, fellow, no problem at all."

He'd said *fellow* instead of *boy*, his concession, everyone at the table supposed, to the award and the dinner and being in a church, a sacred place. But still, there was no evading the word. It was stark and clear. Sirus chose to ignore it and plowed ahead, asking about the councilman's family, his small business, his political goals. For his part, Burnett appeared all too happy to oblige with a pleasant stream of chatter about himself. Every so often he nodded to the others at the table, as if they, along with Sirus, were eager to take in his every word.

Aileen returned the nod but continued to stare at him as coldly as she had since he'd arrived. Look at Sirus go on, she couldn't help thinking, and at this white-trash excuse for a man. She could see that Burnett was not listening to a thing Sirus said. Too busy convincing himself he wouldn't be fooled by Sirus, she thought to herself, that he'd be able to tell the difference between Sirus and a real white man, any day. Why, the nose is too thick, and the whites of his eyes lack the shine and clarity you see in whites, Aileen could see him think to himself. No matter that Sirus had fooled hundreds of them, no matter that he sat with them in their Pullman cars when he traveled north, ate with them in the diners that dotted the back roads from North Carolina to D.C., shopped with them in their stores whenever he chose. No, she thought, Sirus had fooled hundreds, but this Phil Burnett was sure he would not fool him. She could see him filing away every square inch of Sirus's face as they talked, just to be sure.

Mattie, too, was watching Phil Burnett. She didn't like the way he leaned over her father, as if he were bigger than Sirus, when the truth was that her father was much larger. And the way he laughed in all the wrong places, laughing at her father, not with him, she was sure. She also could detect the feelings of everyone else at the table. It was as if an actual cloud hung over them all. Her Great-aunt Viola and her Great-uncle Reggie were talking about the man under their breath. They were laughing softly enough so that he wouldn't hear, making fun of the shiny spots on his ugly brown suit, talking about how little and how fast he chewed his food, just loud enough to reach everybody's ears but his. She could also feel the animosity from her mother, as solid as the chair she sat on. It was like a small, hard ball, thrown with great velocity at Burnett's head, and she almost felt like ducking. And Mrs. Johnson, who seemed to have retreated, pretending as if he weren't even there, the way she could do sometimes when there were a lot of people in the house and she had work to do. And her father, her father. Where, oh, where had the sunny side of him gone?

Burnett and Sirus kept up their idle chatter. The meal itself was a major attraction. Wasn't this meat just the tenderest? Where on earth had the venison been caught? Who had cooked these heavenly rolls? It was the same conversation Mattie had heard millions of times, but with this man, it sounded different.

Everything was too much, the way a teacher could tell you, oh, how beautiful, when you made a painting that everyone knew was silly. The food was wonderful, but wonderful food was maybe all you could expect from the colored. Mattie knew white people thought things like that. Her parents had never told her that, but it was something she had heard other people say, people like her aunt and her uncle.

For his part, Burnett wished the meal would end. Although everything was delicious, eating with these people was not something he particularly enjoyed. He'd come to show white support for the success of "their" colored. (After all, wasn't it somehow a tribute to them?) And to show that he could. And most of all, to attend to a certain matter that he intended to discuss. But as he settled in his chair, the discomfort he felt among the colored was compounded by the array of skin colors assembled at the table. When he'd said he'd be coming to the dinner, some of his friends had teased him, "Going to be some real dark beauties there, I bet," but it wasn't the dark beauties who disturbed him. Like all Southern white men, he knew of the secret and sometimes not so secret mingling of the races, but he was always able to slide his mind over it without its taking effect. Now, though, he had to look at these people and face an uncomfortable truth — not only the fact of white desire, stamped on so many features, but more: the fact that these colored seemed to swallow up all of the whiteness as if it were a small glass of water emptied into a roaring stream. They took it in and went on. Sirus had the features of a white man, wore them like a mockery, and yet was every inch a colored man.

Suddenly, surprisingly, Mattie's water glass dropped to the floor; it shattered, and sprayed shards and water in all directions.

"Oh, gosh, I'm sorry," Mattie began.

"What happened?" and "Watch what you're doing," her mother and father said separately.

The woman who was serving the food appeared at the table in seconds with a broom and a dustpan.

"Just a glass, sweetie pie," she said.

Mattie wished a hole would open up in the floor.

"Are you all right, baby?" her father asked when the glass had been swept away. His voice sounded tired, as if this white man, or something, had drained the life out of him. The glow they'd all had when they first sat down was gone.

"Your husband is quite the raconteur," Burnett said to Aileen.

Aileen hesitated for just the briefest second before she answered him. "Yes, he is," she said.

"He's got a story for everything," Burnett continued.

Reggie added, possessively, "Yes, he's always had a way with words."

"I bet he tells you lots of stories," Burnett said now, looking directly at Mattie.

"Well, yes, lots," Mattie answered.

"And what's your favorite?" he asked, leaning across her father so that his face was closer to hers. Mattie's stomach clutched like a fist around the food she'd just eaten.

"My favorite?" she asked.

"Yes, your favorite," the man repeated. He smiled and looked around at the others. "What's the matter?" he said, laughing, looking back at Mattie. "Cat got your tongue?"

Mattie's face burned with shame and anger. She hated this man. Yet she knew, without lifting her head, that it was toward her that everyone's eyes were turned, with her that they were all silently pleading: "Go on, answer him. Don't let us down; don't let him go on thinking you're stupid." She struggled to clear her head, to make some kind of story come, but it was all a jumble: foxes, rabbits, fields, bridges. No matter how hard she tried, nothing was lining up the way a story or an answer should.

Burnett laughed again and shook his head, lifting his hands in the air, as if to say, "Well, who knew she couldn't talk?" or perhaps it meant, what could he be expected to know of them, of their lives, of their children. They were only colored, after all, and if he blundered, well, there was no way the blame could be his.

To Mattie his hands in the air said, "This is your last chance; you have to speak now or else keep silent forever." So she opened her mouth and said the first word that popped into her head.

"A fox," she blurted out. "And a rabbit." As she spoke she saw one of each: the fox in a field by a rock, the rabbit on a road. "They're in a field. Well, no, just the fox is. And the rabbit's on the road." She saw something else, so she added, "And the fox is lying like he's hurt, with his foot under a rock, and he's calling to the rabbit going by."

"Oh, one of your folktales," Burnett said with pleasure. "Won't my wife be jealous when I tell her this." He smiled at Mattie as if she were a new creature, only recently born, placed here at this moment for his own private pleasure.

"So the rabbit says, 'What?' when he hears the fox, and the fox says, 'Come here please. I need some water.'" She continued, "And the rabbit says , 'I can't do that; if I come close you'll eat me.'" As she said that, Mattie could feel the rabbit's fright; it washed over her like a wave, and she could see him quivering in the road, unable to move from fear.

"'I'm scared,' the rabbit said back to the fox." Her hands were hot against the sides of her seat. The pictures seemed to be moving away.

"And then?" Burnett prompted.

"And then, and then." Mattie's voice echoed in her ears. She strained to make the picture go forward, but all she could see was the rabbit frozen by the side of the road. The silence stretched from now till forever.

"And then," Burnett said, lunging toward Mattie, "the fox said, 'You're right, I will eat you!'" He laughed heartily, at both his joke and the clever way he'd thought of bringing the whole thing to a close. "That's quite a story," he said as he sat back in his seat.

Mattie knew she'd failed. The others laughed, to be kind, along with Burnett. "It's all right, sweetheart," she longed for her father to say. But he was silent. Mercifully, the dinner came quickly to its end. Everyone excused himself from the table, until only Sirus and Burnett remained.

"Well, Sirus," Burnett said, "you folks certainly know how to put on some good eating."

"Glad you enjoyed it," Sirus answered.

"And there's nothing I love more than hearing you people tell your tales," Burnett continued. Sirus was silent. "So it couldn't have been a nicer night."

"Good," Sirus replied.

"Now let me tell you why I really came," Burnett whispered. For a second, his slip appeared to embarrass him, but he turned the gaffe into pleasure and smiled all the more broadly.

"We think you're quite the businessman." He reached over to pat Sirus's arm. "Yes, indeed, think you've done quite well for yourself." He looked around the hall as if it held the confirmation of his statement.

"But there's more, you know, if you know how to get it, if you're smart and the right people come along." He leaned back in his seat as if to make room for his idea at the table. "White businessmen," he announced. "We'd be willing to share in a venture. We've got it all worked out. Shares. Percentages. All the details." Here he paused and reached toward Sirus again. "We'd take care of you; you can be sure of that."

Sirus neither withdrew nor moved closer. "What do you want from me?" he asked. His choice of words was incendiary, and each man knew it. Burnett chose to turn them back onto Sirus.

"Want to help you make a little more money for yourself, boy," he said. "While we make a little something for ourselves." He circled the air with his finger. "See, we've got it all worked out. What have you got? A ready-made market." He laughed. "More of your people than anybody knows where to put them. And who have they come to trust? Nobody but you. Plus you've got an eye for good land, I'll give you that. And your boys, they work real hard and long. For you," Burnett continued with relish. "We'll bring in our banks, back you with some real money. Let you tackle something really big for a change. Plus some real know-how on making a profit." He laughed again. "It's not all selling, you know."

Sirus knew instantly that the thing was rotten, that there was nothing in this man that meant him or any of his own any good.

"I'll have to think on it" was all he said.

Burnett took this for a yes. He had come in person and put it to Sirus because it appealed to some of the other investors' sense of being fair and reasonable. If Sirus didn't say yes right away, there were other ways to bring him to it. As he left, he nodded at the few people who were left in the room, but vacantly. His mind was already racing ahead to contracts and deeds and loans. The lights in the rear hallway flicked on, then off, as he left. A short in the wires, he thought, though it was a signal from those upstairs that the rest of the program was about to begin.

Sirus climbed the stairs from the basement to the front of the church. He could smell the cologne that Phil Burnett wore as it clung to his own clothes, a thin, astringent smell that would dissipate quickly. He wished the rest of Burnett could be as easily shed. He could still feel the touch of Burnett's hand on his shoulder, familiar yet without any warmth, still saw the carelessly calculated look in Burnett's eyes, as if he needn't bother to try to hide what he was thinking. Sirus knew these things could not be dispersed as simply as bad cologne. Already, they were settling in beside other memories equally unwelcome. They coalesced into a single knowing: To them, we are not human.

Sirus recalled the first time he'd been sure of this. It was at the end of that summer in Durham, a wrenching awareness formed of his own experiences, not something passed on to him. It could still bring tears to his eyes. He was able to recognize Phil Burnett as a man, could see what united them, even as he disliked him, but it was a one-sided exchange. Phil Burnett's whole demeanor showed that when he looked at Sirus, or at any colored man, for that matter, he saw not a man like himself, who might hold his wife in his arms in a particular way, who could wield a hammer deftly or not, who ate his grits with butter or with gravy, but something far different and far less, something he refused to embrace as in any way familiar.

When thirteen-year-old Sirus came home that summer from Durham, he told his father what he'd learned. His father grew quiet. His aunt was in the kitchen, fixing them a Sunday meal, while he and his father sat out on the porch. His father's chair, cane-bottomed, squeaked under a shift of weight.

"Who told you that?" his father asked.

Sirus was sitting on the porch steps, shelling the peas his aunt was going to cook with dinner. "Nobody," Sirus said. "I figured it out for myself."

There was more silence; his father's chair squeaked again. "You're every bit as human as they are," his father finally said.

"You have a head on your shoulders, you got a good heart, you got a large soul."

"But why do they treat us the way they do?" Sirus persisted.

Sirus's father looked off into the distance, as if the answer were hovering over his fields. Then he looked at his hands in his lap. "Some men have a need," he began, "to look down on a body. Doesn't much matter to them who; just somebody. And it could be a white man or a colored, could be anybody, so long as they're down and the other man is up. It's like corn liquor, cruelty is. Some men get a taste for it and can never let up."

Sirus had been afraid he'd make his daddy angry if he pressed on, but he couldn't help himself.

"But why us, why me?" he'd asked, his young voice cracking. If he had ever wanted a thing in his life, after his mother still to be alive, it was for his father to come over to him at that very moment, sit next to him on the steps, put his arm around his shoulder, and tell him that people weren't that way. But his father didn't move from his chair.

It was after that conversation with his father that Sirus had resolved he wouldn't acquiesce to such cruelty, no matter what his father said; he could and would build a world of his own design; and his world didn't have to include men like the ones he'd seen in Durham. He could work hard and make things different. He would stay up late, get up early, dream his own dreams, and if he was careful and smart and didn't let up, those dreams would come true.

Now Sirus stepped out of the stairwell from the basement into the main hall of the church. In a row of chairs up on the altar, between the two pulpits, sat Dr. Gant, who was to introduce him, the Reverend Martin, who was going to open the ceremony with a prayer, the Reverend Frankel, who would lead the closing prayer, and Bert Candless and Ezra Stewart, from the bank and insurance company, each of whom was going to

say a few words about Sirus's accomplishments. At the back of
the altar the choir was seated in turquoise robes, looking like
the sparkling water that reflected back from the bottom of the
baptismal pool. And out in the church proper, from the very
front to the rear, were his family and friends. Aileen and Mattie
stared up at him from the first row. Throughout the room, fans
flickered. Sirus took his seat between Gant and Martin, and
people grew quieter. Soon there was just a murmuring sound,
like his own breathing in the middle of the night, rising and
falling in the room.

This is what seals all the other away, Sirus thought to himself.
The Reverend Martin made his way slowly to the right pulpit,
and the choir began to sing softly.

"Let us pray," the reverend began.

Sirus didn't begin his speech with love. He talked about hard
work and persistence and luck, as Aileen had wished. But by
the end of his talk, love could not be denied. "I want to thank
each and every one of you," he said toward the close. He was
standing at the lectern on the altar, where the Reverend Martin
had stood. His deep voice easily filled the church. "Whenever I
needed assistance, some one of you has been right there," he
said.

Sirus towered above the lectern, his hands barely resting on
it. The room was hot by now, and there had been more talk
than people could sit still for. They shifted in their seats, fanning
themselves briskly. But out of respect to Sirus, they coordinated
their movements with his. When he was still, they were still, and
when he took out his linen handkerchief and dabbed at his
brow, people reached for their fans and their tissues. For a
moment Sirus paused and looked out at the audience. It was
already dark outside, but the lights inside the church made the
night seem unnaturally bright. Everywhere he looked was the

gleam of taffeta and cotton in the women's dresses, which glinted in shades of green and yellow and white. Their colors reflected the light so that the room glowed. Next to the women's colors were the dark browns and deep navies of the men's suits, like ballast that kept all the brightness from flying away. Every pew was filled, and people lined the sides of the church and the space at the back.

"You'll never know how much all of you have meant to me," Sirus said.

"We're with you, Sirus," one man called out, and a few people broke into a spontaneous applause. But Sirus waved his arm.

"Just a minute," he said. He thought about all the other things he had originally wanted to say, and he thought about Phil Burnett. "There's one last thing I want to say to everyone before we all go home," he went on. He noticed Aileen smiling at him, and he smiled back. Next to her, Mattie kicked her legs against the base of the pew. She waved at him with her fan.

"Downstairs," he went on, "a man came into our church. A man who is not here now. A man who has never worshiped with us. A man who ate with us tonight, but who would never invite us into his home to share a meal with his family."

Etta Baldridge shifted in her seat and tried to catch Sirus's eye.

"I think you all know the man I mean," Sirus continued. He watched as Etta leaned over to whisper to Ophelia Macon; at the same time, the Butler sisters gave each other a wary look. "And this man said he came here to pay his respects," Sirus went on, "or at least that's what he said at first, but then, I don't know why, but I didn't believe him."

"You better not believe a *word* the man tells you!" Flodie Madison yelled out. "I work for those people, so I know!"

"Well, you just might be right, Flodie," Sirus responded,

"because when the eating was over, well, this man said he had to confess the real reason he'd come."

"To take a look at our fine women," another voice yelled.

"Well, that too maybe," Sirus went on, and here he dropped his voice a little. "The man came to make me an offer." People were suddenly very quiet. "I told him I needed to think about it, which, of course, was what he expected to hear."

"Should have asked him when he's gonna invite you over to his church for supper," someone yelled from the back.

"Yes, I should have," Sirus answered. He looked at the few people who'd been dozing, most of them awake now. "But I didn't. What I did do, however, was lie."

There were one loud cough, and an older woman in the front in a bright green dress sucked her teeth at Sirus. He leaned over the lectern and talked directly to her. "I lied, Mrs. Allen," he said, "when I told him I had to think about his offer, because there's nothing to think about."

"You know it; listen to him, Momma," Mrs. Allen's son added.

"I mean, honestly," Sirus went on, "is there anybody here who needs to *think* about the man. Do any of you have to *ponder* how he feels about you; do you have to *cogitate* or *reflect* on it?"

People began to laugh out loud.

"I mean, is that the stupidest thing you've ever heard, having to stop and think about whether a snake means to poison you if he bites you? I mean, what the hell else is a snake going to do?"

"Preach it, Sirus," a woman in a large hat yelled from her seat in the middle of a pew.

"I wish I could preach it," Sirus answered. "But you folks know I'm not a preaching man. But I'm also nobody's fool. A lot of things maybe, and some not too polite, but not a fool."

"You sure ain't a fool, Sirus," the woman in the large hat yelled.

"Thank you, Margaret," Sirus said. "I appreciate that." He took a swallow of water from the glass on the lectern. "So, what I wanted to say, what I almost didn't say, because I was thinking about this man, is that I love you. Each and every one of you. You, Mrs. Allen, and you, Joe, and Jason and Edith, and Etta, and Melvin and Muriel, and Flodie, and my family, of course, and whoever it is that's been yelling from the back who I can't see."

"It's me, Sirus." A large man stepped out from behind a wall of people to reveal himself.

"And you too, Calvin," Sirus said, smiling. "Each and every one of you. And if I've accomplished something, made something of myself, it's all because of that feeling. It's what gets me up and out of the bed each day."

"Now don't be talking 'bout no bed with me," Calvin boomed out, and the whole room erupted in laughter. The laughter spread like sweet sweat, rolling from one skin to the next, till they were all caught up in it, and then the laughter spread to applause, and people were on their feet, clapping. Sirus stood up straight and let it flow over him. When it quieted, he was very still and quiet too, as if he were holding what they had given him, tenderly, to the center of his chest.

"That's all I wanted to say," he said. "It's late; we're all tired. Even my wife's struggling to stay awake, and she's supposed to want to listen to me, so I know the rest of you would like me to shut up so you can go home."

Some people started to clap again, as if to say no, but it quickly ended. "Thank you again," Sirus said. "Good night. God bless all of you."

1

THE MORNING after the award dinner, Aileen awoke with the sun. She looked around the room, excited. She thought she might not have slept at all. It was as if the dinner and Sirus's speech at the church had begun a new day, and the sun was only now catching up with it. As she surveyed the room, everything had a fresh glow. Sirus's clothes were carefully laid across the back of a chair. Her slip, which she had left on the hook on the back of the door, gleamed like silk. Aileen could easily remember on a morning like this all of the days and nights that had come before, when things were perfect. Sirus, who had spirited her away from her angry home. Sirus, who had stolen her away from herself. Sirus in his glory, as she'd originally seen and known him. She looked at him now, still sleeping. He lay on his back, his mouth slightly open, the covers kicked to the bottom of the bed. Asleep, on a morning like this, he was exactly like the young man she'd married, an open oyster, fresh and translucent. When he looked young like that, she felt young too, and nothing could be frightening or bad. With a young Sirus at her side, the world was transformed, and all of the old expectations were banished.

Back at the beginning, Aileen remembered, Sirus brought all of his dreams to her like a catch from the sea. And she would receive them, excited, as if they were her dreams too. What do you think? he would ask as he spread them in front of her.

"What do you think, Aileen?" he'd asked her once. He was standing at the end of their porch, peering forward as if he were inspecting the lilac bush growing at the side of the porch. But she knew he hardly noticed the bush; she knew that what he saw was something alive only in his mind. They had been married exactly one year.

"The bank takes money in," he went on, "puts it in government bonds, government mortgage paper, people earn interest, but what does that do for us, right here?" He ran his hand along the porch railing. "Now we built this," he said, "out of money I saved. But not everybody can save the money up front. So instead of all of that government paper, why not make our own mortgages? Hell, why not buy our own land, build our own homes?"

"Isn't that risky?" she'd asked, but back then, when she expressed doubt, she rarely meant it. She eventually said yes to everything, if only to see Sirus standing with his head in the middle of the lilacs.

"Risky, I suppose, yes," he'd answer, "but what isn't?"

And then he would saunter across the porch, throw his arms around her, scoop her up, kiss her, enfold her, and everything that he was — big, optimistic, bold — she would become too.

That was how Sirus had been last night, or maybe he was always that way, and it was her seeing it again last night that had been different. He had spoken of love in his speech, and despite Aileen's earlier misgivings, she didn't think it was possible for any one person to be more proud than she had felt. Sirus stirred in his sleep and rolled toward her. Aileen hesitated only for a moment. Then she slid under Sirus like water.

Even before the morning was through, Sirus's words at the dinner had galloped around town, as if by their own momentum. While they brought back fresh dreams to Aileen, for others they stoked a smoldering pride. Etta Baldridge called half a dozen people before she'd even finished her breakfast, and to each of them she said the same thing: "Sirus has got to see this thing through." To Etta, however, seeing it through meant staying on top of every twist and turn and nuance, even if it meant that Sirus should eventually change his mind. The Butler sisters also believed that Sirus should see it through, but they meant that he should stand by what he had originally said. Ophelia Macon agreed with Etta while she was talking with her, and then agreed with her sister, who was visiting, as soon as she'd hung up the phone. "You town folks are just out of practice dealing with those people," Ophelia's sister said. "Down country, we have enough sense to do whatever it is that the white folks want us to do." Still others felt an excitement that was just short of anxiety, an anxiety that could easily change to fear. These others, also rising early, brought the words back for their own particular review.

The Reverend Frankel was one of them. He had been waking early every day for the past week. Today was not an ordinary day, just as none of the days for the past week had been ordinary for him.

Phil Burnett's offer had come as no surprise to the Reverend Frankel. He and Dr. Gant and Bert Candless from the bank had been meeting about it in Gant's office for several days before the dinner. Some white man — Frankel didn't know who — had decided that there was money to be made on the colored side of town, and this thing about the buildings with Sirus, as Gant kept putting it, was just the beginning.

"If it goes through, if Sirus can be persuaded to go along," Gant had said, "why then there are going to be other deals, other plans, and those will be open to us."

At the time, Frankel had felt exultant. A change was coming that would make everything different, a change that would shift around all that was usual. In this future, it wouldn't be only people like Sirus at the head of the town; there would be room for new people, people like him, people who weren't a cousin or an uncle to somebody, people who hadn't gone off to Washington or the North to some big school, people who hadn't always owned their own land so that they were used to keeping and building on all that they earned.

Now, standing at his stove in his undershirt and shorts, stirring grits in a cast-iron pot, Frankel thought back to Sirus's speech and to the townspeople's support for it. On his own he would be worried, but Gant had predicted Sirus's initial response.

"Sirus will be against it, at first," Gant had told him. "And everybody else, too; they'll jump on Sirus's bandwagon. But you don't know this town the way I do. A thing has to fly around town a good two or three times before you can say where it'll land."

Frankel was glad Gant knew things as well as he did. Frankel felt like a plodding child next to Gant, but he didn't care. He would gladly run next to anyone — panting, if he had to — if it was going to help him to catch up and get where it was he wanted to go. He took the grits from the stove, spooned a large ladle of gravy over them, and sat hungrily at the kitchen table.

"There will be those who will stick with Sirus no matter what," Gant had told him last night on the phone. "People like Jason, the Butler sisters, probably some of the men who work out on his sites, one or two of the old-timers down at the bank. And there will be those against it from the beginning. Probably the Macons, the Wilsons, people who wouldn't dare fart if you told them a white person had crossed the horizon. Then there are the rest. We can call them 'the persuadables.' They'll go any which way, depending on what they hear. And some will be persuaded by fear, and some by greed, and some by the desire to go along with their neighbor, but that's who we have to concentrate on."

Frankel finished his grits and served himself another helping. When Gant had first told him what the white men wanted to do, and said that he, Frankel, could be part of it, he had been wary. It was not the kind of thing he would normally do, and especially he would not do anything that might cross Sirus, but he saw that eventually it would be his only chance with Clorissa Macon. He might argue that being the wife of a minister would give her respect and comfort, but he knew that a girl so young and beautiful would demand much more than that. This partnership with the white men would elevate him in a different way. He would be a businessman, a part owner of something — a drugstore, maybe a grocery store — it hadn't even been decided what. But it would be a store, and in exchange for their help with these buildings of Sirus's, why he and Gant would be made partners in the new undertaking.

Frankel looked around the small square room that was his kitchen. When I'm married to Clorissa, he thought, she'll make the hash and the grits and the coffee and fresh juice. And when I want some more, she'll get up to serve me. When he and Clorissa were married, they would not live here; they would be in the parish house, and there they would have a dining room twice the size of this kitchen, and it would be in that dining room that he and Clorissa would take all of their meals. He could already see it. When he married Clorissa Macon, Sirus and Gant and the Reverend Martin and the men from the bank and the insurance company, they would all be there. He would stand at the front of the church, waiting for his Clorissa, and all eyes would be on him and his new bride.

Across town, Dr. Gant was also awake, though rising early was usual for him. He was in his study downstairs, with the door closed. He had just gotten off the phone with Bert Candless, down at the bank. "Are you sure we can turn this around?" Candless had asked. Gant was waiting for others to call. He and Frankel were not the only ones who were behind the deal with Burnett. There was a small group of them — progressives, they called themselves — men who looked forward to the day when nothing would be as it was.

"There are men who live in the past and men who live in the future," Gant liked to say. "Sirus thinks the future should look like the past; that's why he can't understand real progress." Gant understood progress, knew it had a different face from what Sirus imagined. He had given this considerable thought. He leaned back in his chair and looked out his window. He had become a doctor for the very same reason he'd decided to go in with Phil Burnett: it would push out the boundaries of what he knew. As a doctor, he was intimate with bodies in a way that ordinary men were not. His hands had explored not just skin and hair but organs and blood. Where other men knew only what was on the surface, Gant had cut bodies open and touched what was inside.

And he knew white men more intimately. Most colored were afraid of whites, imagined them to have some secret power, but Gant knew they were just men. Gant was eager for the new arrangement. Working alongside the white men would give him a chance to learn even more about them. Up close, he would see exactly how they made decisions, would learn who it was that curried favor with whom, would be able to say for himself that there were white men who looked up to other white men and were afraid of them, just as some colored did with all whites.

For right now, when he met with the white men, he had to hide his intelligence and his watchful observation of them. He had to listen to their insults and their jokes; he had to pretend there were things about contracts and percentages he was slow to understand; he had to pretend to have the same fear and respect that many colored had. But he was not like that at all. The white men thought him their inferior when, in fact, he knew that, with a little more knowledge, he could surpass most of them. One day, not just these white men he was working with, but a lot of white men, would know that. One day, he would learn all he needed to know, and then the tables would turn.

The phone rang, and it was Burnett. He wanted to know how it had gone last night, whether Sirus would agree to the deal. Gant told him about Sirus's speech and about his own belief that the initial sentiment would change. Burnett was sanguine. "What do we need to do now?" he asked. Gant and Frankel had argued about that just this morning, and in the end it was Gant who had prevailed. "I think the way to Sirus is through others," Gant told Burnett. "He's not one to make people he cares about uncomfortable. Any pressure applied directly to Sirus would only intensify his battle with you." Burnett seemed to be in a hurry, and the conversation quickly ended.

"Melvin," Gant's wife called from the hallway as he hung up the phone. She never came into his study. "Melvin, breakfast. Come on now, or it will be getting cold."

"I'll be right out," Gant called back.

Down in the Hay-Ti area, outside Dr. Gerard's drugstore, others also discussed the dinner, but here there was no prior agenda.

Jason stood to the side of an impromptu group that had gathered on the sidewalk.

"Yes, indeed, Sirus told it!" Calvin Brown said to the group. "He may be quiet sometimes," he went on, "but he doesn't take stuff off of no one. Didn't he tell it?" Calvin was excited and proud. He'd been one of the people Sirus had called out to during his speech, and he felt it was his own words that Sirus had spoken. The men with him made a loose circle. Their eyes darted from the ground, up and down the street, then back to one another's faces. Each man danced from leg to leg, as if he was eager to go somewhere, except for the Carter brothers, who stood with their weight planted solidly and evenly on both legs, their feet far apart. All of them but Ed Burns had been at the dinner; he hadn't gone because he'd been nursing a hangover from the night before.

"People clapped when he was through," Jason added. "It was like a revival. You know Sirus isn't that kind of talker, but he was last night. He came striding down off that stage, and people were running over to him like they'd never seen him before, like he was some big guy from out of town. He called Mattie and Aileen over to him, and the three of them were surrounded."

"Yes, indeed," Calvin added, "it was something."

Ernest Adams interrupted. "A whole lot of talk, that's what it was, if that's the kind of something you mean." Ernest owned a butcher shop at the end of Pettigrew Street, and his hands were pinky brown on the inside, like the meat he sold. He waved one wide hand at Calvin. "I was there, man, and I heard him, but I know where he works every day, and where he lives too, and where we all live, and in case you niggers may have forgotten, I don't see none of y'all down there running City Hall. So Sirus can talk as big as he wants; let's just see what happens at the end of the day."

Calvin shook his head and the sunlight bounced off his oiled head. "You're just a sorry nigger, Ernest. Scared if a white man looks at you sideways. Sirus ain't like you. Ain't that right, Jason? You know Sirus real well. When have you known Sirus to act like a fool?"

"Well, nobody said Sirus is a fool, Calvin," Ed interrupted, "but neither is Ernest. Don't need to be a fool to know what butters your bread."

Ernest pushed out his lips in a pout. "That's all I'm saying," he said.

"I wasn't talking to either of y'all," Calvin said. He looked directly at Jason.

"Well," Jason said, "I've known Sirus a long, long time, and I think if he said the thing, he meant it, and he won't be backing down."

There was a brief silence, and then both Mike and Judd Carter spoke up. "He's a strong man, there's no denying that," said Mike. "That's for sure," added Judd. "He's a man who lives by his word." Judd and Mike were twin brothers, in their fifties, each a rounded brown reflection of the other.

Jason went on. "Right, that's just what I mean." He looked around the circle carefully. "And I have to say, for myself, not only do I think that Sirus will stick, but I think he's right to stick. After all, why should we be giving more money than we have to the man? I mean, just damn, doesn't he have enough already?"

Ernest spat on the ground and laughed. "If you don't know that the man can never have enough money, Jason, then you're a bigger fool than Sirus. Besides, every man has his weak side."

"And that means what?" Calvin asked.

"That means," said Ernest, "that there are ways of bringing a man around, any man, and that the more a man has, the more you got to bring him around with. That's all I'm saying."

"Oh, that's sorry," Calvin said. "Ain't that sorry, Jason? I got things to do. I mean, I got better things to do than to stand 'round here and listen to all y'all."

Ed Burns joined in again. "Oh, ease up, Calvin. Now I know I wasn't there, but I've heard the thing, and I think Ernest is right," he said. "Maybe not for the reasons he gave. But the way I see it, Sirus is a reasonable man. Bound to be a whole lot more money in it for him if the white man's in it. They'll come on over, sit down with him, show him the figures; they ain't going to have to be doing no other kind of bringing him around than that."

"I gotta go," Jason suddenly said. A piece of trash blew up on his foot and he kicked it away. "I'll see all of y'all later."

It didn't take long for Burnett to follow through on Gant's advice. It was Jason who got the first call the Wednesday after the dinner. "Just a routine review of your undertaker's license," the man told him. "We pick a few at random, come out and do a site inspection, take a quick look at your books, make sure everything's in order." The inspection and review would not be for another month, but in the meantime, if Jason would come down to City Hall, just for a brief chat, well, then, everything might be cleared up, right then and there.

It was not in Jason's nature to be suspicious, but word bounded back to him, after he mentioned his call to a few people, that he was not the only one. Emma Butler had received a call telling her her teaching certificate needed to be renewed, even though she rarely taught anymore, only as a substitute. And there had been a call to the dean of the college from the building department, saying that a new addition at the college had to be looked into, because a permit had been lost when the addition was put on. There was even a call to a man who had once driven for Sirus, though he now drove for a white man on the city council. This driver was told that maybe he was getting too old to drive, maybe his eyesight was going, even though he was only fifty and saw as clearly as he did when he was twenty. Of course people put two and two together, and word quickly spread that this had to do with Sirus and his big talk the night of his dinner.

It was the driver's wife, Katie, after only a few weeks had passed, who called Aileen first.

"Aileen, you know I wouldn't say a word against Sirus," Katie said. "I clapped like everybody else at the church that night, but my Roy, if he can't drive, we can't eat, and we have seven at the dinner table every night, when we count in Roy's momma, who still, bless her soul, can eat like a teenager." Aileen tried to reassure Katie that things were going to be okay, but really, she didn't quite know what to say. Right after Katie, it was Mary Lou Foster, who hadn't had a call, but who'd heard what was happening and was sure she was going to be next, because she was a teacher, too, second grade. Aileen told her she was sure nobody was going to bother the teachers. Then, before she'd barely hung up, it was Ophelia Macon, calling to say she wanted to chat. But just before she hung up, she said, "Well, I know Sirus is not going to do something crazy."

"People are turning," Aileen told Sirus that night at dinner.

"I know," Sirus said.

"Turning where? Turning to what?" Mattie asked.

"Grown-up talk," Aileen told her. She continued with Sirus. "Four people called just today."

"I spoke to four people too," Sirus said. "Joe Farmer yelled at me from his car at the light on Petrie. Told me that I ought to give the sons of guns a run for their money. And Claudia asked if she could give me her opinion while I was trying to give her something to type, and when I told her yes, well, she never gave it to me. She just kept asking me questions, like, 'Mr. McDougald, suppose, just suppose, you do say no, and then suppose, just suppose, they try and close the bank,' or 'Suppose they call out to my house.' One catastrophe after another she kept coming up with, until finally I asked her to tell me what she thought, and she said, well, no, she shouldn't say; it wasn't her place."

"That girl is simple-minded," Aileen said. "But who else? And all against except Joe?"

"All against except Joe. Claudia, Ezra, and Gordon in finance."

"What are you going to do?" Aileen asked.

"Is this about that white man?" Mattie interrupted.

"I told you, young lady, grown-up talk," Aileen said.

"Oh, let her, Aileen. Hell, people I don't even think I know are calling us up, my own daughter can certainly have an opinion. What's your opinion, sweetheart?"

Mattie made a nest for her peas in her mashed potatoes. She looked at both of her parents. "I don't know," she said.

By the next day, Aileen's happiness of just a few weeks ago was gone. It had slowly dissipated, a little each day, and now it was gone. Everything had changed. All of the applause, melted; all the people coming over to Sirus and her and Mattie at the church to congratulate them and squeeze their hands, gone as well. Even the morning after the dinner, when she and Sirus made love — it seemed months, not weeks, away.

As long as it was the two of them, and people cheering, she had felt lifted above everything, but now she was back on earth again. And back on earth, she had to face the truth about things.

She sat out on the porch, thinking. "If I have told you once, I have told you a thousand times," her father used to say, "people will turn on you just as soon as look at you. And don't you forget it." And her mother had told her, too, that if you

had too much, people would envy you, and if you got too big,
someone would try to take it away, and most important, as they
both had told her every day of her life, you had to be careful
of the whites, every second of every day. She had actually
thought, right after Sirus's speech, when she considered the
white men's proposal, well, how dare they. This thing was
Sirus's, she said to herself, Sirus and the rest of the colored; and
those white men, well, what business did they have coming in
to what wasn't theirs. But she must have been crazy to think
such a thing. Just as her parents had told her, people couldn't
be counted on to stick, and the white people were after them,
just as her parents had warned, and how could she have ever
forgotten everything she knew.

Aileen thought about all of the white people she had known,
which wasn't many, but after all, not a single encounter had
been pleasant. Like that white man whose car had broken
down, just in front of her daddy's church, when she was twelve.
The man had called her daddy over and made him climb under
his car looking for some stone or stick he thought was caught
there. The white man was wearing an old jacket and dirty pants,
and her daddy had on his best preaching suit, but it was her
daddy who had to crawl on his back in the dirt, to fix a car for
a man he didn't even know.

She'd remembered this just last night and told it to Sirus, and
he'd said, "Well, I don't know that things happen that way
anymore." And that was when she had started to be afraid.
Because even if Sirus changed his mind, and decided to go along
with the white folks, he didn't seem to understand the danger, and it was this as much as the white folks themselves that
scared her.

When it came to white people, she realized, Sirus had no
sense at all. Even being from the town where that man, Festus
Porter, was killed, wasn't enough to make him see things clearly.

Maybe his ability to fool white people deluded him, or maybe he thought his prosperity or success was a shield, or, even more crazily, it seemed to Aileen, maybe he thought there was something about his own self that could protect him from them, and to Aileen, this was the most frightening thought of all.

"We ought to pack up and leave town; that's the end of us," she said to him before he went back to work after lunch. He'd laughed.

"Why in God's name would we do that?" he asked her.

"Because there's no way we can win," she answered. "If you tell them no, they'll make our lives miserable. If you tell them yes, and something goes wrong, which of course it will, everyone will blame us. Haven't you heard what's happening? Either way, we're ruined." And then she had started to cry. Sirus put his arm around her and told her not to worry; then Mrs. Johnson came in to clear the plates, and she stopped crying and he went out, as if that was the end to it. But it wasn't the end.

Aileen got up from her seat on the porch, putting aside the magazine that had lain on her lap. She went inside the house, stepped out of her shoes, and undid the top buttons of her dress so that some cool air could get to her chest. She considered having a drink but decided to wait.

What should she do now? The house was quiet. Mrs. Johnson had left early to go out of town to see to her mother, Mattie would not be home from school for another hour or so, and Sirus was not expected home much before five. Dinner was already cooked: a pot roast and potatoes and string beans. Mrs. Johnson had fixed them earlier, so all Aileen had to do now was heat them up in the oven. She looked around the front room, and the house was, as usual, cleaner than she would have kept it herself. She thought back to the dinner on Saturday, how nice it had been until Phil Burnett had arrived. Why did that man have to go and spoil it?

She decided to make herself a drink after all — three fingers of bourbon, lots of ice — and without aiming anyplace in particular, she eventually found herself upstairs in their bedroom.

She took a swallow of her drink, then went into her walk-in closet and pulled her dressing stool up close to the shelves. She climbed on the stool and tugged at a blue hatbox beneath a stack of similar hatboxes piled on the top shelf. The stool wobbled as the box came free, but steadied once the box was firmly in her hand. She sat down and pulled from beneath the cardboard form that held the hat — a small blue velvet cloche — a thin bundle of letters tied with a length of pink satin. They were all of her letters from Sirus. She knew exactly when her fingers grazed the right one, because it was the only one with raised lettering on the envelope. It was one Sirus had written to her from a hotel room in New York. They were just recently married, and there was an insurance seminar he had traveled to New York to attend. Back then, their days apart had stretched on endlessly.

She pulled out the letter and skimmed it quickly, skipping over all of the places where Sirus wrote in detail of how much he missed her. She might be in the mood to read those parts another time, but not today. Near the end was the part she was looking for.

"You will never guess what happened to me today," he wrote. His handwriting was more legible then, almost neat, with a thickness and flourish that was so like Sirus in those days. "I was downstairs in the bar, having a drink, with no one the wiser, if you know what I mean, when a woman came over and sat down next to me. She had dark hair, very long and kind of curly, a white woman I was sure, but she sat down right next to me. 'You're from the South, aren't you?' she asked. 'How could you tell?' I asked. 'I always recognize a certain kind of

Southern man,' she said. Then she winked at me. At first I didn't get it and then I did. She was passing too! We laughed and laughed, and I showed her pictures of you and she showed me a picture of her husband. He's a doctor from Atlanta. He met us later and the three of us had dinner and talked about our time in the city. We both got the biggest kick out of it."

Then the letter had gone back to other things, reminders of things Aileen needed to do, regards to people, and so on. Then, after he'd signed off, there was a P.S., written very quickly, it seemed: "Aren't white folks just the stupidest people on this planet?"

That was the part she'd needed to read. To remind herself that she wasn't crazy, to be clear about the danger she was in. A colored man who thought white men were stupid was a very dangerous colored man to be married to, even to be in the same room with if the time was wrong. She had always loved how big Sirus was, but this was too big, this was the kind of colored man the white man needed to bring to the ground. Why couldn't Sirus see that?

Aileen took up the letter and impulsively tore it to bits. She went into the bathroom and flushed it down the toilet. And she took another sip of her bourbon, and then another. If nothing else, the drink made her feel safe and secure. She drifted back to the bed, glass in hand. She would lie down for a few moments, and maybe while she was sleeping, some answer that would keep them all safe would come.

It was probably an hour later that she awoke. Downstairs, the kitchen door banged as Mattie came in. Aileen got up, checked her hair in the mirror, threw out the melted ice from her glass, and hurried down the back stairs. "Did you have fun with Lily and Elise?" Aileen asked from the doorway near the steps. Mattie nodded, but stood where she was by the table. She always hung back in this way with Aileen, and it always made

Aileen angry to see it, and then guilty. For a second, something huge welled up in her, so dark and gray that she couldn't see Mattie on the other side, and she felt as if she were falling backward. Just as suddenly, whatever it was retreated. She lifted her arms at what seemed a few inches at a time. I haven't always felt this way, she reminded herself. Mattie hurried across the kitchen, and Aileen briefly folded her arms around the girl as she came near. Then she let her go and began to fuss with Mattie's hair, lightly scratching her scalp near her forehead.

"Sit down and I'll fix us a snack," Aileen said. She poured Mattie a glass of milk and put some blackberries and cookies on a plate for the two of them to share. Later, when Sirus came home, he found Mattie on the floor in the living room, leaning against the couch as her mother brushed and braided her hair. "My two girls," Sirus said.

8

THE NEXT MORNING, Sirus drove to his office slowly. He was more worried than he wanted Aileen to know. He tried to make light of the calls from his neighbors, but he knew they were just the beginning. Aileen thought he was naïve about white men, but if anything, he was the opposite. He knew more about white men than he had ever wanted to know.

"You have to think of others, Sirus," Aileen had said to him before he left for work. She was seated at her dressing table, putting on her lipstick. She blotted her lips on a tissue and put on more color. "I mean it, Sirus. People are scared, I'm scared. I know you think you're above everything, but you're not, you can't be." They fought about this often. She thought he didn't put enough store in what other people had to say. "People's jobs, their livelihoods, are at risk. What does it matter to us if they want to put some money in?" she went on. "You'll just build something bigger than what you'd planned."

It all sounded sensible enough, but Sirus knew it wasn't that simple. It was never simple when you had to gather up what people were saying and add in all that you knew. That was always hard and a challenge, hard because sometimes what you knew was hard, and a challenge because sometimes other people didn't want to see what you saw. What people would let themselves see came in layers, and even your own knowing could weave in and out of itself. And then there were the things people refused to think about at all, things that would surprise them later, things they might even regret.

Sirus arrived at the bank and parked in the spot reserved for him at the back of the small lot. He went in the side door of the bank and when he got to his office, he asked his secretary to answer all of his calls. Then he closed his office door.

He sat at his desk. On one wall were pictures of the two founders of the bank. On another was a map of the town. Here were the past and the present. But, closing his eyes, Sirus could see something else. He could see the future. He could see it as clear as day, as clear as that time he'd first mentioned building houses to Ed Menton, years and years ago, as clear even as when he'd been a boy here in Durham that summer. And it was the future that troubled him. He saw it slipping out of his grasp. Each time he tried to hold it, it ran though his hands. It was not going to be built on the past. Instead, it was going to be different, with a different feel and a different shape, and with different people.

Sirus had wanted to explain this to Aileen. He wanted to make her understand that he was not deaf to what people were saying but that he was trying to keep this even more bleak future from coming to pass.

"People are not going to be happy, no matter what I do," he told Aileen. "You said it yourself."

But that wasn't enough of an explanation. That wasn't a true picture of all that he knew.

In just five minutes, the phone on his desk rang three times. He could hear Claudia saying he was busy. Of course anyone who wanted to could walk past the building and see him in his office, just sitting. He opened the door and told Claudia he would take his calls now, and he walked back to his desk. For the first time since he could remember, he had no clear picture of what he should do.

By the Saturday several weeks after Sirus's dinner, there was no longer any confusion in the town. Everything had shifted. Except for the Butler sisters, and Jason and Edith, and Dr. Anson, who was almost ninety now, and the last of the founders of the Federated, it was unanimous. Everyone thought that, just to be on the safe side, the whites should be given their way. People were afraid, or had been convinced by someone else that they should be afraid, or felt there wasn't really a choice, or had picked up which way the wind was blowing and changed their minds to make sure they were on the right side.

"They want everything we got, and when that's not enough, they come back for more," Jason was saying to Sirus as the two men drove out of town. Sirus had called Jason and asked that he make this ride with him. It was late in the afternoon, just as the sun was hanging on its last descent. Sirus was driving Jason to the land he'd chosen for his next project, no matter who it was that did the building.

"That's true," Sirus said.

"I mean, isn't it enough that they own everything, tell us where to come, and where to go? Now they've got to be meddling in the little bit we've got for ourselves."

"You're right," Sirus said.

"You're being awfully agreeable," Jason said.

Sirus nodded. "That, and I'm tired," he said.

"It's been quite a few weeks," Jason said. "It's been a lot of pressure on people."

Sirus laughed. "Pressure. Oh, yes. They know how to do pressure, don't they?"

Jason scratched at a scar on his arm. The skin was puckered and pink. "I got this scar when I was about eight, when we still lived in Bowie. Some little white boy told me it made me look like a white man, right on this scar. He said it like, well, if I had any sense I ought to go ahead and scar up my whole body."

"They're something," Sirus said.

"That's the truth." Jason looked out his window at the landscape whizzing by. "What's worrying you, Sirus?" he asked. "Have you already made up your mind?"

Sirus pulled the car over to the side of the road and a cloud of dust rose up behind them. He turned off the motor.

"Remember those men with the guns?" Sirus asked. "When we were boys?"

"Oh, yeah, I remember, all right."

"Well, you know what's bothered me, all these years?"

"I guess you thought Hank Prinde was going to shoot you. That fool man never had a moment of sense in his head."

"Yeah, I guess that went through my mind. But something else, too."

Jason heard the wind shift through the trees. "What else?" he asked.

Sirus rolled down his window and leaned out. "I thought to myself that day," he said, "this is how people can be."

"Not everybody, Sirus."

Sirus was quiet a long few moments; then he motioned toward the field that spread out along the right side of the car. "Notice anything about this field?" he asked.

Jason stuck his head out his window and surveyed the land. "Well," he said, "it's pretty green, lots of thick grass, and mainly flat, once you get up in there."

"What else?"

"It's got a few nice trees on it, but lots of open space, too."

"Anything else?"

Jason brought his head in from the window. "I can't really say. Other than what I've said, it looks pretty much like all the other fields we passed."

Sirus leaned back in his seat and looked over his shoulder. His fingers rested on the seat behind Jason's head. "Did you notice the rise we came up, and then a dip we made?"

"Not really."

"Or the stream? You can't see it now, but it was along the other side of the road, nearly two miles back. Here it's on this side of the road, but way back, inside those trees that start back there."

"Yeah, okay."

"And you're right about the grass; it's a really bright green. And look here where they built the road, you can tell the dirt's almost sandy."

"Okay, Sirus, I get it. You noticed more than I did about the land. So?"

Sirus turned to look through the front window, his fingers now resting lightly on his knees. "These are all the things I look for in building: water, flat land, not too much space to clear, but trees that will be left for shade, a rise or a ridge for privacy, something that sets the space apart. And now that I've told you that, you could drive around here and start seeing the same things. Nothing mysterious to it."

"Well, it's your know-how, I guess," Jason said.

"True, but that's not the important thing. Must be a good twenty fields I could show you that have got all of these things I said."

"So this one's closer to town or cheaper to buy or something."

Sirus shook his head. He reached over and opened Jason's door.

"No," he said. "Come on, get out of the car." He got out on

his side without waiting and strode around the car, kicking up the small stones that lay by the side of the road. "Look," he said when Jason was beside him. "Out there, toward the middle of the field."

Jason followed the line of his arm.

"Keep looking. Try to throw your mind out there." He felt Jason's hesitation and gestured again. "Go ahead, try, pretend you're standing up there in the middle instead of here."

Jason felt foolish, but he tried. He attempted to shift his senses to the distant point his eyes grazed on. He felt nothing but the pounded dirt under his feet and a slight strain in his eyes.

"It's just a field . . ." he began.

Sirus hushed him. "No, please, quiet," he said. "Look, open your eyes and look."

Jason continued to stare, now feeling uncomfortable as well as foolish. Then, without warning, something shifted. He could smell something sweet, and a sensation of cooler air rose near his feet.

"Feels calm and cool out there, doesn't it?" Sirus said, and Jason nodded, captured by the sensation.

"Voices drift in air like that," Sirus went on. "They sound close up and far off at the same time. Like voices you hear out your window just when you're about to fall off to sleep."

Jason heard Sirus's voice, but within it he heard other voices, too, like the ones Sirus spoke of: a child calling out to her friend; two women's voices fading as they said good night.

"And look how the light is falling," Sirus continued, "right above your head. See how it's sweeping the grass."

Jason looked up as Sirus directed and could indeed see the light moving in a golden arc. It swung over their heads and across the field and then away.

"Light like that draws you up out of yourself," Sirus explained; "makes you feel part of something along with every-body else who's seeing it."

Jason suddenly saw pictures, vivid scenes before him, as if he were being drawn along quickly: the inside of a school filled with children, a barbecue at someone's house, a church supper. They were so real he could smell the sweet sweat of the children, the pungent smoke of a pig roasting, the aroma of a dozen ladies who'd been cooking all day and were now drenched in perfume.

"You can almost see it, can't you?" Sirus said, a thick line of sound along which Jason traveled back to the spot where they stood.

"Yeah, I can," Jason said.

Sirus dropped his arm, then started back around the car and motioned for Jason to follow.

"That's what I see and how I choose," he said. As he reached the driver's side, he took one last look at his field.

Jason climbed in the car wordlessly. They both sat with no sound except that of their own measured breathing.

"How can I share that with people who don't care a thing about what happens to us?" Sirus finally asked.

Jason stared at his friend.

"I mean, about what happens to your kids, mine, someone else's cousins," Sirus went on. "Does Phil Burnett care what kind of light shines in their window, what kind of air carries their voices?"

Jason shook his head slowly.

"No, he doesn't," Sirus said. "And that's why I want to say no. Not because the white people have no right. Not because people are cruel. Not even because I'm sure I can keep it from happening. But right now, today, it's me they're asking. And all I can think about is what's going to come alive in those fields."

Jason sat still and tried to absorb what had happened. What

lingered were the sounds and the smells. They were real. Sirus started the car, and the noise startled him, like a flock of birds suddenly appearing out of a tree. He watched as the light they'd stood in moved like a last gulp of wind across the car, filling the road, and slowly disappearing as it reached the other side.

"Allie, allie, in come free!"

Across town, under a sky growing quickly darker, Lily Baldridge stood, her hands on her hips, peering into a line of trees that ringed an open field. Under her feet the ground was dusty, the grass worn away by bikes and tackles and slides into the spot that, for softball games, served as home plate. She and Mattie and Mattie's friend Elise Senate were taking the shortcut through this field when they ran into two boys they knew from school. At the boys' urging, they'd stopped for a game of hide-and-seek, and now, no one was coming back the way they were supposed to when she called. It was already nearly too dark to see.

"Allie, allie, in come free!" she yelled again. She'd promised her mother she'd be home by dark, and she would never make it if Mattie and Elise didn't hurry up and come in. Just as she started to yell again, however, they both burst from the woods.

"Those boys are dumb," announced Mattie, who slowed her pace as she made for her bike, leaning against a tree behind Lily.

"Where are they?" Lily asked.

"They went home," Elise answered.

"We saw them," Mattie added, "sneaking off like no one would see them. I guess they thought we'd be here all night."

"Oh, that's stupid," Lily said. She also headed for her bike. "They're nothing but little kids anyway." She turned her bike around.

"Want us to ride you home first?" Mattie asked. Lily lived in the opposite direction from Mattie and Elise, whose houses were next to each other.

"Fine by me," Lily replied with a shrug.

They pushed off and pedaled away, the three of them forming a shifting V as they crossed the field. For most of the way, Lily was out in front.

"You didn't call yet about my party. Aren't you coming?" Mattie asked as she pulled alongside Lily. Lily shook her head as she pulled out in front again.

"I can't," she answered.

"Why not?"

"I just can't; that's all."

Mattie struggled to catch up. "But why not?"

"Because she's coming," Lily answered between breaths. She jerked her head toward Elise.

Mattie lost momentum for a second, then regained it. "Why?"

Lily grunted as she pulled out farther ahead. "She said something bad about my mother." She shrugged again. "I only came out tonight so I'd have a chance to tell you." Lily was a good inch or so taller than Mattie, and her bike stood higher as well. Each push of her pedals required at least one extra by Mattie just to keep up.

"What was it?" was all Mattie managed to find the air to say.

"That she drove my father into an early grave," Lily said. With this Lily pulled ahead by a good measure, and Mattie gave up trying to stay level. They were spread out now in a scraggly line, with yards between each one.

"Turn here. I can go the rest of the way alone," Lily yelled as she reached the intersection of Henry and Petrie streets. She veered off sharply to the left; Mattie and Elise turned right behind her. They would circle back when they got to Duke Street.

When Lily got home from the park, her mother called from upstairs, "Lily, Lily, is that you?" She'd heard the back door close, even though Lily had taken great care not to slam it.

"Yes, Mother," Lily called back.

"Thank God you're home," Etta said as she came into the kitchen. She held a piece of furled paper in her hands. "Look at this." She sat down at the kitchen table and pushed a stack of newspapers off to one side. "It's some kind of bond of your father's," she said, her fingers moving lightly across the crisp paper. "Come look," she repeated, patting the seat beside her. Lily reluctantly took it. "Read what it says here. Do you think we can cash it?" she asked.

Lily tried to focus on the words printed along the top and bottom of the page. This was exactly the kind of thing Elise had teased her about her mother: always after something, her hands and fists clenched tight around something as if she intended never to let go. Was it any wonder people said she'd driven her father to his grave?

"It looks as if you could cash it any time from maturity up until ten years later. Maturity, I think, was just this year. See, it says right here, 'Maturity: January 1947.' So it could be any time from then until almost ten years from now."

"How much do we get?"

"I'm not sure I can figure that out. There's something called the issue price, and I don't know what that is, and something called the face value." She pointed along the top: FACE VALUE, TWO THOUSAND DOLLARS was printed in a thick, florid script. "Maybe that's what it's worth now," she conjectured.

Etta moved her mouth over the other words on the page. Lily watched for a few moments, then took a sip of the orange juice she had poured herself. She stared out the window over her mother's head. The light of day was nearly gone, and one lone blue jay balanced on the top of their circular clothesline, a contraption that looked like a large parasol strung with heavy rope. Even when it was filled with clothes, the breeze, if it was full enough, would spin the clothing around in a mad whirl.

"I could ask Sirus to put this in with what he's doing on his next project," Etta said. Lily swirled the juice in her glass so that the pulp clung to the sides like tiny seeds. She captured one with her tongue and pinched it between her teeth; a tart, sweet taste burst on her tongue. "Or I could put it in the bank for later," Etta continued. "Or I could ask Ezra or Sirus to see about something else, another bond or something. But those things make me nervous. At least with what Sirus does, you can drive out there and see what your money's doing."

"What about the white man?" Lily asked.

"Why do you ask that?" Etta asked, startled. "What have you heard? Did Mattie tell you something?"

Lily swirled the juice again and drained it. "No, it's just what they're saying at school." She shifted in her chair and brought one foot up under her thigh. "Someone was yelling at Mattie that her daddy was going to make all the colored men lose their jobs. They said he was acting like that because he's so light, he thinks he can get away with it. And Mattie started crying, and she and this girl almost got into a fight. Then the teacher called us all in from the playground early, and took each class, first mine, then Mattie's grade, and explained there was no call for everyone to be fighting. 'Just a difference of opinion,' she said."

"But what did she tell you about that man?"

"Oh, that. Well, she said it wasn't that anyone was right or wrong, only that some thought it was best not to get too mixed up with the whites, even if they start asking. And some who thought it would be good to, you know, oh, shoot, what did she say? Oh, right. 'Break down the barriers between us.'" Lily felt, for a second, very grown-up.

"Well, did she say whether this man could be trusted?"

Lily shook her head. "She didn't say anything about him really, just that he'd asked. She talked mainly about Mr. Mac and the other people in town who all have been talking about it."

Etta took back the bond, rolled it up, and tapped it sharply on the table. "Well, what do you think?" she asked.

Lily found a last bit of pulp in her mouth and bit down on it. It was almost sour, she thought. She looked at her mother in her house dress, the top button open showing the beginning of the red freckles that covered her chest. Her hair was in four sections, as if she'd divided it to oil it and then stopped. Her face was scrubbed clean of makeup.

"I think Mr. Mac ought to decide," she answered.

Etta looked red and raw. "Really, do you think so?" she asked.

"Umm-hmm," Lily said, her thoughts beginning to cohere on the subject. She pictured Mr. Mac on his porch, his hat in his hand, looking off down the street. "See, up till now, Mr. Mac's done it all on his own, just with his friends and neighbors. Right?"

"Right."

"So now this man comes along, and it's like he wants to join in. But you can't come in in the middle like that, I don't think, unless Mr. Mac says yes."

"I guess not."

"No. Because if he wants to join in the middle, the one who started it, and that's Mr. Mac, he's got to say yes." Lily saw Mr. Mac and the white man now looking at each other, each standing and watching the other from where he stood. The white man finally waved, and Mr. Mac turned and went back inside his house.

"That's what I think," Lily finished. She looked back toward her mother, whose eyes were beginning to fill with tears.

"Oh, Lily, I'm so worried," she said, her voice hoarse.

Lily got up from her chair and tugged at her mother's arm. "I'll make you a nice foot bath with some Epsom salts, and then rub your feet for you," she said softly. "Come on." She pulled Etta up from her chair and led her across the kitchen. "It'll make you feel better, and then you can go right to sleep."

Back on Fayetville, though it was only eleven on a Saturday night, Aileen had already been asleep for an hour. She'd had a headache, so she'd gone to bed, but now she was wide awake. She could hear Sirus's voice from downstairs. He was talking to Jason. Jason must have dropped by while she was asleep.

"So I guess that's it," she heard Jason say. "Are you going to call him tomorrow?"

Aileen could hear them clearly, though they were trying to keep their voices low. There was a particular way the two of them spoke with each other, probably because they had been boyhood friends, so that even if she hadn't heard Jason's voice, she would have known he was the one Sirus was talking to.

"Yeah, tomorrow," Sirus answered.

"And are you going to call people here and tell them too?"

"People like who?" Sirus asked.

"Oh, just a few. Gant, Dr. Gerard, people down at the bank."

"They'll probably know before I hang up the phone," Sirus answered.

"How so?"

"Because Frankel and Gant, they have some kind of deal with the whites after this."

"You're kidding."

"No, I wish I were, but I'm not. They don't know that I know. One of my men, a plumber, he drives for a white man on the weekends. Heard the whole thing while he was driving one day."

"Why didn't you tell people? If people knew, I bet it would change their minds."

Sirus didn't answer for a while. From the pause, and then from the sweet smell of tobacco that wafted upstairs, Aileen knew that Sirus was fiddling with his pipe. He rarely smoked it, and when he did, he spent most of the time trying to keep it lit. He would draw on it, tamp down the tobacco, then light it again. He always had a look of intense concentration on his face as he did that, and Aileen thought it had more to do with the tobacco itself, the smell of it bringing back growing up on a farm, than anything to do with trying to keep his pipe lit.

"It doesn't matter," he finally said.

"What do you mean?" Jason asked.

Sirus still didn't answer. Oh, you could drive a truck through his pauses, Aileen thought. She remembered once, shortly after they were married, when she'd asked him something about his mother, and he had paused like this, as if time could march on and leave him behind; if it took ten minutes or ten years for what he meant to say to come to him, he would take whatever time it took. She saw the farm boy in him in those pauses, as if he were still in a small town or a field, and had all the time in the world.

"I mean what I say; it won't change things. Gant and Frankel have made up their minds. Other people have made up theirs. If I told about the other thing, it might change things for a day or two, but basically people came down where they did because it was what they wanted to do."

"Oh, I don't know about that, Sirus. You should give people more credit than that."

Sirus began laughing, though it sounded almost as if he were crying. Aileen suddenly regretted that she hadn't stuck by him. How this must hurt, she thought; not Frankel, but Gant. He'd always thought of Dr. Gant as his friend.

Both Jason and Sirus were quiet for a while. Aileen could hear each man fiddling. Sirus puffed some more on his pipe. Jason shook the ice in his glass.

Sirus broke the silence. "Did I ever tell you about the time, when I first moved to Durham, how I made a wrong turn driving, and I ended up in a white part of town?"

Aileen knew Jason must have shook his head because Sirus went on.

"It was that little section at the back of the tracks, where all of those poor white people live. Those shacks are just like the ones some of our people live in, so I didn't even know I'd made a wrong turn. Until this woman came out and waved down my car."

"Oh, Lord," Jason said.

"Exactly," Sirus went on. "Her boy was sick. And she thought I was a white man. And since I had a car, she was hoping I might be willing to drive her and her boy over to the hospital, because she was scared how long it might take her to get there walking."

"What'd you do?"

"I took them. Her whole family. The boy, who was about five, two older twin girls, about Mattie's age, a teenager, a boy, another man, I think someone who was an uncle. They were all squeezed on top of each other's laps. And none of the children would even look at me, because I was a rich white man to them, and they shouldn't be looking me in the face, and the mother kept thanking me over and over, and wanted to know where my house was, so she could bring me some vegetables from her garden as thanks, and when I didn't tell her where I lived, I could tell it was because she thought I didn't want any poor white trash coming to my house."

Jason let out a long breath. "Imagine. Did you ever tell them?"

"No, but I started to. I started to tell them, just as they got out the car. I wanted to yell, hey, you shouldn't be so quick to judge people, now that it's a colored man who maybe saved your boy's life. But I didn't. Right at the last minute, I didn't say a thing."

"Why not?" Jason asked.

Aileen heard Sirus strike a match. "Because it wouldn't have made any difference. Just like now. Those poor people didn't have a pot to piss in, but they could say to themselves, each morning, thank God, at least I'm not a nigger. And people like Gant and Frankel, they have their reasons too. And other people . . . Ernest Adams, Bert Candless, Ophelia Macon. If you're a person who looks out at the day and says, well, what's in it for me, or what have I got to look out for, well, then, that's all you're going to see."

Aileen heard Sirus walk to the front door and open it. There was no traffic, just the sound of the crickets growing louder.

"I respect you, Sirus," Jason said, "but I have to say, you don't sound too happy with what you've decided."

Aileen couldn't hear what Sirus said, if, indeed, he answered. Whatever he said must have gone out onto the porch and been swallowed up by the wind.

9

IN FOUR SHORT WEEKS after Sirus gave his decision to Phil Burnett, Mattie was dead. The morning she died was like any other morning. Her mother went down to the hospital for her volunteer shift; her father left early for work. For separate reasons, each parent left without saying goodbye. Both times Mattie heard the front door close, just in time for her to run to the window and see, first, her father's head disappearing into his car, and then her mother's back as she paused on the walk to adjust her slip. Her mother hitched her skirt up, unself-consciously, and smoothed down the material with both hands. Mattie watched them leave, and each time, as she turned from the window, she played the scene over differently in her mind, and saw each look up at her and wave goodbye.

After she'd had her breakfast, she went outside to play. She played first on the porch with her dolls, and then went back inside to get her skates. While she skated, less than two blocks away, the Reverend Frankel and Dr. Gant sat on Gant's porch, talking. They could hear, off in the distance, the sound of

Mattie's skates on the sidewalk as she skated to the end of the block and back.

"There are men who live in the past and men who live in the future," Gant repeated to Frankel. "Sirus thinks the future should look like the past; that's why he can't understand real progress."

The two were still talking about Sirus's decision. Even though it was early morning, the reverend was enjoying a second piece of peach pie.

"Me, I live in the present," Frankel said. He took one more bite. "There's no other time but that." He was already full, but the pie was so good, he even considered a third piece.

"More pie?" Gant asked when the plate was empty.

"I couldn't, but thanks," Frankel answered.

The men were silent. Each pondered the events of the last few weeks and the road that lay ahead. All of the uproar following Sirus's decision had passed. Burnett had called Gant when Sirus first refused his offer, cursing both Sirus and Gant, but then Gant was able to convince him that it was only a momentary setback. Burnett calmed down after he conferred with his partners and found them perfectly content to wait. "Ease up; let him buy the land. Once he's made the investment, he'll have no other choice but to go along if he'd otherwise lose it," Gant suggested. Burnett thought that a good idea, and for the time being it was decided to ease up on all the pressure.

"Amazing, the way they just backed off," Frankel continued. "I'd love to have that kind of power."

Gant watched as the reverend searched for any last crumbs that might have escaped to his clothes. He wasn't sure who he was the more contemptuous of, Frankel or Burnett.

"You know, when all of this goes through," Frankel went on, "the housing project, and then the drugstore, do you know what I'm going to do?"

"No, what?" Gant asked.

"I'm going to ask Clorissa Macon to marry me."

"Think she'll have you?" Gant asked.

"Once I'm the equal to anyone else in this town, why wouldn't she?" Frankel replied.

Gant didn't think Frankel would ever be anyone's equal, but what he thought of him didn't matter. Their spheres of influence were different but complementary, so they were useful to each other. He left it at that.

For others in the town, the sudden let-up had come as a large surprise. There were no more phone calls, and those which had come before were miraculously explained. "A clerical error," all the recipients of the calls were told.

"You'd think they could at least come up with a more original lie," Ernest Adams complained to a few people, but no one took him up. Everybody was just plain relieved and grateful that the crisis seemed to have passed. "Who cares if they lie plain or fancy?" someone said to Ernest.

About the only person, besides Sirus, who was still uneasy was Etta Baldridge. It was nothing specific, just a lingering fear.

"White people never let a thing go so easily," she said to whoever would listen, but not too many people would. There were enough things to occupy people's minds other than something they believed was shut in the past.

As for Sirus, even now that all the commotion was over, he still couldn't get out of his mind the outlines of that disturbing future he'd glimpsed. Although he'd put in a bid on the piece of land and gone out to the site with one of his builders, and though he'd begun to work the numbers for the financing with the building department down at the bank, he felt unsteady, in a way he was rarely unsteady, each step of the way. He felt as if the ground were shifting under his feet.

This morning, he drove out to the site before he went on to

his office — just to get his footing back, he told himself. He got out of his car and walked from one end of the site to the other. He looked up at the trees, felt the ground rolling under his feet, heard both the birds and the wind, and yet none of the voices or feelings would come. Nothing surged up from the ground as it usually did. It was as if the earth itself were shut away from him. The ground, the earth under your feet, is what sustains you, his father used to tell him. Find a patch of ground that feels right under your feet, and you can go anywhere in the world from there. Sirus knew this was true; he had learned it a hundred times over. When his mother died, it was the fields outside his window at home that had saved him. It was the air that blew across them that had given him the courage to wake up in the morning, and it was the thud his feet made as he ran across them that had convinced him his mother's heartbeat hadn't been silenced forever, and it was the trees that spread their roots from one end of the field to the other that hinted at all the things he had left to do.

And here, here in Durham, he had found a different kind of field, a field that had a thousand dreams spilled onto it, with a ground of progress that was built over the ground, and with buildings attached to the earth that could sustain the people who lived here like trees.

But it was changing. He could see blood and heartbreak and worse, a horrible tearing, his hallowed ground caving in right under his feet.

Sirus returned to his car. The closed doors further muffled the earth. He drove back into town, and even as he drove through the streets, normally so vibrant, the uneasy quiet prevailed. He was sure he would be of little use in this future.

Just as Mattie made her last turn at the corner, her skate broke. It was her left skate, the one that was already hard to keep on.

She'd had to keep tightening the clamp on the front, but invariably it loosened again. She was just past the Senates' house when it happened again, the metal grip giving way, hanging uselessly below the platform that held her shoe. As Mattie pushed off with her foot, she slipped from the top of the skate and, losing her balance, fell to the ground. This had happened a dozen times or more in exactly the same way. It will never be fixed, she thought to herself, never, never, never. She ripped the worn leather strap from her ankle to release the skate, and as she neared her house, in a fit of pique she threw it into the bushes. She clumped unevenly into the house with her other skate still on, and angrily banged up the stairs to her room. Once there, she sat on the side of her bed, slowly loosening the skate with the key.

Mattie rolled the skate under her bed, out of the way. She would put it away later, or maybe she'd leave it there, since she couldn't very well skate with just one skate. It didn't occur to her that perhaps the broken skate could be fixed.

She left her room and went back downstairs, trailing her fingers along the bannister. She slid them along the back of her father's chair in the parlor, across the sofa in the living room, over the surface of the dining room table and the kitchen counter. Then she left the house. As she walked out the back door, she said to Mrs. Johnson, as casually as always, "Going outside."

In the yard, she climbed the steps of her slide for the next-to-last time in her life. There was no one around. She sat at the top of the slide and held on to the bars at the top, pausing for a moment as she always did before pushing off and flying along the slick warm metal. She thought of her mother and father, of all the arguing that had gone on in the past few weeks, of how the arguing had ended, and then she let go. She flew down the board and her sneakered feet skidded across the sand at the bottom. A cloud of dust rose up and settled along the sweat on the back of her neck and her arms. She was filthy by now, she was sure.

Tears suddenly sprang to her eyes. She wished her parents would get along the way she always hoped they would; she wished that people in the town wouldn't argue with one another; she wished that all of the white people on earth would just disappear. She'd said that once to her father — that if she were God, she would wipe them off the face of the earth, since they were so mean to the colored, and her father had said, "Well, if we got rid of them, things still wouldn't be perfect; there would be some other bad thing we'd have to deal with. You can't get rid of evil."

Mattie had no idea why she'd suddenly thought of white people — she just did — and she climbed her slide again. She stood up at the top, though her parents had always warned her not to. But she did it sometimes anyway, because she believed she was much steadier on her feet than they did.

If I were God, I would make a perfect world, she thought. No reason that I couldn't. No white people, no mean people period, no arguing, no fighting, nobody dying until they were really old and had lived a happy life. She held her arms out at her sides. She thought of Phil Burnett and that night at the dinner.

Before he'd come and spoiled it all, why, that night, she'd really been happy. There was no reason her world had to have people like him in it. A bird flew by the slide and she followed its flight. It was a cardinal. She loved cardinals, with their bright red flash that came out of nowhere. She'd better sit down, she decided; the sun reflecting on the metal was making her dizzy. Besides, Mrs. Johnson might look out the window and see her. Just then, there was a loud crack behind her; it sounded as if someone was coming up the slide behind her, or maybe it was a squirrel. Before she could think, she started, and jerked around. Her feet slipped out from under her and her head made a long arc toward the ground. Oh, boy, that was so stupid, she thought — and then her neck snapped, like a twig, as her head slammed into the concrete that steadied and secured the base of the slide.

III

AT
THIS TIME
OF THE
YEAR

10

"A WHITE MAN didn't throw Mattie from her slide," Sirus said quietly. "And there wasn't anyone creeping in the bushes."

Aileen was on the bed, sobbing.

"How do you know?" she said. "I saw a white man drive past our house today. He was smirking out his window. It could have been him."

"Aileen, please," Sirus said. He stood at their bedroom window, staring out as he put on his tie. He'd said the same words over and over. There was no white man. There was no one in the yard. "It's been almost a year," he said. "Next week, next Thursday, it will be a year."

"Do you think I don't know. Do you think I don't know how long it's been?"

"I wasn't saying that; I was only saying it's been a year. And there was no one in the yard. You have to let that go."

"No, you let it go, you let it go. I wasn't the one. It wasn't me making out to be a big man. Didn't people warn you? Etta warned you. Didn't I warn you? Oh, God, Sirus, why did you do it? Why didn't you listen, our baby, she, oh, God, our baby, why didn't you?"

Sirus finished his tie. He fingered the knot and rocked it back and forth, making it tighter. Aileen's sobs started again. She thrashed about on the bed, and suddenly she was still. He turned to get his jacket from the back of his chair and looked at Aileen, who lay face up. Her face was wet but the tears had stopped. She was staring at him.

"There wasn't any white man," he said.

This morning, it was just the white man, in the yard. Other mornings, it was a white man in someone else's yard. After all, someone would have seen, would have noticed a white man in their yard. This white man could have hidden better over there, could have projected an unseen missile to make Mattie lose her balance.

"He could have thrown something," Aileen would say. "It could have been a rock, just a little pebble, something that hit her in the eye, on the back of her head. Who would have noticed a tiny little bruise at a time like that? It could have been there all along and no one ever saw it."

Other times there was a man with a mask, a mask that made him look colored, until he was right there beside Mattie. "Then he pulled the mask off; he frightened her to death," she'd say. "That's why no one would have seen a white man around. Because of that mask."

"Who's ever heard of a mask to make you look colored? What kind of market would there be for that sort of thing?" Sirus had replied once, but that was senseless. Why would he even think to argue with what she was feeling?

What had started it this morning? Sirus couldn't remember. All the days blended together, all the mornings that Aileen burst into tears while brushing her hair, or the afternoons she spent hiding in the bed, or the meals where they sat silently across from each other, the quiet at the table a weapon that assaulted each of them. The days were all the same — tortured and empty.

This morning had been no different from all of the rest. Sirus awoke to find his legs entangled with Aileen's, as if their bodies sought a comfort unmindful of the distance that otherwise lay between them, and as soon as they were awake, they moved apart. Before Mattie's death, it was usually then that they would roll toward each other, still half asleep, the erection Sirus often awoke with, the longing Aileen usually sensed when still asleep, drawing them together into the other's need, before Mrs. Johnson had arrived or Mattie was awake, even before the sun was fully up. This morning, however, each rolled away, as on every morning of the past year. Sirus reached for his shorts to cover himself and Aileen rubbed her hip where the weight of his leg had mottled her skin. Then Aileen had gone to the bathroom, begun to get dressed while he showered, and when he came back to finish dressing, she was on the bed, half dressed, crying.

Outside, on his way to work, he couldn't believe it was September again. A whole year since Mattie's death. A year of longing without end. A year of accusations. He always said, "There wasn't any white man."

But he was careful never to say, "It's not my fault."

Because he now was convinced that it was. The specifics didn't matter. He didn't happen to believe there had been anyone crawling about their backyard or in a neighbor's yard, but in the end, it didn't matter. Even if it was nothing more than a bird, even if it was nothing at all, it was still something, and that something was the most horrible thing that had ever happened to him. It had to be evil, and in this he'd finally decided Aileen was right: evil always came for a reason, and if it came, it was because you'd done something wrong. He gave in to the whites when they later renewed their offer, not that he could change what had happened, but because he'd finally learned the truth of what Aileen had been saying: that horrible things happened to people when they got too big. He would never be big again. He would never imagine that he could go against the grain of things, that he could set himself apart, that his will might be something he could use to act on the world. He may have been full of pride and arrogance, but he was not stupid. Stupid would be not to understand that he had been knocked down by what happened and that he should stay down, like a person with some sense.

In one way, it was a relief. The world was at last lifted from his shoulders. He could finally be released from his dreams. Now, nothing mattered as it once did. He went to work at the bank and the insurance company, as always; there were the board meetings at the bank; there was the club in the evening. Friday nights they often went out to dinner, to a friend's house, or they had people in. Aileen had her work at the hospital, on the committee at the college, the tutoring, her card playing. Occasionally someone would drive to New York for a show and music up in Harlem, and she would go along. No one suspected what went on in the house.

Sometimes he wanted to tell someone, but what would he say? Our house has rotted? There's nothing but decay and death inside? It looked the same. He looked the same. Who would believe him? He could drive out to any one of his projects, sit or stand in the fields with the men who spun something out of their hands and backs with their glinting, shining tools, but everything he saw was at a remove, no longer of his making. His hands were in everything and nothing. Even the workers he hired seemed wooden. He heard their hammering and the whine of their saws, and at the same time he heard nothing. He smelled their sweat, and the odor was dry and flat, like flowers in which no oil remained. Even their hands on his were dry and paper thin.

By now the large housing project was nearly completed. It had proceeded with both investment and considerable advice from Phil Burnett and his friends. The passage of time, by itself, seemed to have pushed things along. Time, in fact, had pushed a lot of things along. Just as Aileen had predicted, the very people who were at first relieved that Sirus had gone along with the whites now resented it. They complained to him about the way some of the white investors drove across town out to the site, faster through a narrow street than they should, about how they hated seeing those pink faces whizzing past their houses before they were fully awake. And other things too. The deal that Melvin Gant and the Reverend Frankel had struck with the whites was to build a new drugstore, and everyone was afraid it would take business away from Dr. Gerard. Also, Gant was so busy with his new meetings that he was rarely at the hospital anymore. And finally, the Reverend Martin had died, and the Reverend Frankel was now the sole pastor. Frankel had asked Clorissa Macon for her hand in marriage, and most people thought Clorissa was waiting until a decision was reached about making Frankel's appointment official or until the drugstore actually went through — or maybe both — before she gave her answer.

Sirus felt as if all this news was stale, as if he were reading in an old newspaper about people from a distant town. That these had once been his friends, that he had once had an intense interest in their lives — now it felt like a persistent memory. So he noted in his daily paper: the formation of a committee to protest the closing of yet another colored school was stalled; Etta Baldridge was enrolled in a course at the college; and Cora, Mrs. Johnson's eldest, was about to be married. Sirus had learned that he could respond to all of these things with only a small piece of himself, and no one seemed to notice; if anyone did, there was no comment on the change.

He neared the housing project. The only work remaining was details of trim and paint and hardware. Viewed from the southeast, which was the way he came to it from town, it sprang into view nearly all of a piece, the tarred roofing slick and almost ominous, the red brick nearly indistinguishable from the earth.

He had remarked to Jason one day when they passed by that the day-to-day drama was over; he contrasted the slow progress during the last three months with that in the beginning, when entire frames were strung across the empty land like so many circus nets, and three, four, sometimes five apartments emerged each day, so that by the end of the third week the entire structure, skeletal and frail, was clearly visible. Now, the progress was slow and incremental, with what seemed like few rewards for the effort expended. It was always this way in building. Workers still swarmed over the site, the architect occasionally visited with his blueprints, and the investors, of course, were occasionally there — they liked to come and stand in the sun and watch how their money was being spent — but the guts of the building were embedded, hidden, so that the grade of the wood in the beams, the resistance and amperage of the wires, the alloys that were mixed in the pipes could no longer be seen.

What anyone saw, sitting solid, brought to life on the grassy meadow that he'd chosen, was what looked to be a dream come true: a nest of homes, clean and complete. It would be at least another month before the homes were finished, but people were already calling him, stopping by the office with their checks. They were all eager to sign the papers that said that these sweet dreams would be theirs.

Sirus parked his car at the site. His foreman came over as soon as he saw him. "I've been waiting for you," he said. "There's something I want to show you."

Back at home, just as Sirus arrived out at the projects, Aileen poured herself a second cup of coffee. She was now completely dressed. She sat at the table in the kitchen. So far, it had not been a good day. Good days did not start out this way. On a good day her mind was filled to the edges so that there was no room for Mattie to sneak in. On a good day, she was fast and alert and could veer away from the things that would hurt. On a good day, she could get from the back stairs to the stove in the kitchen without looking out into the backyard. On a good day, she didn't hear muffled giggles coming from under the stairs. On a good day, she didn't smell the lilacs or the honeysuckle or the roses, or any of Mattie's favorite flowers. But today was not a good day, and she'd been caught before she'd even made it out of her room.

Today, it happened when she put on her slip. She had her arms up over her head, and as the material slipped down over her body, just the feel of it passing over her head and her shoulders and her hips made her remember that night, right after Sirus's dinner, when everything had still been wonderful. She and Mattie had both been here in the kitchen in their slips. It was a hot night and they were excited, and neither of them had wanted to go upstairs. So she told Mattie that they could do something she and her sisters used to sneak and do. They took off their fancy dresses, laid them carefully over a chair, and had ice cream out on the back porch, just in their slips. She knew it felt to Mattie the way it had to her when she was that age, daring and free, to be outside, and a little undressed, with the cool night air resting on her skin. She remembered too the glow they both had, that shiny white of their slips, reflecting all the moonlight, and also how skinny Mattie was in her slip, no difference between her body and that of a young boy, except how delicately thin she was, with maybe a promise of something to come. But this morning, as she'd put on her slip, Aileen was forced to remember how nothing else would be coming. She felt her own body under her hands as she smoothed her slip, and her body felt like a curse. Feel how full my body is, she cried to herself; look at these hips and these breasts, Mattie will never run her hands along her own body like this; nor would she know the rest of it — the boys who would admire it, the pleasure it could give her, the husband, the children, damn it, just the weight of being a woman; how that felt, standing, walking, lying down in bed at night.

Aileen stirred sugar into her coffee. That was how things went on a bad day. Reminders were everywhere. Sometimes, when they got too bad, she drove over to the white part of town, to one particular schoolyard where she knew the schedule, and she'd wait for recess. A door would open and forty or fifty children would tumble out. The playground would go, in an instant, from empty to full, and the children were all pink and happy. She could hardly stand to see a colored child of Mattie's age, but she could watch these pink and white children. They would never grow up to know what she and Mattie had known. They would never be told, you have to live over here, you can't sit there. No one would ever spit at them, call them nigger; and when they grew up, no one would steal across town and kill one of their children. I'd just love to see the day when their parents come home screaming and end up crying for the rest of their days, Aileen would think to herself, but she knew that wouldn't happen. Things like that didn't happen to white people. Only to the colored.

But at the same time, Aileen knew that Sirus was right. She knew there had been no white man in their yard; she knew someone would have seen him. She also knew that the kind of white men who were after Sirus were not the kind who crawled around in the bushes, throwing little colored children off their slides. It was not that they cared; it just wasn't the kind of thing they would do. The kind of white men who were after them did other things, killed children in other ways, like putting their parents out of a job and not caring whether they had worked for someone for a hundred years and had debts and mouths to feed. They were the kind who wouldn't even look at you when you got up and gave your seat to them on the bus; who sashayed in and out of a front entrance and didn't even notice you standing by a back door. That kind of white person went to church on Sunday, was always, in his mind, kind to the colored, held no malice against them in his heart, but knew, after all, what kind of people the colored were: not bad really, just childlike, and a little irresponsible and untrustworthy. There were the other white men who did the actual killing, if things came to that. But Aileen was not crazy. She knew that Phil Burnett and his friends were not that kind.

So why did she say what she did to Sirus every day? She didn't know. She'd tell herself, I have got to stop saying that; one of these days someone is going to think I've lost my mind. But then, as on a morning like this, she'd find herself yelling it at Sirus, or even worse, saying it to someone else, and other people didn't bother to argue with her the way Sirus did. When she talked about the white man in the yard to other people, they nodded and added their own ideas. Other people always went along with the whole thing and sometimes went her one better. And then she'd be through and she would say for the hundredth time, that's the last time; I'm going to drop it. And she'd really mean to, until there she was, saying it again.

She swallowed the last of her coffee. As always, it was too sweet at the bottom, but she drank it anyway, the little puddle of sugar pausing for just a moment like sand on her tongue. She got up and searched for her purse. There was no choice but to push on with her day. She got her car keys from the hook in the cupboard where she kept them and rushed out of the house. Only when she was a block away did she decide where she was going. She would drive out of town to the site of the projects.

When the buildings were in view, she pulled over to the side of the road and looked down at the attached houses. Nearly two hundred of them. They twisted and turned over the ground as if they had grown there. They were nothing but brick and wood, but Aileen knew that it was because of these houses that Mattie was dead. That was how she viewed them. It was the same as looking at the slide in the yard, which Sirus still hadn't arranged to have taken down. Both were malevolent objects. It was terrible to have them so linked in her mind, but she couldn't untangle them. They seemed to have grown together more each day; at first, almost by happenstance, they were linked in time; then, more clearly, their true nature had been revealed. If it hadn't been for these buildings, if she and Sirus hadn't been distracted by them, if they hadn't been arguing, if other people hadn't been so concerned with what the white folks were going to do, then perhaps something, just one second, would have changed, and that second would have led to another and another, so that finally the moment of Mattie's fall would have been different.

Aileen could see Sirus's car off in the distance. She knew he was shut away from her forever. Whatever comfort there might exist in the world to ease them had passed them by. She guessed they had already been given and had spent their allotment of happiness. Oh, there had been long days and months of such moments, more than she'd counted at the time, but now all those moments were locked in the past. She watched Sirus as he came around the corner of one of the buildings. He was walking with someone, she couldn't make out who, and he held his hat in his hand.

Down at the site, Sirus waved a fly off his arm. He was hot and tired, and it wasn't even nine yet. He tried to concentrate on what his foreman was telling him, something about holes and fresh plaster.

"Just since yesterday, somebody patched 'em," the foreman, Hal, was saying. "I don't know who. But before they did, I peeked inside all them places."

Hal was sweating. He didn't do physical work anymore — he had a weakened heart — but he sweated all day as if every job he supervised was something he were doing himself.

"What? Holes?" Sirus asked.

"Right. I'm trying to tell you. Yesterday, I was about to call you when I seen the holes, but two of the men was here and they said, nah, might as well wait till you come on out today."

Hal never called the white investors anything other than "the men." To him, they were an amorphous, indistinguishable group.

"Okay, now I'm here. There were holes? At least now they're patched."

"But I didn't want 'em to be. That's what I'm saying. Oh, it's not good, Mr. Mac, that's what I'm saying. I seen things, seen things you oughta have seen."

Sirus looked past Hal's head. From here he could see the spot on the road where he and Jason had once stood, looking out on this place when it was empty. He would never have believed that this was where the future would take him.

"And I tried to talk to that other fella the men got here every day, that John fella; you know the one I mean. In fact, I told you, Mr. Mac, a job like this don't need two foremen; something funny in that. And sure enough, he acting like I'm some sort of crazy. 'You sure you saw some holes?' he says. 'Looks like just some plastering over seams to me.' But you saw them places. Ain't in no line like a seam, and 'sides, they seamed that one up a week ago and that plaster in there now ain't even half dry."

There was a light breeze, and Sirus thought he heard a sound traveling right inside, right next to the sound of the wind.

"You listening, Mr. Mac?" Hal asked.

"Yes," Sirus answered, "I'm listening. Sounds like you're taking care of things real good."

"That's not what I'm saying, Mr. Mac. It's what was behind them holes."

Sirus put his hat back on. The sun was starting to beat down. "Like I said, Hal, I'm glad. You're doing a real fine job."

Hal kicked a clump of dirt with the toe of his boot. He looked around. A couple of workers acted as if they hadn't been listening; they turned back real quick to what they were doing when he looked their way. "I guess I better get back to the men," he said.

Sirus thought of his office, where he would at least be cool. "Yeah, you do that, Hal, and keep up the good work. I'll be out here again in another day or two."

The problem was that a day or two never came. Hal lived a few doors away from Mrs. Johnson and he spoke to her the following Saturday afternoon, while she picked hydrangeas in her yard. He came over and sat on Mrs. Johnson's front steps, and he didn't beat around the bush with her, the way he had just a little bit with Sirus.

"They is something wrong with them places," he told her, "and not just one thing, but one thing on top of another."

Mrs. Johnson had a nice bunch of hydrangeas to put in the house, and there were still a lot of the big blue flowers left on the bush. "You want some for your table?" she asked.

"No, thank you," Hal answered. "My wife does roses, and they blooming now too."

The street Hal and Mrs. Johnson lived on was nothing like the street where Sirus and the Gants and the Baldridges and the Macons lived. It wasn't Fayetville or Lawson or even Dupree or Petrie. It was Cottie Lane, and there was a whole network of such lanes, and only sections here and there throughout them were paved. There was no order to how the lanes were laid out, and both the houses and the yards seemed to run in to one another. There weren't any trees to speak of along these lanes, and as a result, trying to get things to grow took more patience or time than most people had. Most people, at the end of their long days, found the effort to keep something growing too much, and their yards were little more, in the summer, than dusty pieces of ground. These dry patches of earth seemed easier to decorate with folding chairs or old washtubs, or anything else there wasn't a whole lot of room to store in the house, than to try to grow something.

But Mrs. Johnson was one of the few on the block who had her small plot of flowers and vegetables. It meant spending every morning and evening, both before the sun was up, and later, when it started to go down, watering things and tending and sprucing and pruning; but Mrs. Johnson thought she would not have the strength to get up and go out to work each day if she didn't at least have some flowers to look at on her way out and in, and if there weren't some fresh vegetables she could look forward to at the end of the day. Hal's wife also had a garden. Partly it was because Hal made enough so that he could pay a boy to come and water his wife's garden a few days a week, and then of course his girls did it some, so his yard was one of the few others that also had something blooming.

"So what I'm saying," Hal went on, "is that I could tell somebody had been down there poking around, and now I know who it is."

"Who?" Mrs. Johnson asked.

"Paulie Peters. Tricia Peters's son. He live up north some-where. D.C., I think, and anyway, he down here to see his momma last week, and she telling him 'bout these places, how she so excited to be moving out there with the trees and all, and he being a city boy, and into building, well, he don't leave nothing to no one, so he just carried himself on out there for a peek."

"And what did he see?" Mrs. Johnson asked. She put her pruning scissors in her apron pocket and set the flowers in some water in a can that sat on the side of her porch.

"That the thing," Hal said. "It stuff I been seeing too, but I wasn't sure, 'cause every time they been getting to something like that, why them men, they come up with some long outa-the-way thing they want me to do. And I been telling Mr. Mac, but every time I say something, seem like he off listening inside hisself to something that ain't what I'm saying at all."

Mrs. Johnson didn't respond. Hal pulled out a piece of yellow paper, on which Paulie Peters had written down all that he'd seen. Next to each item, Hal explained, his wife had written for him how things were usually done.

"Why're you giving this to me?" Mrs. Johnson asked.

"You work for him. Maybe when he at home, you can get his attention."

Later that evening, Mrs. Johnson pulled out the list. Her little house now smelled like tobacco and lemons, and there were sticky rings on the furniture where people had set their glasses of lemonade. Word had spread fast, and before she'd even gotten her supper dishes cleared off the table, there was a whole crowd, standing outside her front door.

"Can we come in, just for a spell, Wanda?" Bertie Anderson had asked.

"Why sure," Mrs. Johnson had told them.

Bertie, like all of the others who came, and like Mrs. Johnson herself, had already signed a contract and put money down to live in one of those houses that Sirus was building. And this thing with Paulie Peters had spread fast. Not many understood the things he spoke of, but all of them knew about unsafe: fires, children falling through railings, holes in the floor where you lost things if you were lucky and a leg if you weren't. To be safe was one of the things that led them to the homes Mr. Mac was building. They'd all visited his projects in town, had seen for themselves that things shut the way they were supposed to shut and opened the way they were supposed to open. Those, and the little things you couldn't even point to that made the places feel like home. The people who tried to duplicate what Sirus had done may have been at a loss to know what it was that made them sell, but for the people who lived in his projects, there was no mystery.

"Look, I'm not accusing anyone," Bertie had said, once everyone was inside Mrs. Johnson's house and settled. "I'm just saying we got a right to ask and have our questions answered." Bertie had finished what she had to say with a big nod. Mrs. Johnson had to smile as she remembered it. When Bertie nodded, it was like something huge shaking, since her head was nearly twice as wide as her hands. And right after that, Mrs. Johnson noticed, there was a split almost exactly down the middle of the room. All the women who worked for the whites were quiet, and all the women who worked for the colored, except herself, agreed with Bertie.

Fiona Madison was the only one, however, who had something to say.

"They got a bus and all. Take us right to work," she said. When she spoke, she kind of swayed back and forth, as if she were already seated on that bus.

"So?" Bertie said. "Who said nothing 'bout that bus?" She looked at the others, exasperated. "We talking 'bout the houses theyselves, unless this still ain't clear to someone."

Both Fiona and Bertie, like Mrs. Johnson, were day workers. They all had to get up before dawn. Those who worked for the whites had to get up the earliest, because their trip was the farthest. Fiona herself had to change buses three times. But there was to be a special bus from the housing project that would travel straight to the white residential part of town, making two or three stops; and arranging for this bus, which would drop off the workers who worked for the colored as well, had been Sirus's idea. That, and the financing available through the colored bank, had all made the houses themselves that much more desirable. And there would be another bus to carry workers to the mill and the tobacco-sorting plant, each only a little more than a mile in the opposite direction. Fiona's husband, Albert, was one of the workers — a sorter whose job it was to divide the leaves by size — who would travel that way.

When Bertie finished, she waited for someone else to speak up, but no one took the challenge. "Okay, then," she concluded. "We just got to choose someone to ask out our questions."

The business part of the meeting had finished shortly after that, with Mrs. Johnson chosen as spokesman, but the socializing went on for at least another hour. It was awkward socializing, with lots of stories begun and only half finished, words broken off before they could provoke a fight. It was rare that the two groups — the women who cleaned for the colored and the women who cleaned for the whites — got together aside from church or some civic work. It was not a large barrier, but it existed. Unspoken were the assumptions beneath each woman's choice: to clean for your own was demeaning, whites were dirty, your own paid better, the whites gave you more things. But the contest over these assumptions was fought with half gestures and words: "Been saving a little"; "Missus Reynolds give me it"; "No dirt like white dirt"; "Wouldn't stoop so low myself."

"Plain ridiculous," Mrs. Johnson muttered now that her house was empty. "Grown people sparring over whose toilet it

was more an honor to clean." She had never told it, but back
in Hollister, where she was from, she had worked for the whites,
and what she'd hated was having to hold herself in, never
feeling at ease. She never told herself, well, it's more right to
work for the colored, but it was the only way she could do it.
She liked to cook what she knew, and to have familiar smells,
and that meant working for the colored. Some, she'd found,
were as mean as the whites, but when it came right down to it,
she felt lucky that the Macs — mainly Mr. Mac — were the
kind of people they were. She didn't fool herself with long
speeches about working for the colored being some kind of
noble thing; it was just what she could do and be comfortable
doing.

Besides, she thought to herself as she stacked the empty
glasses and plates in the sink, if truth be told, what all of them
would like best would be to have what the people they cleaned
for had — not just their cast-offs, but the whole kit and caboodle. She could do with a few of Mrs. Mac's clothes for one,
and she wouldn't mind having those bookcases that were in
the front parlor. Her eldest loved to read and had had books
stacked everywhere while she was growing up. Bookcases like
those would have looked nice in her own living room, and
would make a lovely wedding present to her daughter now that
she was about to get married. But nobody wanted to say that;
it would sound too greedy, and silly, too, since it wasn't about
to happen anytime soon. Instead, they just tossed their envy
back and forth in their little squabbles.

Of course, the whole kit and caboodle would mean just that,
and it was here that Mrs. Johnson was glad she could draw the
line. She had loved Mattie to death, and missed her something
terrible, but if she even thought of something like what had
happened to her happening to her own daughter, or to one of
her two boys, well, what coursed through her she didn't even

want to think about. So what she always said to people when they started complaining was, well, you have to look at the whole picture, because you just never know, and it was best to look around at your own life and count your blessings rather than to be always worried about what somebody else had.

Of course, just because she felt that way didn't mean she was all too happy about this spokesman thing. It had happened before she'd even had a chance to think, and now it was too late to take back.

"Wanda Johnson is the one should do it," Fiona had said. "Can't nobody else be sashaying over to the McDougalds' house and on up to the front door. Wanda is over there every day, and besides, she can pick the right time."

"Fix some light biscuits that day," somebody said, but Mrs. Johnson couldn't remember who.

"She ain't got to fix nothing but her words together in her mouth," Bertie yelled. Right, it was to Betsy Morris that she yelled, because that was a pretty funny thing coming from Betsy, considering how everybody knew she was a terrible cook. Mrs. Johnson was sure the white people she worked for must be nothing but skin and bones if they had to live on her cooking. But Bertie was right; it wasn't going to matter what she cooked that day. It was what came out of her mouth, and that was something she had better get to thinking on fast.

She looked around her. Her kitchen and house were clean once again. She sat in her front room, which was both parlor and living room. She loved sitting down in a clean house. At the new houses, it would all be fresh paint, and that would make it even easier to get and keep the rooms clean. And there were lots of trees around, and that would make growing things so much easier. And she'd have a cool place out in the yard to sit. It made her sad to think that her daughter's growing was all done, and that it had all happened here, where there weren't any trees, but she had played a lot at the Macs' house, and they went down to the country every summer, so it wasn't like a yard with no trees was all that she knew.

She thought again about what to say. Cleaning might be the way to get Mr. Mac in the best of moods, since he loved a clean house almost more than anything, but didn't she do that every day anyway? Certainly she did. Besides, she was pretty sure that now, since last year, she could have dumped dirt onto the floor instead of sweeping it up, and no one in that house would have noticed. That was something people were respectful about, but they had concerns too, and after all, it had been a year.

Oh, it had to be someone, Mrs. Johnson finally acknowledged, so it might as well be me. She still didn't know what she'd say, but she was sure some words would come to her when the time was right.

The next day, Sunday morning, Jason was driving along the road out of town. It was right after church, and he had a visit to make.

"Give Emma and Satha my regards," his wife told him when he left her and the kids at home. The kids were all out on the sidewalk, begging to go. "I'll be back before you know it," he told them. "Besides, out at the Butlers', you'd all get bored, with nothing to do."

"We certainly appreciate your dropping by," Emma Butler told Jason when he arrived. He was glad he'd come. He liked the Butler sisters. Besides, they were about the only people he thought he might be able to talk to about Sirus. Ever since Mattie's death, it was as if Sirus had drifted away. And now with the problems at the projects, Jason wanted to say something to him, but he didn't know what. Yes, the Butlers would be a good choice. Not only were they good at thinking things through, but they were also about the only people in town who could hold a secret in place.

Their house was at the very edge of the town, a good mile between it and the next house, and unlike the other houses out there, it was set back from the road. It wasn't in the country, really, but it had that feel to it.

"If you can't see your neighbor, why then they can't see you" is what old man Butler always used to say. After their father died, most people had urged Satha and Emma to move closer to town, especially because of Satha's affliction, but instead, they hired a man to help get Satha in and out of the car when they wanted to go somewhere, and there was a woman who came two days a week to help cook and clean. Emma said they didn't need any more help than that. Besides, she used to tell people, she and her sister were both too old and too set in their ways to move.

Jason had come to see them at their request. Though neither was much out of her forties, still, they were planning for their deaths. It was a bit premature by a long shot, Jason told them, but Emma said, "Well, it's bound to get here one day or another; might as well be ready. Besides, if you make the drive out," Emma had promised, "I just bet we'd have some fresh blueberry cobbler that we'd need some help with eating. Anyway, the whole thing shouldn't take too long. Satha and I have it all written up, type of casket, flowers, music, and so on. We could go over it with you, to be sure that we haven't left anything out." Jason had to laugh to himself. There surely weren't too many who did it this way.

"Who's to say I'll even be here to carry out your wishes?" Jason had asked her, and Emma had laughed.

"Oh, you'll be here, Jason," she said. "People in the town will have to stop dying when you go."

They sat out on the porch to do their business, and when they were done, Emma brought out the blueberry cobbler she'd promised.

"This sure is good," Jason said when he tasted the cobbler. "Are these blueberries from out of your garden?"

"They grow wild out in the back," Emma said. "I picked a couple of quarts. You could take some along with you for Edith, if she likes to bake with them or put up some jelly."

"She loves to put up blueberry jam."

"Then it's settled; you'll take home a quart."

"Why, thank you," Jason said. He looked out across the front yard. It was filled with flowers, with barely any space left for grass, just flowers and blooming trees, and here and there, scattered throughout the yard, were painted chairs, benches, little settees. Some were the size for a child; others were for an adult to sit in. When old man Butler was alive, he liked to sit out among the flowers, and when Satha had started to get sick as a child, he had made small benches and chairs for her all over the yard, so that she could walk as far as she could go and then sit down. Jason could remember coming out here to visit when both Mr. and Mrs. Butler were alive and all four of them could be found perched one place or another, all over the yard, each one busy with something — weeding or doing needlework, or Mr. Butler might be at work painting or refurbishing a new chair.

"Y'all still sit out in the garden like you used to?" Jason asked.

"Oh, yes," Satha answered. "Every chance we get."

There was another pause in the conversation, but it was always this way with the Butlers. They were content to let time slip in and take a chair in the middle of what anyone was saying.

"Have you seen Sirus and Aileen recently?" Emma asked when time had had enough of a visit. "How are they doing?"

Jason thought about them. As between the two of them, he thought, Aileen looked better. She had an almost haunted look in her eyes, particularly when she saw other children, but at least it was a look that seemed alive. It was different with Sirus. "He looks like he's the one who died," some people said about him. "He ain't dead, just grieving," Jason would say to defend him, but as all these months had gone by, Jason himself felt less and less sure. He didn't want to admit that Sirus was failing, but he had seen it enough times in his work. You could tell it sometimes right out at the interment, right while somebody stood over the grave. The preacher would throw a piece of earth on the coffin, talking about dust to dust, and for some, it was as if they'd been slapped, and they'd let out a yell. They'd fall to the ground, screaming, and their kinfolks would have to drag them up to their feet. Sometimes they'd be like that all the way to the car, moaning, clutching at other people's hands. Later, they were the ones who did just fine.

With others, it was as if the sound of that clod of earth was a voice calling to them, and they'd hear it and turn and then something inside them would climb down and lie beside their loved one inside the grave. And after that, all of the light in their eyes would be gone. Other children, parents, even husbands or wives couldn't reach those people who'd climbed down into a grave after their heart. He worried that this was what was happening to Sirus. "They're holding up," he finally answered.

Satha rolled her wheelchair closer to him.

"Are they really?" she asked.

Jason looked at Satha's face, straining, as it always was, from the effort it took to both talk and control her expressions. Even sleep, Emma had once confided in him, wasn't easy for Satha. She had to awaken several times in the night just to have her position changed.

"I guess I can't lie to you ladies," Jason said. "The passage of time don't seem to be helping them. Particularly Sirus."

"That's what we've heard," Emma said.

"What is this we hear about the projects?" Satha asked.

Jason didn't want to carry the tale, though he supposed it was all over town, about the troubles Sirus's foreman Hal had been seeing, and what it was that Paulie Peters had found.

"Well, there's bound to be some problems in a building," Jason said cautiously.

Satha rolled her wheelchair forward and back, quickly. It was a gesture she sometimes made instead of speaking.

"We know all about what's been found," Emma said.

"Well, I didn't want to be the one to be spreading it," Jason said. "Sirus is just about my closest friend, you know."

"We do know," Satha said.

"That's the real reason we asked you to come out," Emma confided. She and Satha both looked at him, as if checking for a response, and when he gave them none, Emma went on.

"Look, Jason," Emma began, "you haven't lived here all your life like us. You and Sirus came here nearly grown, and it must be hard for the two of you to understand some things about the town."

"Like what?" he asked.

"Like the way people make up their minds," Emma said. She looked out over the porch behind her, as if she were looking back in the direction of town. "Now maybe out in Carr or Bowie, well, maybe there people can settle on something right away." She turned to look back at him. "And some people here, people who are kind of on the outskirts of things, well, maybe they can do that too. But most times — well, it takes a bit of things going around."

Satha rolled up as close to him as she could get. "My sister and I," she said, leaning forward, "you too maybe, we look at things a little different. Death sometimes clears things up. Pain and hardship too. But other people are not so blessed."

"Blessed?" Jason asked.

"What Satha means," Emma said, "is that burdens, they give us . . ." She waved her hand in the air. "What would you call it, Satha?"

"Well, sight, I guess I'd say," Satha replied. She paused a moment to get her breath together for her next words. "I mean," she said, "just seeing, all clear, how the hard times . . . fit in with the good." She leaned her head against the back of her chair. "You must see it, Jason, every day, in your work." She was nearly out of breath from the effort. "People in love, a little baby, of course, little Mattie," she said.

Jason felt tears spring to his eyes.

"You see what we mean." Emma reached toward him and put her hand on his arm. "But other people, like with these buildings. I know people have been all up and down the bend, and they're just coming back, and you must think, Sirus must think, well, what's the matter with these folks, didn't I tell them, now here it is coming true, but it's not like it is in the country. Here, well, sometimes things have gotten so good, at least for some, that it's easy to think that life has lost its hard edges."

"And it hasn't," Satha said.

"Exactly," Emma continued. She took her hand from his arm. "What we're hoping is that you'll talk to Sirus. He musn't give up. If it's taken people a while to come back to what they know, well, you must help him."

Satha then leaned so far out of her chair that Jason worried she was going to topple into his lap.

"Grace has to come," she whispered. "That's the thing. Isn't it, Emma?"

Emma nodded.

"You just tell that to Sirus," Satha instructed. "Tell him to wait. And then, just when he least expects her, she'll come."

"Grace?" Jason asked.

The two sisters looked at each other and then back to him. "Yes," they both said.

11

WHEN MRS. JOHNSON arrived at work the following morning, the Macs were still sleeping. It was just as well, she thought; it would give her more time to think about what she was going to say. All morning Mrs. Johnson rehearsed her words. She planned to start in as soon as Mr. Mac came downstairs and had had his coffee. No point in waiting till the words burned a hole in her head. And she wasn't going to mince words either — she would be straight with him, the way she always was. She was on her third run-through when he came down the back stairs.

"Morning, Mr. Mac," she said. "You sleep well?"

"Fine, Mrs. Johnson, and you?"

"Oh, pretty good," she answered.

"What kind of day is it outside?" Sirus asked. He looked out on the back porch.

Mrs. Johnson poured his coffee and set it on the table.

"A good day," she said. "Nice, real nice. Still warm. And sunny."

Mr. Mac came to the table and sat down. Mrs. Johnson decided not to wait until he'd finished his coffee.

"I've got something to talk over with you," she said, sitting down at the table across from him.

"Of course," he said.

"It's about High Ridge," she began.

"Umm-hmm," Sirus said, sipping the coffee.

"A group of us were talking Saturday night, and, well, what I have to say is something you may not like, but you know I've always spoken my mind."

"Of course."

"Well, one of us, I can't say who, had a relative to look the place over. He's into building up in the North. And I know he had no right without asking, but he did it anyway, said sometimes it's the only way to get the plain truth." Mrs. Johnson waited for a nod or a frown, but when neither came she continued. "So anyway, I'm not excusing it, but the thing is, now, to deal with what he found."

The grease in the griddle Mrs. Johnson had left on the stove began to smoke. She got up, turned the flame off, and sat back down.

"There are things he said he found that are not right, not safe," she said. "Wiring, vents, beams, that sort of thing." Mrs. Johnson folded her hands on the table and looked at them. She felt accusatory but believed there was no other way. She let the words sift into Mr. Mac before she went on.

"Unsafe?" Sirus repeated. It was the first time she'd looked closely at him since he'd come downstairs, and she saw that he still looked half asleep.

"Yes, Mr. Mac, unsafe. Now I can't talk technical. But he — this person I'm talking about — wrote it all down." She pulled a piece of yellow paper from her apron pocket and handed it to Sirus. She pointed at the paper. "He put what he found to one side, and then Mr. Hal, he wrote what was usual on the right. Now this man, he can't say where everything was, for sure, because he only, I guess, peeked in through some holes in places. But he said they're the kind of things you usually find throughout."

Sirus looked at the list. There were about seven items, taking up less than half a page. Written down, they looked quite small, unimportant, like a schoolboy's pledge not to dip a pigtail in ink, written over and over again. But as soon as Sirus saw the words, he knew their weight. Substandard wiring, loosely welded fittings, misplaced vents; his mind could translate each thing into its vivid counterpart, the manifestation of that particular item's flaw: burned hands, shorts and blown fuses, a smell in a bathroom that won't go away. And worse: fires in the wall if a family rigged the fuses to keep the radio and two lights on at the same time. It happened all the time. And it was amazing how fast electrical fires could spread.

"Who wrote these things down?" Sirus asked again.

"Well, on the one side is what this man, this relative wrote. And the other is what Hal, your foreman, wrote."

"Hal wrote this?"

"Well, yes, he was the one who first brought the paper to me."

"And who else has looked at it?"

"A whole group of us," Mrs. Johnson went on. "There was about fifteen people or so out to my house."

Sirus looked at Mrs. Johnson sitting across from him at the table. Every day, five days a week, and half a day on Saturday, she came to his house. She fixed his breakfast, washed his dishes, cleaned his house, and up until a year ago had taken care of his child — so many years of intimacy between them. And yet, when he considered it, they were strangers. He had been inside her house only a few times. When he gave her a ride home in the rain, he let her out from the car. He found it hard to imagine fifteen people squeezed inside her small house.

And the idea that they would be there meeting and talking about him . . . he didn't know what to think of that. He had no way of knowing what Mrs. Johnson might have said about him in such a context. He thought they had a good and fair relationship — he'd always tried to be fair — but still, if he thought about it, there was that doubt. She might think things and never say them, for fear of losing her job, and even if it wasn't that straightforward, there was an undercurrent, something that would always be there.

This was one slim example of his power, and one, up until now, he'd never really considered. How could he have missed such a simple fact? And, of course, with these houses, how much greater was his power? There were two hundred houses. How many lives was that? Three hundred, four hundred people? How many children and old people and young couples and hardworking people like Mrs. Johnson might that be? Weren't these people dependent on him? They could be safe or not; their children could grow up injured or intact; and it could all turn on decisions he made. He thought of all those times on this job when Hal had tried to pull him aside to tell him something. And he hadn't listened. Even as recently as a few days ago.

He felt like shaking his head. He didn't like where these thoughts were carrying him; they seemed to be pulling him in a direction he didn't want to go. Like thinking he should step in and save people. Or imagining that it was up to him to change the way things might go. Those were exactly the thoughts that had undone him before. No, he was finished with crazy thoughts like that. Like thinking that he ought to be a big man. Or that he had a particular burden he should carry. Hadn't fate shown him the truth? Hadn't he been as knocked down by it as all the rest? He felt a slight muffling in his ears, as if he were going up a steep hill. What was it called, that thing that divers got when they went to the surface too fast? Right, the bends. It was as if this conversation was bringing them on.

"This is a short but powerful list," he said to Mrs. Johnson. "Do you know what these things mean?"

Mrs. Johnson shook her head. "Well, not to the details, but I think everyone got it pretty clear that they could be serious." She sat looking at him, expectant.

"I don't know what I can do," he began. "I mean, there are things to be done, that could be done, but they would be hard at this stage. Too many things are out of my hands." He looked at his hands now, large and pale. What he was saying was true. Why was Mrs. Johnson staring at him as if he had some magic to offer her?

"Are you all right?" she asked.

He shook his head. He felt tired but agitated, as if his feet wanted to move but were bolted to the floor. He wasn't sure he could stand up. But when he pushed himself away from the table, he did stand, and as he did, Mrs. Johnson's face seemed to recede. "I have to go out," he said. He backed away from the table and turned and hurried across the room. Mrs. Johnson watched as he nearly ran out of the house.

A few blocks away, Etta Baldridge was visiting Ophelia Macon when Sirus's car drove by. There was no mistaking the sound of his well-tuned Cadillac, and both women looked up just in time to catch a glimpse of him as he drove by.

"Why, there goes Sirus," Ophelia said, peering over the top of her reading glasses.

"I wonder where he's off to so early on a Saturday," Etta said.

"Maybe out to those projects. This is the way he usually goes," Ophelia suggested.

Etta tapped the church membership list on the table in front of Ophelia. "You better get back to your list."

Ophelia smiled the smallest smile, and there was no way Etta could miss it. She had been smiling like this a lot lately. It was a triumphant smile. Things are changing around, is what Ophelia was saying with her smile. The problems with the projects were all over town, and there was nothing that Sirus could or would do. People had conveniently rearranged events in their head, so no one seemed to remember that Sirus had initially said no to the whites. "He is just plain messing up, getting in with those white people and then giving them a free hand" was what people were saying.

Etta knew Ophelia was glad to see it. She was happy, as she'd put it to someone, "to see Sirus brought down a peg." She hadn't dared say it to Etta, but it had gotten back to Etta nonetheless. Etta knew that each peg that Sirus went down Ophelia saw as a leg up for herself and her family. After all, it was common knowledge, from way back when, that Sirus didn't have too high an opinion of the Reverend Frankel. And since the deal with Burnett, things were very strained with Gant, too. So if Clorissa said yes to Frankel, as Ophelia had confided to Etta she would, then it was all to the good for the Macons if Sirus were not so high up anymore in the town. Already, Gant and Frankel were talking about how they would keep a tight check on the whites, how they would not repeat Sirus's mistake.

Ophelia went down the list of the membership of the church. Though Clorissa hadn't made her acceptance official, Ophelia was already deciding who would be invited from the church to the wedding reception.

"Of course Sirus and Aileen," Ophelia said, putting a tiny check next to their names.

"Of course," Etta replied.

"And of course Dr. Gant and Muriel. Though it wouldn't do to have them seated near Sirus."

Now Ophelia outright chuckled, and Etta felt her forehead

tingle. She sometimes turned bright red right between her eyes when she was mad.

"You are going to be laughing out of the other side of your mouth one of these days," Etta said.

"What do you mean?" Ophelia asked, arching her eyebrows up over the top of her glasses.

"You know very well what I mean," Etta said, hoping her threat would carry some weight, though she knew Ophelia wasn't bothered in the least. After all, she was right: What in the world was there that Etta could do? There was no way she could save Sirus if he wasn't going to save himself. And he didn't seem likely to do that. He acted as if he didn't care what happened to him, or to anyone else in the town. He had to know what people were saying. Where was his pride? How could he give things over to people like Frankel and Gant?

"I have a headache," Etta told Ophelia abruptly. "I have to go home."

Ophelia offered to drive her home or to fix her a cool spot inside the house to lie down, out of the sun, with a cold compress for her head, but Etta insisted, no, she had to get home. "We'll have breakfast one day next week and we can go over the list then," she said when she left.

Once she was home, Etta went straight upstairs to her room. She closed her door and pulled down the shades; she needed a little quiet to think. She lay down on her bed. This threatened upheaval was just what she'd feared, right after little Mattie's death, and here it was, coming to pass. Her stomach tightened and tightened. People like Gant and Frankel couldn't be trusted. With them at the head of the town, everything would come falling down.

Twice this week, already, someone had passed her out on the street without speaking. At Dr. Gerard's when she left with an ice cream and her prescription. And at the meat market, after she'd chosen some pork. It was small, barely noticeable, but what kind of town would it be if people didn't stop and speak to each other?

Oh, people like Gant and Frankel had their place. Every town needs a cold man and a fool. But it couldn't be a place at the head; even a child would have more sense than that. How could anyone think of following people like them? At the head you needed someone who could put things together, someone like Dr. Anson, who had started the hospital after the insurance company, someone like Jonathan Carter, way back when, who had started a school. It wasn't just brains and ambition. You needed something beyond all that.

That extra was something that Sirus had once had. Etta knew that extra thing well. Oh, she didn't have it, but she could see it, and it was something her Charles had had, and maybe even Lily would have when she grew up. It was something the Butlers had too, only they wouldn't use it often, and that made Etta mad. Of course, Charles never had the ambition that Sirus did, or quite as much of Sirus's smarts, but he had had that other, that looking out and into the heart of things.

"How can I save Sirus?" she asked herself out loud. She got up from her bed and paced back and forth across her room. "He's grieving, but I know grief. He's in despair, and I know that too." She picked up a picture from her nightstand. It was a picture of Charles that Lily had drawn. She looked at it closely; it was such a good likeness of Charles. To think, her Lily had drawn it. She put down the picture, walked to the window, and peeked out. She'd been so surprised, when she'd found that box in Lily's room the other day, all the way at the back of her closet, filled with pictures like these — some sketched in pencil, others more carefully done, like this one, with colored pens, even a few done in watercolor, with that set Charles had given Lily that Etta had never seen her use.

Etta had told Lily later that night after dinner, "I found these," and held out a stack of the pictures. To Etta's surprise, Lily hadn't seemed angry or upset, just resigned, as if she knew she couldn't hide the pictures forever. Of course Etta didn't have to guess why the pictures were hidden. As soon as she found them, she knew that Lily had not wanted her to see them. She had pushed them as far away from Etta as she could. But why? Etta loved Lily, wanted only the best for her. Why would Lily hide from her something so lovely? She walked back to her nightstand and looked at the picture again. Charles stood alone, under a clear sky, with nothing else in the picture; it was just Charles. He looked young in the drawing, almost younger than Lily could have known him. Etta compared the picture to her own recollection of Charles. She had never seen him so solitary. She always saw herself in the picture with him, or she saw something else there — Lily, him at his job, him at the club or at church. She thought that Lily would have wanted to put herself in the picture.

It was very precious, she thought, this space that Lily had surrounded her father with. It was as if she were asking nothing of him. For herself, Etta realized as she stared at the picture, she had seen this much space around Charles only once in their lives, on the day they were married, as he stood at the front of the church. She had looked down the aisle at him, and, for a moment, everything around him had receded: the music, the smell of the flowers. There he was, just Charlie. Standing there, a little shy, boyish, well intentioned, smart but not too smart, energetic, but not overly so. After that, in fact, as soon as she began down the aisle, she filled in the space around him. She saw the two of them together; she imagined all of the great things he would do. She saw the house they would live in, the children they would have, the job at the insurance company, the clubs, the cars, the house.

It was as if Lily knew that her father longed for space, so here, in the picture, Lily had given it to him.

Was it that obvious, Etta thought, that a child would see it? She thought of that woman in Mobile. Hadn't that been an example of Charles's taking some space? She had to marvel at his determination. As his wife, Etta may have surrounded him, but Charles had kept enough of his own to defy her. That was what that woman in Mobile was about.

But of course, she realized, it was the same with Lily. That was why the pictures were hidden. Lily didn't want Etta to know that she could see things and capture them this way. Maybe there were hundreds of things she had hidden. A horrible image suddenly came to Etta. She saw herself as a strangling creeper, snaking through the house, attaching herself to everything that lived in it, until the only safe place for Charles was all the way out of the house, all the way down in Mobile, and the only safe place for Lily was tucked away, as far and as secret as she could get, at the back of her closet. Etta shuddered. She loved Lily, loved her with all of her heart, just as she had loved Charles, and here she was, threatening to choke the life out of her.

She put the picture down and folded her arms over her chest; she took some deep breaths. All she had ever wanted was the best for both of them. The best for her friends. The best for the town. She laughed at herself, and then, suddenly, she began to cry. Who was she to think she could help Sirus or save anybody? What a ridiculous notion. Look at the mess she'd made of her own life. Her Lily and Charlie, running from her, both struggling to get out of her grasp. And maybe Charles had even been driven to stop his own heart, just to be free.

She couldn't stop her tears. They made a mad dash down her face, and she feared she might cry forever. She cried first for all she had kept Charles from having, and then she cried for Lily, and at last she cried for herself. She hugged herself tighter and tighter. "Is there time for those of us who are living?" she finally asked Charles's picture. His face seemed to be looking back at her clearly.

On the last mile to the project, Sirus drove quickly, passing many of the slower cars. How often in the past year had he driven this road? The landscape, so numbingly familiar, looked foreign, as if he'd never seen it before. Has that curve in the road always been there? Has that tree been leaning so far over all this time? How long has that tractor been abandoned at the side of the road? Sirus couldn't answer any of his questions. When he reached the buildings, he went straight to the house Hal had shown him, pulled a small screwdriver from his pocket, and poked open one of the holes that had been plastered over. Peering inside, he could see one of the wall beams, just to the left inside the hole, and sure enough, as the list had indicated, it was not the right width for a building this size. Down near the floor was another hole, and he poked through that as well; here he could pull out some of the wiring. It was like the wiring used in a lamp, not that which was to be used in a wall, to carry the main electrical circuits. In the bathroom, he saw pipes that were haphazardly soldered.

Everywhere he looked, there was something substandard or makeshift or unorthodox. He poked out all of the holes, and through each one he found more of the same. He put his screwdriver away and walked outside, up the rise at the back of the houses. A large stand of trees hadn't been cleared, and from there he looked down the hill at the project.

Every day of his life, since he'd been a grown man, he had been able to look squarely at his actions. When he'd made a mistake — and there had been many such times — he could review his decisions, find the flaw in his judgment or skill, and rectify it. Nothing rose so high that he could not see over or through it. Nothing before had threatened to sweep him away. But this year had delivered more than he could bear. His beloved Mattie was gone, and he believed that his arrogance had caused her death. And now there was this nightmare of houses, sprawled across the landscape where his dreams should have been. Any one of these things made a wall so high and thick that he could not get past it. On the other side was Aileen, and people calling to him, and their children, crying; yet there was nothing he could do to reach them. There was only this thick wall and a roar in his ears like the sea.

"Daddy." A quiet voice spoke from the other side of his pain. "Daddy."

The voice was inside his head, but he blinked his eyes and whirled around. "Daddy," it called again.

He looked up at the trees. It was as if their branches were whirling; he felt dizzy, watching them spin. The ground seemed to be falling away, and he grasped one of the trees to hold on — and then everything stopped. He felt as lucid as he had in a year. Off in the distance, a child beckoned to him. He could see the youngster as if he were standing a few yards away, and the child was the boy he had been, and next to the young Sirus stood Mattie. The two seemed as near to him as the houses behind him. They stood quietly, close to each other, their hands lightly clasped. As Sirus watched, they said and did nothing, merely stood across from him, silently urging, as if he were resisting, refusing to let go.

"My children," he whispered, and he wanted to run toward them, back to all of the innocence they sheltered, but his feet remained planted. He was caught and he trembled, and the air thickened and held him until he was surrounded in its taut circle of light. The light reflected his past and future, and it cupped his present as well, a present that was vibrant with life.

It felt like hours, the time he stood there. He let the light wash over him and fill him, and slowly all his resistance flowed away. The air shuddered around him like a million hummingbirds, their wings like tiny razors that splintered the light, until every-thing was subsumed in its magnificence — all that he could recall of dignity and perseverance and grief and even the mo-ment when he learned of Mattie's death. He stood as if rooted; slowly, imperceptibly, the feeling that was Mattie began to fade, melted into the air. It melted the way his kisses had done on her cheek when she was a baby, melted the way her sweet humming had faded away when she had drifted off to sleep, melted the way the memory of the exact color of his mother's eyes had left him when he was grown.

And Sirus heard the voices again, softly, then more insistently, calling him. Aileen's voice. And Etta's. And Jason's. And Mrs. Johnson's. A hundred other voices. And when he came back to himself, he hurried into town as fast as could.

Back at his house, Mrs. Johnson stood at the counter in the kitchen, seasoning ground beef for meatloaf. She held it in her hands and squeezed hot sauce, salt and pepper, and spoonfuls of brown gravy through it. She wasn't thinking about her con-versation with Mr. Mac, not right now, nor did she think of the chores that lay ahead. She simply felt the meat in her hands, and listened to the wet sound it made as her fingers moved through it. As she spooned more gravy into the bowl, suddenly she was aware of how much her legs ached. It was startling, this pain, as if she had just now done something agonizing to them, but she was merely standing on them as she always stood. Then again, her legs were always tired; there was never enough time to rest them. They were stiff in the morning, and no amount of rubbing them with Vaseline would ease the stiffness. They throbbed as she sat at her kitchen table, where she had her first morning cup of coffee; and later in the day, when they were almost numb, there would be a sudden spasm or tear as she reached for something: Mrs. Mac's earring under a table, perhaps. Day in and day out she stood, walked up and down stairs carrying laundry, things from the freezer, or ran after Mattie or her own children. How many times had she really felt this pain? A dozen times out of a thousand? How often had she actually stopped in the midst of what she was doing to acknowledge, as she did now, oh, my God, how my legs are aching. And as she thought this, it was clear to her that if her own legs were sometimes a stranger to her, how much easier for these people she worked for, these people who were certainly not as near to her as her own legs, how much easier then for these people to be strangers.

Who'd she been kidding, she thought, with her belief that she knew Mr. Mac, that she knew what he might do, how a thing would strike him? Who had sat at the table staring vacantly as she'd described something that could ruin their lives? Who had run out of the house like a child? She thought back further, to the day before, and the day before that. Where was the Mr. Mac she thought she knew?

The thought spread in her brain like a weed. She was seized with the idea that there might be hundreds of these unknown things right in front of her, things she was blind to. Had she ever known Mr. Mac? Were her images of him as good and fair only descriptions she'd created? She sat in the chair at the table and looked around the kitchen as if she were seeing it for the first time.

Slowly, methodically, she ran over the situation again. What else was here, right under her nose, that she hadn't seen? And then, of course, it was obvious: Mr. Mac was not recovering. Time was not healing his wounds. He was sinking deeper and deeper into a pit from which he might never escape. That is what is going on, has been going on for months. And Mrs. Mac, too, she thought. She could drink herself to death or have one of those fits nervous people sometimes have, and that would be it for her forever.

Mrs. Johnson knew, as firmly as she had felt her legs, that these were not conjectures — they were the way things were, concretely, around her. As soon as she recognized this, more appeared. For example, didn't Mr. Mac often take a thing too much to heart, as he had when the town went against him with Phil Burnett? Or the way he was with Mrs. Mac herself? Didn't he tiptoe, almost always, around a great hole that threatened to open between them?

Her mind raced. Who was going to come to his aid? Which of his friends would find the right words to save him? Or were there no words, at this point, that could heal? She didn't flatter herself that she was the one to say them, but there was one thing she could offer, and that was prayer.

Sweet Lord Jesus, she prayed, ease their sorrow. Guilt is eating them alive, guilt and grieving over what can never come back.

Etta rode in the car with Lily, on the way home from Lily's dental appointment. Lily watched out the window quietly, rubbing her jaw.

"You still feel numb from the injection?" Etta asked.

"Just a little," Lily answered.

Etta looked at her daughter. She had shot up in the last year, but she still looked very small in the large expanse of the car. She's been through so much in these past few years, Etta thought, first losing her father, and then her best friend. Etta thought again about the pictures, so much of herself that Lily had hidden away. What other kinds of things did she hide? Etta glanced at her again, quickly, so that Lily would not catch her staring. Her light hair was beginning to darken, her face had a more defined look, and right between her eyes, exactly where Etta had them on her own face, were the beginnings of two worry lines.

She's not even thirteen, and she worries this much already, Etta thought with dismay. But hadn't she herself been the same way at that age — her own fear when she was ten, for example, that she would lose her voice as a punishment for being so loud. Was it possible to pass such a thing on, Etta wondered. She stole another look at Lily. When exactly had those worry lines appeared? It could have been months, even a year, and she had to admit that she'd been so preoccupied with her own worries that she wouldn't have noticed. When she did think of how Lily was faring, she'd tell herself, oh, Lily is fine, she's so steady. Now she wondered if it was true.

She suddenly wanted to know more than anything how Lily really was. She never talked with her daughter about her feelings, and as she considered it now, she worried she would do it badly. Then she remembered Charles once more. She was being given a second chance, and she wouldn't let her fear of failing stand in her way.

"Are things okay, dear?" she asked tentatively.

Lily looked up at her with surprise.

"You mean my tooth?" she asked.

"Well, that too, I suppose. But no, what I meant was, in general." Etta adjusted her hat. "Your father and Mattie and all."

Lily stopped rubbing her jaw and grabbed the hand tightly with the one in her lap. "I suppose," she said; then more quietly, "Sometimes, I worry."

Etta wanted to squeeze Lily to her as tightly as she could, but she only reached over and stroked Lily's clenched hands.

"You worry?" she asked.

Lily nodded.

"I know what you mean," Etta said. They approached the corner of Fayetville and Lawson. "We're near to the McDougalds'," she said.

A look close to fear passed over Lily's face, and as it did, Etta remembered how Lily had fainted at Mattie's wake, and the nightmares she'd had for weeks afterward, and the strange questions she still sometimes asked, about God and punishment and forgiveness. The pictures, and Lily's reasons for drawing them, suddenly made sense.

"Let's stop by and see the Macs, what do you say?" she asked, and Lily gingerly agreed. They hadn't been over to the McDougalds' together but once since Mattie's funeral. "Turn here; I want to go by the McDougalds'," Etta told her driver.

Lily watched her mother shyly, but with a certain excitement. Etta searched in her bag for the envelope she had put there this morning. It was another of Lily's drawings, a drawing of the McDougalds and herself and Lily. When Etta had told Lily she'd found the pictures, she had asked whether she might keep this one, along with the one of Charles. She had put it in her bag without even thinking, and realized now that maybe she'd had this plan all along. She pulled the picture out and looked at it again.

"It's so lovely," she said to Lily, and Lily smiled in a way that Etta rarely remembered. "I think when we stop by we should give it the Macs. What do you think?"

Lily looked at the picture as her mother held it. In it, she was standing under a tree, and to one side of her, sitting on the ground on a picnic blanket, were Mr. and Mrs. McDougald and her mother. It was a blanket like one you'd sit on at the beach, with broad stripes. Off to the other side, a little smaller and farther away, was Mattie. She was smiling a happy smile, and she was waving. She had a basket of berries, one of her favorite treats, at her feet.

"Yes, I think that's a good idea," Lily said quietly.

"Why, Mrs. Baldridge, Lily," Mrs. Johnson said when she heard the door on the front porch open.

"Hello, Mrs. Johnson," Etta said as she stepped inside. "Are they home?"

"Umm-hmm. They're still upstairs, though. Mr. Mac was out for a while, but I think he may have gone back to bed."

"Sirus, back to bed?" Etta asked.

Mrs. Johnson was quiet, fearing that maybe, already, she'd said too much.

"Well, you know what Lily and I are going to do?" Etta went on. "We're just going to sit right out here in the parlor and enjoy this nice breeze, and when they come down, well, then, here we'll be. Will we be in your way in here?"

"No, I'm on my way back to the kitchen, just getting supper ready to leave for them. Can I get you coffee, maybe iced, or some tea?"

"Iced tea, two glasses; that would be wonderful, Mrs. Johnson," Etta answered.

Mrs. Johnson left to go to the kitchen and Etta looked around the room. She hoped this was really a good idea; she suddenly doubted herself. Maybe she was doing once again the very thing she'd been telling herself to stop, filling up other people's lives with her own imaginings. Maybe this was the same. Just because the picture of Charles that Lily had drawn had helped her, did that mean that a picture of Mattie was going to do the same for Sirus and Aileen? And was it really a good idea to bring Lily to this house again? But they were here, and she couldn't very well run out of the house now. Of course she could make up another excuse for why she was here, but she had told Lily what she was planning to do, and maybe Lily would be hurt if she didn't give them the picture. All of this thinking was so new to her, it made her head hurt, but she remembered her promise to herself and her entreaty to Charles, and she resolved to see it through.

She heard footsteps at the head of the stairs. It was Sirus and Aileen together. They looked as if they had just awakened. "Halloo, good morning," Etta called out to them. "I know you must be surprised to see us."

"What a pleasant surprise," Aileen said as she reached the bottom of the stairs. She kissed Lily on the cheek first and then Etta. Sirus followed her, kissing Etta first, and then Lily.

"You two are up and out early," Aileen said. She sat in one of the side chairs and Sirus sat in the other. "I see you've gotten something to drink. Can I get you something to eat? We have some ham left over. Mrs. Johnson could heat it up with some salad and heat some rolls."

"We're stuffed. We had an early lunch just a little while ago. Lily had a late morning appointment with Dr. Taylor."

"Not too many cavities, I hope," Aileen said.

"No, just two, and they were little ones. But he said I have to come back in six months instead of a year," Lily said.

"Well, you have to keep at it; you don't want to lose that pretty smile," Aileen said.

Lily smiled in spite of herself. She hated when she did this, offering a smile just because an adult said she had a pretty one, but she couldn't help it. Besides, she had always liked Mrs. Mac.

There was a small pause in the conversation, not enough for anyone to grow uncomfortable; a minuscule one. But enough time for Aileen to steal a glance at Lily, whose legs reached the floor easily now from the divan, enough time for Etta to notice how embarrassed and almost guilty Lily looked under Aileen's sad gaze, and time enough for Sirus to notice how longingly

Aileen looked at Lily. Lily knew what it was that Mrs. Mac felt, and she felt sure about what she was going to do.

"I made a picture," she suddenly said.

"A picture?" Aileen asked, but Lily didn't answer. She was looking down at her hands, shyly.

Etta had no choice but to step in. "Lily draws. Pictures. Very nice ones."

"Oh, how lovely," Aileen said.

"That's quite a talent," Sirus added.

"And she made a beautiful picture of our Charles," Etta said. "Really, very beautiful." Etta certainly hadn't intended to cry, but her eyes were filling with tears. "I can just see him," she went on, "you know, the way he was, still a young man. Oh, Lord, forgive me." She searched her purse for a handkerchief but couldn't find one, so she let the tears run down her face.

"Momma likes it a lot," Lily interjected. "I do too. When I look at it, I always think of Papa lifting me up."

Etta went back into her purse and grabbed the envelope with Mattie's picture. She handed it to Sirus. "Open it," she said. "Lily drew it. We thought it was something you might like to have."

Sirus hesitated. He hesitated often these days. He hesitated whenever he came into the house, whenever he left it. Opening something was the worst thing. The car door, the door at his office, even the top of a jar. Whenever he was about to open something, it brought him back to that day, opening the screen door at the front of the house. And what had been on the other side. It was so minute, his hesitation, hardly more than a second; anyone watching would not see it. But it was always there. And in this hesitation, in this brief respite, lay all his hope. All that he had ever wanted or expected or wished for in the world was now compressed into that microsecond. It was compressed into a single desire: that Mattie be alive; that he come through the door and find her in the house as she always was, her voice calling out to him, her face hurtling from the darker reaches of the house, the smell of her, a smell he didn't even know he was aware of when she was alive, rising up to greet him. In his million hesitations she came alive and died again every day.

So he hesitated, and his hesitation came back to him, a sweet expectancy, a waiting peace. It felt gracious, this unexpected reprieve. He opened the envelope and took out the picture. At first he didn't even see Mattie in it, off to the side. He recognized Lily by the golden bush of her hair, and then he saw himself and Aileen and Etta, Etta with her mouth open, Aileen with her hand running through her hair, his own hand holding his pocket watch, holding it open. And then he noticed Mattie. There were the two scars on her knees, little patches of beige in the midst of the brown, and there were her pigtails, and most of all like Mattie was her hand on her hip. Her other hand was in the air, waving.

Tears came to his eyes and he couldn't escape. This was his life, he thought to himself. In this picture and in this room. He wasn't going to be given any other. Here was Lily, not much older than his daughter would have been, if she'd lived. She was growing up, getting taller every day, coming into her own. She sat across from him, staring at him with private intensity. And here was Etta. Etta who was here because she had to be, because she couldn't stay away if she tried. And here was his wife, Aileen, wounded, struggling, watching him, waiting for something from him, waiting for help to arrive. And Mrs. Johnson was in the kitchen, waiting for his answer about the houses. And his beloved sweet Mattie was gone. Outside was the porch that framed their house, and beyond it was the street that ran in every direction and tied his house to his neighbors'.

"It's a beautiful picture," Sirus said. There was nothing else he could say. Etta wanted to take his hand but didn't, and Lily made sure she didn't put the bottoms of her shoes against the sofa as she drew her legs in closer. Aileen watched Sirus for some sign of what he was feeling, and she saw a look that was totally new. Briefly, she almost had a feeling of hope. Sirus then handed her the picture.

That night, in the midst of a dream about Mattie, Lily awakened. There was a bolt of lightning and then a loud crack of thunder that shook her room. Lily was, at first, confused. She had dreamed about where Mattie had gone; and now that she was awake, her room was alive with shadows and flashes of light and then a blackness as one thick cloud after another raced across the moon. On her wall and ceiling, spreading as if it were growing there, was the shadow of a tree, swaying wildly, illuminated and then obliterated by the flash of light. Her windows rattled as the sound of rain and the wind's howling rushed through the room. She pushed her sheet aside and ran to the window. It was a violent late summer storm. The rain poured from the sky in thick sheets, and the wind screeched down the street like a banshee. Her mother had told her, a dozen times, never to stand near the window in a storm, but the dark howling was mesmerizing. She pressed her face against the glass. Across the street, one tree's branches swayed and shook, now a towering figure, screaming, its arms upraised, now a dancer, swooning in the wind's embrace. The wind shook and shook and seemed to rattle the tree to its core. Suddenly, one branch, no more than ten feet from the ground, turned back on itself in an unnatural arc until it cracked, snapped from the trunk like a tooth broken off at the gum. Lily nearly screamed — but she felt excited, electric. All of that turbulence outside, and here she stood, dry and warm. Just like her dream about Mattie. All that stillness in the other place, and here, where she was, her heart raced, her feet pressed into the floor. She could smell a small scent of herself, like must and secrets, on her hands, and she felt unexpectedly, wildly, happy. She was alive. Another flash of lightning lit the sky, followed by more distant thunder. She felt released from a secret sadness. After all of these months, it was gone.

She thought back to Mattie's funeral, to all the night dreams she had had of Mattie's body, so cool and still under the ground, and all of the times that she had worried that something bad would also happen to her. She hadn't been able to tell a soul, yet she had waited for it, expected it, as if she would be punished for remaining alive, and now it was all gone. No matter how sorry she was about Mattie, no matter how much she missed her, she still had this, this wild howling in the midst of a storm. It is so wonderful to be alive, she thought. The slimness of her thought amazed her; it stood at her center, like a slender sapling. To have these feelings, to plant her bare feet on the floor, to look out on a night unexpectedly beautiful, all of these things were a miracle. No matter how close she and Mattie had been, it was Mattie who had died, and she, Lily, was still here.

She sank into the chair by the window and ran her fingers over the objects on her desk. She saw Mattie's death fanned out in front of her, and she saw her own life forking, and going another way.

Lily thought back to the night before Mattie died, how they had sat and talked on Mattie's front porch. They had been swimming after school, the last evening swim of the summer. Lily was a good but lazy swimmer. She liked to cling to the sides and splash her legs, or make brief forays halfway across the pool, where she would stop and tread water and peer at the divers from below. Mattie, on the other hand, was one of the divers, one of those who stood at the end of the board again and again, like a little metronome gone awry. She would dive into the water, scamper up the ladder, climb the steps to the high board, peer into the water, and dive off the end again. She alternated between the high board and the low board, one dive following the next. Lily had watched Mattie dive as she treaded water near the side of the pool and could see her as she sank to the bottom.

"Why do you dive like that?" Lily asked her later as they sat together on the porch at Mattie's house. The porch light was off, and a light shining from Mattie's parents' room upstairs created an arc that seemed to seal them in darkness. Mattie shuddered before she answered. Her mouth and nose and chin appeared smaller than Lily remembered them to be, perhaps stunted by the warmth and darkness.

"Like what?" Mattie asked, her teeth beginning to chatter.

"Oh, you know," Lily had said, slamming her hands together in imitation of the splash Mattie invariably made. "Up, down, up, down, up, down."

Mattie's eyes began to glisten. "I don't know," she said, staring at the light that ended just beyond her reach. "It's just how I do it."

And Lily thought now of herself, her own circumspect approach to things, so much less bold than Mattie's, so quiet, yet with her own heart, which leaped and danced and dived. And she realized that she could still have that, understood that Mattie's death, just like her father's, was horrible, but it had happened to them, not to her. She felt set free. There was nothing she had to be afraid of anymore. There was no angry spirit that she had to appease, no one, not even the Macs, she had to apologize to for being alive. She took out a sheet of paper and her oil pencils. In the newly quiet sky, there was just enough light from the moon to see. She drew fast and sure, a picture of herself and Mattie. She decided it would be the last picture she would ever draw of her friend.

.   .   .

A few blocks away, both Aileen and Sirus were also awakened by the storm. Neither of them moved. Each hoped the other would think him or her asleep, yet each knew the other was awake. Sirus could tell because of the change in Aileen's breathing; and Aileen could feel Sirus's alert thoughts. They heard the thunder and the rain, and from his side of the bed, Sirus could see the dark clouds roll away from the moon. From her side, Aileen could see the shadows the clouds made on the wall as they sped across the sky.

Aileen thought of the picture of Mattie, and of Lily's having drawn it, and then she faced the inescapable fact that Lily was alive, to come into her own in this way, and her Mattie was not. If she could, would she ask that their lives be switched? She thought of Etta. No matter Etta's faults, she couldn't wish this much heartache on another soul. But what of Sirus? What heartache did she wish on him? What about all those times she had accused him?

Sirus was strong, she'd always thought to herself. But was he? If he was so strong, where had the man she married gone? If he was so strong, what was that look on his face this afternoon when he'd opened the picture of Mattie?

"We can't go on like this, Ailie," Sirus suddenly said.

"Sirus?"

He rolled onto his back. "I mean it. We can't. I can't."

Aileen didn't want to move. She wished one of the clouds she'd been watching would envelop her and carry her away.

"I know you're awake. Please, Aileen, we have to talk."

She rolled over so that her face was in her pillow, and she bit into the feathers. Then she rolled toward Sirus, her head tucked into the corner of her arm.

"I can't, Sirus," she began.

"Aileen, sweetheart," Sirus said.

"Sirus, don't," she said. "Don't humor me."

He reached out his hand toward her and then pulled it away.

She sat upright in the bed. "I know what you're thinking," she said.

"What, Aileen?" Sirus asked. "What is it that you think I'm thinking?"

She put her hands over her face and pressed her eyes. "You know," she said.

"I don't," Sirus answered. "Please, tell me."

"You can never forgive me," Aileen finally breathed into her hands.

"Forgive you? Forgive you for what?" Sirus asked. "I'm the one. I was going to make the world over. I'm the one; you've said it."

Aileen interrupted. "No, not you, me. I just say that." She began to whisper, "It was me, me."

"You?"

"For being jealous of Mattie," Aileen said. "For envying her. For being jealous that no one was trying to crush her. God heard me. God punished me. If I had loved her the right way, she would never have died."

Sirus thought of the right way to love, or the right way to live, and knew he would never count on either again. Because there was no secret pathway around pain. "Aileen, never, never, I never," he said.

Aileen pulled her legs up to her chest. "You had to, Sirus. She lit up for you. I was never that way. I couldn't. Whenever I heard her . . . When she would — The way she smiled, I couldn't. I wanted to. Honest to God, I did. But it would — Oh, God, and she would, and you, Sirus, believe me. How I wanted. If I could, just for one second. Oh, God, Sirus."

"Ailie," Sirus said, but Aileen didn't hear him. He tried gently to pull her hands away from her face, and then tried to move her legs from her chest, but Aileen resisted, and as he tried harder, she pulled herself tighter. So they stayed like that, their tensions and strengths equal, neither moving, until Sirus took his hands away and let them hover above her, stroking the space between them. He poured all of his love into that space, using everything these painful days had forced him to know, and he circled her around with his love, which was open to heartache, and cruelty, even death, stroking the air between them, around and around, slowly, ever so slowly, closer and closer, until just his fingers brushed her skin, feathering across her. He trailed one finger slowly after the other, and soon, as she let him, his touch grew a little stronger, so that he was stroking her, then kneading her skin, then taking her face in his hands. He cupped his hands over hers on her face. "Ailie, look at me," he said.

She let her hands drop and slowly looked up. In her husband's face she recognized the child they had birthed together and had lost.

"You're so soft," she said, and as she said it, she suddenly knew it was true. As she looked at him, she saw, as if she had never seen him before, that he was as soft as she was, not at all strong the way she'd always imagined, but soft at the center, soft at the center of his eyes, at the center of his heart, where anything and everything could pierce him, just as things pierced her, and his strength was just muscle and bone that shielded his soft heart.

"Hold me," she said, and Sirus took her into his arms. He held her against his chest, where she could hear his heart beating, and she wrapped her arms around his chest and up to where she could stroke his face. She could feel the pulse behind his ear and he could feel her breasts against him and she could feel his breath in her hair and he could feel her eyelids moving across his chest. They held on to each other, each melting into the other, all the grief and the anger and the reserve and the guilt melting, until there was nothing left in either of them but a hole into which they were both opening.

"You loved our child, Ailie," Sirus said.

Neither of them moved. They kept their arms tight around each other until the sun came up, each falling slowly, deeper and deeper, closer and closer to the center of the other's heart.

12

THREE WEEKS LATER, Sirus and Aileen stood on their porch after church, expecting visitors. The Reverend Frankel and Clorissa Macon were the first to arrive.

"Reverend, Clorissa," Sirus said, extending his hand.

The reverend took Sirus's hand, though it meant letting go of Clorissa's, and he retrieved her hand as soon as he could. This was their first social visit since she'd said yes to his proposal of marriage, and for the briefest of moments, just as they stepped on the porch, Clorissa looked captured, as if it suddenly dawned on her, seeing herself in Sirus's and Aileen's eyes, that there was no escape. Within a few moments, however, her face relaxed and she slipped her hand free from the reverend's, took hold of his arm, and began the process of setting him forward in the light in which she wanted him viewed.

"We heard about what happened," she said, "and Leroy and I wanted to be the first to tell you that we think you did absolutely the right thing. Don't we, Leroy?" she said.

"Well, yes, absolutely," the Reverend Frankel said. "One thing doesn't have to ride on the other." He looked to Clorissa for her reassurance that he had done as she asked, and she gave it to him in the form of a squeeze on his arm.

"Well, I'm glad there are no hard feelings," Aileen said.

Clorissa shook her head with a practiced abandon and laughed what she hoped was an engaging laugh. She looked at the reverend again. He might not be perfect, but he provided her with plenty of material to work with.

Sirus and Aileen escorted Clorissa and the preacher inside. A few minutes later, the Butler sisters arrived. It took a while for the man who helped Satha to get her and her chair up the stairs, and meanwhile more people arrived. Within minutes, there were half a dozen people gathered out on the porch.

"He did right," Bertie Anderson said, putting one hand on her hip. "I knew Sirus would come through," Fiona Madison added. Fiona's husband, Carlton, looked around as if he were searching for food. "You ain't starving," Fiona said to him under her breath. For their part, out of respect, the Butler sisters were quiet. They had, after all, made their views known all along, and anything they said now would sound like bragging. Mrs. Johnson, on her way in, had stopped on the porch. She was here to help out with the food, but even if Mr. Mac hadn't called her, she would have found an excuse to drop by. She smiled now, listening to what people had to say. She knew all this pride might be momentary, but it was nice while it lasted. By the next day or next week, people would have had a chance to think over what had happened, but right now there was a heady consensus, and an obvious joy in what Mr. Mac had done.

Sirus had said nothing for nearly two weeks after Mrs. Johnson told him about the problems with the building, except to reassure her every morning that he hadn't forgotten what she'd said. Then, all of sudden, this past Wednesday, with Jason, he'd driven to see every person who'd put money down on a house.

With the same yellow sheet Mrs. Johnson had given him, he had told each person what he knew.

"The wiring is not up to grade," he said, patiently explaining from one house to another what that meant. Some people, like Grandma Tracey, waved her hand and told him she didn't need to know nothing from a piece of paper, that if Sirus said it wasn't fit, well, then, that was all she needed to hear. After he explained what he thought, each person asked, "Well, what do you think, Sirus?" And he'd said, well, he wouldn't take it, not himself, not for his family, unless there were significant changes. When each and every person said, well, no, then they didn't want it either, but what could they do, Sirus had pulled from his briefcase the contracts they'd signed. He had all of them with him — those which wouldn't fit in his briefcase were lined up inside a large box in the car. And when anyone said he didn't want the place anymore, he ripped up the papers, all the copies, tore them up, along with the checks for those who'd given him a check, and gave the paper to each person to burn. To people who had paid in cash, Sirus handed the money he had withdrawn from the special account he'd set up at the bank.

No one had thought about it before because it was so simple. Sirus had all the contracts and all of the money. The white folks had had him do all the talking, and the contracts, with the down payment checks still attached, were in his safe at the office. So he'd taken them all out, and ripped them up when the buyers said no. By the time he'd gotten to the third house, most had already heard what he was doing. The phone calls, of course, had preceded him; but still he didn't rush his way through it. He took the time to say hello, go over the problems in as much detail as anyone cared to hear. It had taken him a good four days, all the way through Saturday, to get to everyone, but he visited each person, and everyone agreed with him that it wasn't a fit place in which to live.

What people wanted to know now from Mrs. Johnson was this: Had she seen it coming? Had he told her what he was going to do? Had there been any calls yet to the house from the white men? Had he given any indication of what he was going to say when they called? They peppered her with questions, and when she didn't have answers, they asked for the details — the endless pieces of expressions and moods and habits that would allow them to deduce things for themselves. Is he still eating like always? Have you seen any cars swinging past the house? The town was filled with a million detectives, piecing together the likeliest scenario from what they had to go on.

Mrs. Johnson went inside the house and back to the kitchen. She was glad she had left it as nice as she had on Saturday. She hadn't known what was coming, this little impromptu party, but she was glad that the house was ready. It was clean and the beds were made and there was coffee cake in the pantry that she could heat up. She put the coffee on to brew, a large pot. As people arrived from church, handbags and Sunday shawls piled up on the bed in the back room, and more people moved out onto the porch to escape the mounting warmth in the house. There was the *tap-tap-tap* of Sunday best shoes across the porch and between the rugs as they passed from the living room to the dining room to the kitchen and back again, trailing the thick smell of Sunday perfume and powders and aftershave and coffee.

It was like a baptism, all of them declaring by their presence that the official mourning was over and a new life had begun. They were dedicated now to the future rather than the past. It's over, you've survived, and we've survived, their presence seemed to say, as if a great worry had been lifted from their shoulders, even as new burdens were being taken on.

Standing in the kitchen, Mrs. Johnson felt as if this new light that had been turned on in her head had spread and spread until now there was hardly a thing that was safe from its glow. It was not that she'd previously thought life to be easy. In fact, she had never thought of it as being either hard or easy — it just was. But now, in this vast new light, she saw that it was something else entirely. It was as if everywhere she looked she saw that there were these things: hard and soft, horrible and easy, cozied into one another. Her daughter, with her new husband, would have a life that was like the one she herself had had, both blessed and, if she was lucky, tolerably hard, and the happiness everyone had always imagined to fill this house was now a happiness that had been tested by pain.

Jason suddenly appeared in the doorway, his shirt sleeves rolled. He had insisted on accompanying Sirus on all of his rounds to tear up the contracts, said someone should be right with him, shoulder to shoulder, and he peeked in the kitchen now, as if he wanted to be sure that Mrs. Johnson was alone.

"Afternoon, Mrs. Johnson," he said.

Mrs. Johnson could see just the smallest bit of tension in his face, like two small screws at his temples.

What, Mrs. Johnson thought, would this new light of hers reveal if she trained it on Jason? He stood where he was, his palms sweaty, the front of his shirt rumpled. She offered him coffee. He came to the stove and poured it himself, drinking the first half of it by the stove.

"Well, if they call," he said suddenly, "the white folks, that is, and he's got to go over there to answer to them, well, by God, I've decided to go too." As he spoke, the coffee misted his cheeks with steam.

"That's decent of you," Mrs. Johnson said, "but I'm sure everything's going to turn out all right."

Jason seemed to shiver without moving, the brown of him settling like dirt into a fresh hole. He both shook and nodded his head, and the cup he held rattled in his hand.

"Well, yeah, but you never know. I just hope we don't have to go across town. If we do, like I said, I'm going, but I do hope we won't have to go over there."

Watching his hands move, Mrs. Johnson saw, with simple clarity, how across town, "over there," where the white folks lived, might just as easily have been Mars or Jupiter. How perfect, she thought, his hands are for sealing bodies and burying the past, for preparing for worms and earth, for re-creating a familiar pose. And how unsuited they were for holding still in his lap as he sat in a strange room with unfamiliar voices and white faces. He was like an old rock or a tree, so at one with its place that, once it was rooted, it was unimaginable that it should be moved. How could she not have seen this before? Now that Jason had settled himself here in Durham, he was of this place and these people. The statement filled her. What did it mean to be of a place, a people, a time? The three so fitted together in your bones and marrow that you were seamless in the moment, inseparable from the conjoinings of blood and dirt and marrow which spawned you. Did the first fish floundering on the land, its gaped mouth gulping in the unimaginable, inhospitable air, its fin legs unfolding, did it look as startled and fiercely out of place as she imagined Jason would be if he were forced to live out the rest of his life "across town"?

"I'm so glad Sirus has come back to himself," Jason said. He spoke quietly, as if to himself, and Mrs. Johnson saw another piece slide into place. And the piece that now so easily fell into place was Mr. Mac and Jason's friendship, the fit of it. Mrs. Johnson saw how Jason was a man born to settle in just one place, while Mr. Mac was a man who might belong anywhere, and who thus had to work to fit where he was. It was as if Mr. Mac was always working to send out shoots that only tentatively took hold, but all Jason had to do was stand in one place long enough and he would be as rooted as an old oak, the system so deep and interlaced that to move him would require special handling. And, of course, what one had the other one needed, and so they walked side by side, each getting from the other precisely what it was that he lacked.

Mrs. Johnson's head ached, and she felt like muttering, Lord Lord, this new sight is a strenuous burden. What she said instead was, "It's a relief for all of us."

Jason said, "You just don't know."

Mrs. Johnson pictured Sirus and Jason as children, walking across an open field. They held their hats in their hands, and they moved through goldenrod, wild wheatgrass. It was dusk, and a country moon was just beginning to rise.

"I can imagine," she said.

Later, as evening began, Sirus and Aileen and Etta and Lily sat quietly on the front porch. Everyone else was gone. Dr. Gant and his wife had left early. Jason and his wife and children had given Mrs. Johnson a ride home. The Butler sisters, even though Satha was tired, had stayed to the end.

As the people departed, they had gathered first in a group on the porch, their voices musical in the clear air. Have you got my shawl, women asked their husbands. Who needs a ride home, men asked each other. Y'all take care, both the women and the men said to Sirus and Aileen. Then, slowly, they descended the steps and from there flowed out to the street. Once there, as if no one could bear to be the first to break away, they moved in a tight circle. They stood close together like that, all of their friends and neighbors, out in the street, as they waved goodbye to Sirus and Aileen up on the porch. It was an improbable sight, Sirus thought, everyone in his Sunday best, waving and calling out from the middle of the street, as if it were a country road.

Now it was starting to get dark, and fireflies in the yard flickered their lights, searching for one another. Etta and Lily sat together on the swing while Sirus and Aileen sat in their gliding chairs. The chain on the swing squeaked as Lily pushed it back and forth with her feet. Etta swirled the remains of ice in her glass, and Sirus's and Aileen's chairs added their own contented whine.

As the dusk came closer, the katydids began to sing. They always sang at this time of the year. Sirus marveled at the sound.